BEIGE PLANET MARS

'We just did what we had to do to survive,' General Keele was saying. 'Of course, we should never have needed to, if we hadn't been betrayed so bad. Sure taught us not to trust civilians. No offence intended, York.'

'None taken,' Phillip York replied quietly. The old man was clearly paying him little attention, lost as he was in the past.

'Yeah, we were shafted good and proper,' muttered Keele. As the old general stared into the distance, into his own past, Phillip mumbled some platitude and backed away. The old man made dismissive noises.

As Phillip walked away, he heard Keele mutter a name, undiluted hatred seeping into every syllable. It was a name Phillip, like every other resident of Mars, knew well.

'Tellassar,' snarled Keele, digging his fingernails into the bar's varnished surface.

BEIGE PLANET
MARS

Lance Parkin
and
Mark Clapham

First published in Great Britain in 1998 by
Virgin Publishing Ltd
Thames Wharf Studios
Rainville Road
London W6 9HT

Bernice Summerfield was originally created by Paul Cornell

Cover illustration by Mark Salwowski

ISBN 0 426 20529 4

Typeset by Galleon Typesetting, Ipswich
Printed and bound in Great Britain by
Mackays of Chatham PLC

The authors gratefully acknowledge the assistance of
Cassandra May and Rebecca Levene.

Mark's Credits

Dedicated to my mother and father, for endless help through
a difficult year.

Thanks also to:

Jim Smith, for ideas and read-throughs.

Fitzrovia and Beyond: Lee Binding, John Binns, Simon
Guerrier, Mark Jones, Jo Kemp, Jonathan Miller, Jim
Sangster, Alan Stevens, Gareth and Guy Wigmore, Tat
Wood, and all those people who've asked 'So; done any
work on it yet?'

At SSEES: Megan Blair, Grant Cooper, Mirja Dillen, Saqeb
Mueen, Abby Pulfer, Sean Semple, Peter Siani-Davies, a
whole lot of first years including the 1998–99 Union
Committee, and anyone else who took an interest.

At Connaught: everyone who suffered my 'distracted
behaviour' during the writing of this book.

Dave Stone and Emma Scott, for inspiration and star quality.

Karen Tvedt and family, for the years I wasn't getting
published.

Sarah and Orlando, for being.

Last but not least, Andrew Plummer, Merri Snyder and
Monica Piercy; a better gang of friends I could not imagine.

Lance's Credits

For Cassandra May.

Thanks, as always, to Mark Jones, Mike Evans, Rebecca
Levene, Kate Orman and Jon Blum. Thanks this time to
Alyson Shuttleworth and Charity Stonier.

WORLD OF THE WARS

Everyone knew by the last years of the twentieth century that human affairs were being watched keenly and closely by intelligences greater than man's and yet as mortal as his own. As men busied themselves about their affairs they had come to know that there was life on Mars.

With infinite complacency most men went to and fro over their planet, going about their affairs without giving a thought to the older worlds of space. If they thought of Mars at all, they did so only in daydreams and stories: idle fancies allowing an escape from the real world, that brightened the time between renewing their car insurance via direct debit, arranging to open a current account with a building society or fretting about the rising price of unleaded petrol.

At most, terrestrial men fancied that *one day* there might be men living on Mars. The means to get to Mars existed, the technology had been there for some time, tried and tested, but the will was not. It would cost hundreds of billions of dollars to go to Mars. Better to use the money to sort out the problems here on Earth, the people said. And so those hundreds of billions, and many more besides, were spent on stealth bombers and old-age pensions and paying back the national debt and tax breaks for the middle classes. So, for more than a hundred years, mankind spent their time living normal lives, with proper jobs, and they invested their billions the way they wanted to, on lottery tickets and alcohol, cigarettes and DIY.

In 2086, the Martians destroyed Paris.

The method used was very simple: they dropped an asteroid. The Martians didn't worry too much about the target, aiming it at Europe and letting chance and gravity decide exactly which city would be obliterated. It could have been Prague, Milan, Geneva, London, Manchester or Rome. But the asteroid struck Paris, and wiped clean centuries of history in an instant. A million people died at least, and mankind mourned them almost as much as it mourned the loss of the *Mona Lisa*, the *Venus de Milo*, Notre Dame and EuroDisney.

Humanity quickly worked out *how* the Martians had done it, and didn't stop to ask *why*. That would be a question for the historians and the archaeologists in the centuries to come. Before that, the Martians had to be destroyed. This was something that humanity understood, and now, abruptly, the will to reach another planet was there. There were men on Mars in eight weeks: United Nations soldiers parachuting down through the thin Martian atmosphere, setting up bridgeheads and command posts. Space stations arrived above Mars, watching over the battlefields with godlike disdain, selecting targets, coordinating the fight, relaying the television pictures back to Earth. Many men died fighting the Martians, but the *greenies* were driven to the brink of extinction in exactly a thousand days. When the war was over, mankind found that it owned another planet.

Swords became ploughshares, and colonization efforts began in earnest. UNASA rockets brought supplies, robots and satellites prospected for minerals, astronauts laid foundations. The canals and river beds of Mars flowed with water once more: first a trickle, then a torrent as the human race melted the Martian ice. Mars was a place of innovation, pragmatism and uncompromised excellence. Mars had deuterium, palladium, gallium and silver in abundance, but its greatest asset proved to be its citizens, a young population more motivated and trained to a higher level than any previous human society.

In the year 2095, the University of Mars was founded to celebrate all that the planet was, and all that it would become.

Tiny settlements quickly became great cities as the very best and brightest that humanity had ever produced flocked to Mars. It was a time for heroes, for great leaders, for men of vision, for scientists, for explorers.

FIVE HUNDRED YEARS LATER

PLANET OF WAR

21 June 2595

Five hundred years is a long time, Professor Bernice Summerfield observed as her shuttle craft approached Martian airspace.

Five hundred years before the first American space probes had reached Mars, there had been no America. The land itself was there, of course, and there were people there, but they weren't *Americans*. Amerigo Vespucci was still a young boy, and it would be a generation before the Europeans discovered the continents which would come to bear his name. Vespucci was born into a world where the printing press and cannon were still at the experimental stage and the fastest way to get around was on horseback. Botticelli and Michelangelo were alive, the ceiling of the Sistine Chapel and the *Birth of Venus* were modern art. Columbus, da Gama and Magellan had not yet set foot aboard a ship. There were no laws of gravity, or of natural selection. At this time, Earth was surrounded by concentric crystal spheres, and every living being was linked in a chain that started at the foot of God and ended with the lowest forms of life. Human beings had seen Mars moving across the night's sky since prehistoric times, but had only a glimmering of what it might be. It was fifty years before Copernicus' time, a hundred before Brahe would use his observations of Mars to formulate his Laws of Planetary Motion.

And five hundred years after man had first arrived, the Mars that Bernice and her two hundred fellow passengers were approaching was a very different planet from the one that space probes had first photographed and mapped. For one thing, this world was as familiar to Earthmen of the twenty-sixth century as Brighton was to a Londoner back in the twenty-first, and the journey to Mars was just as routine. The old place names were the same, but they held little mystery now: there was a yachting lake in Utopia, a casinoplex in Deucalionis, vineyards in the Mare Sirenum. She could see them all from space. Even the old Native Martian sites were just stops on the tourist trail now, complete with handrails, electric lights and concrete ramps so that no one stumbled on the uneven ground.

The most obvious change was the ocean at each pole. This close they dominated the Martian landscape. There hadn't been an ocean on Mars until mankind arrived, let alone two. The terraforming of Mars had been the great human endeavour of the early twenty-second century, the greatest engineering project since the building of the pyramids. It was the reason that the two major Martian spaceports had been built where they were. Both at Carter in the south and at Ransom in the north, space freighter after space freighter had arrived from Earth and the Belt, bringing prefabricated machine parts and the construction workers who would assemble them. The second generation of Martian colonists had built a string of mile-high geothermal power towers to thaw the polar ice caps, they'd reclaimed the ancient canals, they'd planted great forests on the shore and around the new cities. New landmarks and features were added to the maps, and on a clear day any kid with an optical telescope could see them all from Earth.

It had taken a couple of centuries or so, but now the Borealis Ocean in the north was a vast freshwater sea feeding the canal network, supplying the entire planet with its water. There was water in the Southern Sea, too, but mostly there was carbon dioxide. Just as precious, the released CO_2 thickened the atmosphere, helped Mars to retain the Sun's heat and sustained the Martian forests that, in turn, produced the oxygen that the population of Mars breathed.

As the shuttle passed over the south pole, it was just possible for Bernice to see some of the power towers through the thick, perpetual, ocean fog. When they had been built they had been harsh, angular structures. After five hundred years standing in the steaming Southern Sea they looked like vast stalagmites, dripping with lichen, not something man-made at all. She'd read in her in-flight magazine that no one ever went out to them any more: each tower was maintained by its own small colony of robots.

Anyone looking out from the observation lounge of Carter Spaceport and staring out to sea would have seen Professor Summerfield's shuttle as four small white lights, high in the fog, growing brighter. Gradually the sound of rocket engines would be becoming more and more apparent.

The small shuttle craft drifted down, turning slightly on its axis. The shuttle curled into the landing position, its antigravs fired once and it touched down into its docking cradle. Outside, gangway tubes slid into place, locking on to the three exits. Robot cargo loaders whirred into position. Inside, the passengers, Bernice included, stood up, got used to the gravity, collected up their hand luggage.

A hundred metres behind them, another shuttle curled into the landing position, its antigravs fired once and it touched down into its docking cradle. Noachis Spaceport handled about 60 per cent of the planet's commercial flights – a ship arrived every fifteen seconds or so. There were facilities for larger ships: military ones, usually, or diplomatic service ships. Most of the arrivals were much smaller: shuttles and boats from the big interstellar ships that stayed in orbit, or privately owned yachts and merchantmen.

A million people a day arrived on Mars, half that number departed. Those statistics might suggest that the population was increasing, swelling even, but that was because the figures didn't explain why so many people were coming to Mars in the first place.

They were coming to die.

After living long and prosperous lives, there wasn't a

better place to die in the whole of Earthspace than Mars. From the earliest days of colonization it had been clear that Martian humans lived longer than they would have done on Earth. The low gravity lightened the load on the heart, made it easier to get around; it even lessened the effects of arthritis. The pure, dry, processed air contained few bacteria, few pollutants, few contaminants, few carcinogens. The regulated climate and beautiful landscape were the icing on the cake. For many years now, the people of Earth and its colonies had come to spend their autumn years on Mars.

Just as the Martian land had adapted to its human inhabitants, as the forests and gravity nets spread, as the seas and canals swelled, its frontier economy also evolved. The elderly population ranged from the wealthy to the very wealthy, and they demanded the best in medical care, the best in residential care, the best security. The whole infrastructure became geared to meet their demands.

There were young people here, there had to be. There were some jobs a robot just couldn't do, or rather there were some jobs that the robots refused to do. Menial jobs, demeaning jobs, washing and wiping and pretending to care. There were some young people who really wanted to help: nurses with genuine vocations, doctors keen to find breakthroughs in geriatric medicine. But most of the young were here to make some money. Demographics were on their side: there were barely ten thousand babies born on Mars a year, and the children of Mars didn't want to stay around the dying planet. First chance they got, they went to Earth or its Moon, or the Belt, or the Jovian Archipelago, or they left the Solar System altogether, never to come back. Mars was one of the few places you could go these days if you wanted a job but didn't want to go to college first.

Barney Durham was one of six hundred who had the job of Welcomer. In days gone by, he'd have been called a Customs Officer or an Immigration Official. But that was a unionized job, a profession, one with a salary well over minimum wage. Welcomers were cheaper than Customs Officers. There was high staff turnaround, but the recruiting drones didn't find it difficult to drum up applicants. Even the least enterprising job seeker coming to Mars managed to find the spaceport.

It was a simple job: wear a camel-coloured coat, walk among the crowd of arrivals and welcome them to Mars. A friendly, personal service.

Behind the scenes, of course, all this friendliness had a purpose: every single individual would be stopped for the regulation eighteen seconds, just long enough for the scanners embedded in the floor to get a complete reading. The computers upstairs would know straight away what the arrival had brought with him, from smuggled drugs to genetic disorders. It happened from time to time, and when it did, Barney Durham's job was to direct them towards the security drones, preferably without tipping the smuggler off, and preferably without the smuggler pulling one of those ceramic pistols – the ones that the weapon scans didn't pick up – and blowing him away. Three weeks ago that had happened to Jeff Mett, ten metres from Barney's spot, when a Chelonian pilot had pulled a burster from his – or her, it was very difficult to tell with three-metre humanoid tortoises – shell. It was a crappy job, and Barney had only taken it because it had sounded like a good way to meet women.

It wasn't.

The typical specimen was several years older than his gran, and even the younger ones were still in late middle age. Take the example confronting Bob Caius ten metres to his left. She was large and lumpy as a brick pressure shed, and the yellow wool coat she wore didn't help. Her wig . . . well, it had probably said 'henna' on the box.

'Two weeks,' she said, for the third time. As she smiled, three more chins were added to her already copious collection.

Was that really his best prospect? Bob, with an eagerness born from true desperation, was even trying some of his best lines on her. Jesus.

Barney shook his head, and turned. The woman he bumped into was slim, with long legs. If she was as old as she looked – somewhere in her thirties – then she was four decades younger than the Martian average. Her black polo-neck shirt and denim jeans stood out in a sea of beige, tan, fawn and tweed. She was also the first woman through here for a week who could be described without using the word 'sagging' somewhere. She had a small canvas rucksack slung over one shoulder. She wasn't from Mars, even though she was perfectly at home in the low Martian gravity. Like a lot of offworlders she was wearing dark glasses. Even in the acclimatized areas the UV levels were well over Standard tolerances. If you were going to live on Mars for any length of time you had your cornea fixed – a simple enough operation, but not worth doing if you were just visiting. Barney had paid for the op with his first wage packet.

He smiled, but even at point-blank range she hadn't noticed him.

She was looking around, taking it all in. Not many people stopped to do that any more. When it had been built, Noachis Spaceport had been one of the greatest human architectural achievements of the early twenty-second century, right up there with Golden Dream Park or the Lunar Tower. Barney had been told at school that many of the first generations of colonists had settled on Mars because they had been told that the whole planet looked like this. But nowadays there were countless human colony worlds, each with its own native and man-made attractions. Bizarre to think that this had been the most exciting place in the universe a few centuries ago.

But while just about everyone else was content to join the orderly queues for the transmat cubicles, this woman was staring up at the monorail as if it was the holy grail, instead of a museum piece.

Barney made his introduction, the woman's details flashing up on his lenstop screen as the central computer matched her face to its immigration records. 'Good afternoon, Professor Summerfield.'

He gave his best Welcomer smile.

As she stepped up, the scanners dotted around the concourse had already found out everything there was to know about her. This was Professor Bernice Summerfield of St Oscar's University on the planet Dellah. Even before she had taken off her sunglasses, Barney knew from his readout that she had blue eyes, and that she was here for the quincentennial celebrations at the University.

'Welcome to Mars.'

'Hi. Call me Benny.' She had high cheekbones, a wide mouth, ruffled black hair. She wasn't as movie-star stunning as she'd promised to be from behind. But there was something about her smile and the way she cocked her head.

'Not your first visit?' he asked her, as the computer answered him.

'No. I'd forgotten how beautiful Mars is. I was twenty-four the last time I was here. Now I'm –' She stopped, trying to work it out.

'You're thirty-five. Today. Happy birthday, Professor Summerfield.'

She checked the giant clock that was suspended over the main concourse and seemed genuinely surprised by the date. Interstellar travel did that to you, or so Barney had been told. Something to do with travelling faster than light, or spending so much time on planets where the days and years were the wrong length.

'Gosh, time flies, doesn't it?' she said. 'It doesn't seem five minutes since I was celebrating my thirtieth. A thirty-fifth birthday's nothing special, though, is it? Hardly worth mentioning, let alone celebrating. Er . . . I'd love to stop and chat, but –' She held out her hand, wanting to know where she should be heading.

'The transmats are that way,' Barney told her, pointing out the queues.

She shook her head. 'I want to *see* Mars,' she told him. 'I could transmat straight to The Hotel, but I'd miss out on the scenery. Same with a travel pod. The windows on those things are so small that –' She paused. 'Does that monorail work?'

Barney smiled. 'Sure. It's –' He waited a few seconds for his lenstop to feed him the information. Benny waved her hand, trying to jog his memory.

'Sorry. Yeah, it's part of Martian heritage. It has been restored by the Martian Trust. Based on linear induction, the first hovertrain tracks were laid in 2093. It's powered by atomic fusion, and capable of speeds of two thousand kilometres an hour. At the time it was built –'

'Right,' she said, cutting him off. 'Sorry, but looking at that board, it says that I've got five minutes to get from here to there. So I'll have to dash. Bye!'

She flashed a smile at him that he'd never forget, and then ran off, following the signs to the monorail terminal. She'd vanished into the crowd before Barney realized that he hadn't told her the most important thing about the monorail.

Perhaps if Benny Summerfield had been concentrating on something other than running she'd have wondered why no one else seemed to be in a hurry.

If she had noticed, though, she'd probably have dismissed it as infirmity – she was just about the only person who was able to reach the platform without sticks, crutches, frames, chairs or exoskeletal help. Because she was in a hurry, she saw every single one of her fellow passengers as an obstacle in her way: something to dart past, dive between, weave around. Intellectually she knew that there was nothing deliberate about their doddering, but it was very difficult not to feel that there was some conspiracy of duffers, all trying to prevent her from catching her train.

An easy five-minute stroll was becoming more and more frantic as each second passed. She could tell she was getting nearer to the platform: it was getting cooler as she reached the outskirts of the temperature-controlled arrivals lounge. She was so focused on catching the train that when she arrived at the platform and the train was still there, with people still boarding, she felt relief on a scale usually reserved for the civilian population welcoming a liberating army. Happily, she let a small group of pensioners on ahead of her, and then stepped aboard.

The interior decor was all moulded plastic and formica surfaces. Benny took her place at one of the tables, alone for the moment at least. She looked out through the window. From here she had quite a vantage point: the monorail track was supported by elegant metal pylons and was about twenty metres above the ground. It had been laid parallel with one of the canals, presumably at the same time the canals had been reclaimed and filled. This close to the poles, the water was crystal clear and flowed freely. Benny could see the reflection of the train in it. Water still looked alien on Mars, like some morphing, writhing CGI effect in an old movie.

The monorail was yet another expression of the up-and-at-them belief-in-science age during which it had been laid. The train had already been out of date for decades when it had been approved. There must be some story behind its construction, a story that Benny didn't know, but which probably involved a corrupt mayor and some overenthusiastic engineering students. The first few decades of Martian colonization had been characterized by youthful dynamism, as the crème de la crème of the scientific and academic community on Earth came to Mars to forge their utopia, funded by the big aerospace and information technology companies. For a generation, Mars had essentially been a huge Californian-style campus, a place for fifth-generation hippies and fourth-generation net.utopians to come and build a society based in absolute faith in the future. Their legacy was still obvious from some of the place names on the rail map above her head: Picard, Moderation, Applemac, Ddeb. Words redolent of a lost golden age.

There was a soft *bing-bong* and the conductor announced that departure of the train would be delayed for an hour. There would, he promised, be further announcements.

Benny looked around, hoping to share some communal sense that the people who ran this shoddy organization should be shot, but no one had even looked up.

'It's always an hour late,' she heard someone say. 'They should change the timetable.'

Benny checked her watch to see what time they might expect to depart, then realized that she hadn't adjusted it to Martian time. She could see the giant clock in the concourse from here. The train wouldn't leave until two, and she hadn't got anything to read. She'd brought a couple of books with her to Mars, of course, but she hadn't realized that the flight here would take quite so long or be quite so uneventful. She'd

15

polished them off before the freighter had even reached the Terran Sector.

She decided to mount an expedition to the bookstall that she'd seen as she hared past on her way to the train. She was looking for a couple of local history books. She checked her purse and discovered that she had about twenty Martian sovs. Enough money.

She made her way off the train and down the stairs to the shop and back into the warmth. The first thing that caught her eye was the newspaper stand. A few of the usual titles, written at some central news monitoring station and then fast-lined to the major planets, where some poor sod of a subeditor would add a couple of columns of local sports news and alter the masthead. *Mars Today*, *The News of the Worlds*, *South Chinese Daily*. Mars also had a couple of newspapers of its own. Always keen to absorb some local flavour, Benny bought a copy of the *Martian Chronicle*, before making her way to the bookshelves at the back of the shop. There was a small group of businessmen carefully vetting the pornography, with the help of some old women.

One snaggle-toothed old crone thrust a book into Benny's face, so close that she couldn't read its name. She gathered enough from the blurred impression of stockingtops, pink letters, cleavage and tentacles that it probably wasn't the sort of thing she'd be listing in a bibliography.

'Ooh, you should read this.' The old woman cackled. 'It's pure filth, of course, but I love a bit of sex now and then.'

Benny grimaced, a number of witty epithets springing immediately to mind.

'Not my kind of thing at all,' she assured the woman, gently moving her out of the way.

There was a gratifyingly large archaeology section . . . that is to say there was a shelf and a half of choice, wedged in between the space operas and books about Jack the Ripper. There was another old woman at the bookstand.

'Excuse me,' Benny said gently.

'Young people, always in such a hurry.'

'Well, in theory at least,' Benny said. The old woman

looked up and smiled at the joke, which immediately put her in Benny's good books. She was a smartly dressed human in her late sixties, with short, steely grey hair parted at the side. Her eyes were a dark brown, incredibly wide and deep, windows on a soul that had experienced much. Benny noticed that the woman was flicking through a copy of E. K. Trinity's *A History of Mars*.

'Don't read that,' Benny said, eager to educate. 'The author treats her readers like morons.'

She felt a bit ashamed pushing a copy of her own book *Down Among the Dead Men* at the woman, but it really was the best popular treatment of Martian archaeology. Besides, she got 7.5 per cent royalties, ten Martian sovs in her pocket, if she persuaded the woman to buy it.

'Look, it says on the back, there: "Professor Summerfield's work is thoroughly absorbing and very imaginative . . . she conveys her information with a ready wit".'

The woman did something odd: she went straight to the copyright page. 'Sixth printing, this paperback edition,' she noted approvingly. 'The author must be rich.'

'I hear,' Benny confided, 'that she spends all her royalties on alcohol and Belgian chocolates and she spends most of her time totally skint.'

'She sounds like excellent company,' the woman said, smiling. 'Professor Summerfield, I presume?'

Benny bit her lip and giggled. 'It's a fair cop.'

The old woman held out her hand. 'Professor Elizabeth Trinity, visiting professor of areoarchaeology, King's College, Cambridge. I treat my readers like morons.'

There was one of those awkward pauses that occasionally punctuate conversations with people you've just met.

Then Trinity smiled, an expression which was clearly as near as she ever got to laughing. 'You should see your face,' she said.

Trinity bought a copy of Benny's book, Benny bought a copy of the latest best-seller to challenge the orthodox view of the evolution of life in the solar system, *Martians Are from Venus, Venusians Are from Mars*. Together they made their way back up to the monorail – Trinity's preferred method of transport.

They took their seats and Benny took out her book. 'A comic romp . . . a real delight,' the quotes on the back promised. She read the first paragraph, flicked through to the middle, started chapter ten and then tucked it back in her rucksack, all before the train had left the station.

The monorail began powering up, lifting slightly. The doors hissed closed, and then they were underway.

'The train's nearly empty,' Benny observed.

'It's a museum piece,' Trinity replied. 'Every couple of years someone in the Rotariat suggests that the monorail should be closed down, but no one really has the heart to go through with it. They wheel out the excuse that some people are still transit phobic, so they can't use the transmats, but . . . well, they could just take travel pods, couldn't they?'

The train slid out of the terminus, nudging its way out between the various terminal buildings and hangars. From her vantage point high up on the monorail track, Benny looked out, saw the spaceport with an archaeologist's eye. Typical architecture from the early colonial period, the sort of stuff that the textbooks called premodernist. Anyone from the late twentieth century would see the sort of bold use of concrete and glass that fell out of fashion after about 1975. It looked like a university campus, or a nuclear power station. The sort of place Dan Dare would feel at home. But over centuries, the bold intent had faded, the hi-tech styling of the pyramids, domes and skylons had grown quaint. Supermodern was all a bit old hat these days.

They were clear of the spaceport, riding over one of the forests that surrounded most of the major conurbations. Benny got her first sight for many years of the Martian landscape, indescribably older than that of Earth, where even the oldest mountains were only hundreds of millions of years old. Five centuries of terraforming had barely altered a tenth of the terrain. The belt of forest petered out ten or twenty kilometres away, yielding to the rusty Martian desert. On the horizon – so much nearer than the horizon on Earth or Benny's home planet of Dellah – there were hints of mountains and mesas. It looked a lot like Arizona or Nevada, only the geological features were so much larger than anything that Earth had to offer. This train journey would take them along the Valles Marineris, four times deeper and ten times longer than the Grand Canyon, and would terminate in Jackson City, on the slopes of Olympus Mons, three times taller than Everest.

'It's beautiful out there, isn't it?' Benny said.

'Beautiful and dangerous,' Trinity replied, a little melodramatically for Benny's tastes. 'This is the planet of war, after all.'

'The Thousand Day War in 2086 to 2089; the Invasion in 2157; the Battle for Mars fifty years ago,' Benny said, counting them out on her fingers. 'Three wars in five hundred years is a pretty good tally. A lot better than Earth over any period of human history you'd care to mention. And the last two of those were started by the Da–'

'I know my Martian history,' Trinity snapped, clearly annoyed to be contradicted. 'There were wars here long before humanity arrived,' she continued softly. 'The native Martians were warriors, you know that. Just over the horizon that way is the Argyre crater. In the late twentieth century there was a massive nuclear explosion there which completely wiped out the local clan.'

'Mmm, yes. I know my Martian history, too,' Benny said.

'It's filled with water from the Southern Sea now. The sunrise over the Argyre Dam is really quite beautiful to behold. The real estate prices over there are the highest on Mars. The scars heal over.'

The premise of Trinity's book was coming back to her now: Mars was a planet with a long and bloody history and prehistory; humanity had tamed it; now it was beautiful. Her book was thirty-five, forty years old and it represented – no, Benny was being unfair, *it had shaped* – the orthodox view of Martian history. The version where the noble humans had freed a magnificent planet from its backward and savage natives. Students of Benny's generation had rebelled against people like Trinity, reinterpreted their evidence, tried to see both sides of the argument.

'This train passes through Tharsis, I take it,' Benny asked gently.

The dying Martian civilization had been bombed to the verge of extinction during the Thousand Day War, and the heaviest fighting had been in the mountainous Tharsis region.

Trinity gave a flickering smile. 'Only three wars. Three wars too many. Perhaps this is the planet of war because we remember the past.' She paused. 'Is that a good thing, I wonder?'

2

LOBBY POLITICS

The sun was sliding beneath the horizon as the monorail passed through Jackson Forest, Lake Jackson and into the outskirts of Jackson City itself. Olympus Mons had been dominating the landscape for over an hour. Now it completely filled the horizon in front of them, its peak poking above the Martian atmosphere. Benny remembered reading somewhere that it covered an area the size of Colorado, but she had no idea how big Colorado was, so the comparison lost a lot of its impact.

Trinity was dozing on Benny's shoulder. She'd fallen asleep around the time the train had been crossing the Noctis Labyrinth, possibly the most dramatic part of the journey. But Trinity had made this journey dozens of times, over decades. Chaotic terrain and pink dust storms were as mundane to her as lorry yards and rainclouds would be to an English commuter. Long before they'd reached Noctis it had become clear that their academic differences weren't going to stop them becoming friends. They'd cracked open an overpriced bottle of winterberry wine bought from the restaurant car, and mulled over the state of academia, corporate funding and the publishing industry.

The monorail was at a forty-five-degree angle now, although thanks to its artificial gravity field Benny wouldn't have known without looking out of the window. Terraces had been cut into the base of Olympus, making it look like an open-air theatre for giants. Despite that, the city layout was similar to

21

every other place since the industrial revolution: suburbs wrapping around the central business district. Two or three hundred years ago, the suburbs of Jackson would have been dull, nothing to write home about. Just the typical suburban sprawl of an era when the population of all the colonies skyrocketed. But Mars had always been an affluent planet. There was elegance here in the way the roads, canals and moving pavements had been laid out. Many of the original pressure domes and brick structures still stood. When they had been built, they had housed whole communities: hundreds in their bunk beds and dorms. Now they were the houses of rich individuals and their families, poking from the suburban landscape. There were large expanses of carefully irrigated parkland, although no one seemed to be using them. There were people walking along the banks of the canals, congregating around the pubs that had probably once been lock keepers' cottages.

Benny nudged Trinity, gently waking her. 'Nearly there,' she said.

The train had slowed to a crawl as it became just another cog in the city's transport network. It allowed them a better view of the city.

'What's that pyramid?' Benny asked.

'No need to get excited. Olympus Opera House,' Trinity said. 'Or rather it used to be. A bingo hall, now.'

Benny nodded. They were running parallel with a canal again, and she was watching two gondolas, apparently racing. A few dozen spectators on each bank were cheering them on. The movement of the two robot gondoliers was fluid, graceful, but their craft were barely travelling at walking pace.

'Our hotel,' Trinity said. 'Or, rather, The Hotel.'

It had no other name, such things being rather sparse on Mars back when The Hotel was built. Even when the Hiltons, Imperials and Tannazakas started appearing on Mars, this place remained The Hotel. Benny couldn't help being impressed when she first saw it, favourably back-lit in the bloody dusk. It was typically ostentatious for its period: a vast double helix, which would once have been shockingly reflective, its curves picked out with neon highlights. Time had made it less tacky, years of wear and corrosion rendering its sleek metallic surfaces a rich bronze veined with pale green.

The train slowed to a halt, and the platform folded up to enclose it. Trinity was already on her feet, trying to remember where the luggage carriage was. Benny had travelled light, and so her own disembarkation was a lot easier. Benny let her aged fellow passengers disembark first; or, more to the point, she stood back as they jostled, elbowed, and generally fought their way off the train and on to the platform of Central Plaza station. She was content to wait for the turnstiles to process their elderly blockage, and instead of joining the queue she dropped her bags and just stood on the platform, feeling the cool evening breeze and looking up at The Hotel.

A seventy-two-floor spiral. Benny hoped she wasn't going to be installed on one of the higher floors; one drunken stumble and she would roll all the way to the bottom, bumping down a curving flight of stairs for dozens of floors, reaching the ground a purply bruised mess. Even with the lower Martian gravity, a fall like that wouldn't do her much good. She shook her head; this was ostensibly a business trip, and her paper still needed work. She would probably have very little chance to leave her room, never mind get disgustingly smashed on the local booze. The room would have a minibar, but Benny had never seen the point of the things.

'All work and no play...' she muttered to herself, picking up her bags and strolling over to the now unblocked turnstiles. She slipped her ticket into a slot, and the turnstile thanked her politely for travelling InterMars as she stepped through. She emerged into Central Plaza itself, one of the earliest urban developments on Mars. Disappointingly, she could now see that The Hotel's lowest couple of floors were fairly normal, a red-brick structure that paled in comparison with the grandiose design of its higher storeys. Between Benny and The Hotel there lay a great mosaic of multi-coloured paving stones, all polished and gleaming in the fading light. The other buildings scattered around the edge of the plaza seemed mundane by comparison. There were

23

shops and offices, and all the other elements of any small town centre. Humans and aliens scurried in between these, clearly trying to beat the closing times, making preparations for the weekend ahead. Even after all this time, humanity still lived by the old traditions, Saturdays and Sundays never losing that magic they gained during Earth's industrial revolution.

The centrepiece of the plaza was the ruin of Brusilov's statue. Colonel Brusilov had been the first UN soldier to hit the Martian soil during the fightback of 2086, and had famously elected to stay on after the war. In 2545 the statue erected in his honour had much of its head and right shoulder melted away by an enemy plasma blast during the Battle of Mars. The government had elected to not repair it. So, while masons had hand-carved the slabs to re-lay the plaza, and metal workers had used arc-lasers to repair the damage to The Hotel's spirals, Brusilov had retained his injuries. Benny checked her guide, comparing the pristine version in the brochure with the liquefied, wrinkled face that stood there now. What had been an unremarkable memorial to a hero had become a poignant monument to the damage done in the ancient and recent past, a wreck in the centre of an otherwise immaculately kept square.

Benny remembered her own sacrifices during the last War: her mother's death, her father's disappearance. That was what the Galactic Wars meant to her, the loss of two people. Was that selfish? Entire worlds had died in the fire that had swept an entire galaxy. Colony worlds of a billion people destroyed in an hour of atomic bombardment, fleets of ships wiped out. Genocidal policies on all sides had wiped out a dozen alien races, leaving nothing but ruins. That was just the first year, 2540, and the War would run intermittently for over thirty more like it.

The forces ranged against humanity had been utterly ruthless, thriving on conquest and extermination. They had a hundred thousand slave races on a million colony worlds, a thousand battle fleets. Four hundred years before they had made an easy conquest of Earth, using only limited resources. Within five years the enemy had reached the Solar System, and seemed to be on course for total victory. But the enemy had underestimated the humans. The War had reached Mars, but only a few biogenic weapons managed to get as far as Earth. The enemy had failed to reach humanity's homeworld, this time. The human race had grown. As the enemy armada swarmed into the Solar System, the human race was ready for them with an armada of its own. More than that, humanity had formed secret defensive alliances with a thousand planets throughout the galaxy, and each of those planets had fleets of warships. Against all logic, against all they had planned for, the enemy found themselves outnumbered and within a decade they were retreating to the safety of their own territory. But for years Earth Intelligence had been sending agents in to train the slave populations in the art of guerrilla warfare and terrorism. The enemy returned to find an entire empire in revolutionary turmoil. For two decades the war was fought on enemy territory, and the War ended on a decisive note with the destruction of the enemy's home planet.

But not before the enemy had killed Claire Summerfield in an air raid, and not before Isaac Summerfield's ship, the *Tisiphone*, had been lost over Bellatrix.

So much had been rebuilt in the decades since the War ended, but the greatest injuries could never be truly repaired.

Deciding that her thoughts were becoming far too maudlin, Benny began to make her way around the great mass of the statue. As she headed towards the brass-plated revolving doors of The Hotel, a familiar figure was weaving his way between the liveried doormen, politely refusing any help with his few items of luggage.

He was a blue-skinned humanoid in an elegant pin-striped suit. As he and Benny approached each other across the shining plaza his mouth cracked into a broad smile, revealing a set of small, but very sharp, teeth.

'Professor Summerfield,' he said. 'A pleasure to see you.'

'And you, Mr Saldaamir,' she replied. 'It's been far too long. Just leaving?'

'My business here is concluded and I'm expected back in San Francisco this evening. I gather you are here for the Mars Conference.'

'Afraid so,' Benny confirmed. 'I'm even presenting a paper, for my crimes.'

Mr Saldaamir laughed. 'Nothing too anachronistic, I hope.'

She smiled. 'I shouldn't think so.' She grimaced. 'To be perfectly honest, I haven't even finished writing it yet.' Or started it, she added to herself.

'Well, good luck,' he replied, as they began to drift apart, he to his train and she to The Hotel. 'And watch out for Professor Scoblow; the academic grapevine tells me she was a bit of a pollen fiend in her youth, and has never been quite right since.'

Benny watched him disappear into the station. Where did she know him from? It was on the tip of her tongue. She shook her head and strode towards The Hotel's imposing entrance.

Gerald Makhno flicked his fringe out of his eyes irritably. Life was not good. It had seemed such an easy job: be a greeter at an academic convention, brushing up on your knowledge of Martian history while notching up a few credits. The perfect job for a lazy post-grad looking to suck up to his academic betters.

Of course, back then he hadn't known who would be in charge of the event; he had not met Scoblow. Neither had he realized the chaos, the long hours and the sheer effort that went into making an event like this run even remotely smoothly. So here he was, standing in the lobby, sweating into his cheap suit, grinning inanely and handing out ridiculously complex sheaves of leaflets and programmes to the arriving academics, fielding their ludicrous questions about lost baggage and inequitable room sizes, all the time wishing he had taken a job as a gravedigger out in the suburbs instead.

Makhno was just trying to explain to a delegate from Alpha Centauri exactly why the air-conditioning was unlikely to suck people up and spit them out on to the concrete below, when he spotted Scoblow striding across the lobby towards him. While one hemisphere of his brain devoted itself to dealing with the delegate's query, the other half decided to engage in blind panic.

Eventually, the delegate nervously wandered off, and Makhno was left alone with his superior. Professor Scoblow, Emeritus Professor of Human History at the Santa Diana University on Mars, was a Pakhar, a metre-tall humanoid rodent. If this wasn't disturbing enough, she was a total humanophile, both intellectually and, alas, sexually. She had even changed her name from the original Sk'o'bel'ou, to make it more comprehensible to human ears. She wore a tight-waisted tweed suit, with gold-framed pince-nez balanced on her snout and an oak pipe permanently installed in the corner of her mouth. She twitched her little nose in what Makhno sincerely hoped wasn't supposed to be a seductive manner. She looked like a Beatrix Potter character, but one who had grown up, had a couple of unsuccessful marriages and then spent the eighties in rehab.

'Now that's what I call *Homo erectus*,' she said shrilly, indicating the departing hexapod and tweaking Makhno's cheek with her paw. Makhno laughed half-heartedly, the other half sinking rapidly. And she smelt of sawdust.

'Well, how's my little Gerry?' the giant gerbil continued, her little black eyes squinting at Makhno over her glasses. She blew smoke out of the side of her mouth and flicked one of her long whiskers. She leant close. 'If any of the delegates get too naughty, you just tell me. I'll sort them out.'

Makhno nodded mutely, secretly hoping that spontaneous rodent combustion was possible.

'Of course, if it's *you* being naughty, you have to tell me that too.' Scoblow giggled girlishly, a high-pitched squeak that made the lobby's crystal chandelier ring. Makhno looked around desperately for any potential distraction.

One of the newcomers was a human woman in her mid-thirties, slim and boyish, with dark bobbed hair and wearing jeans and a black polo-neck. Makhno recognized her from the back of one of his textbooks. One of his favourite textbooks. This was something he hadn't expected.

'My Goddess! Isn't that Bernice Summerfield?' he asked, starting to flick through the guest list for confirmation.

Scoblow took another drag on her pipe. 'Oh, that's her all right,' she replied, bitchy acid seeping into every syllable.

'Unfortunately, we need cheap, small-time academics like her to fill out the schedule at a convention like this, offset the cost of the real talent. More's the pity, that's what I say.'

Makhno ignored this slight on his academic heroine, and grabbed a registration package. This was going to make up for all those other horrid delegates.

Benny looked around the lobby appreciatively. 'Lush' was the only word to describe it. Vat-grown ivory floors. Gold brocade. Tapestries and paintings depicting ethnic Martian history on the walls. Actually, 'lush' wasn't the only appropriate word: 'vulgar' would do just as well.

Benny barely had time to take all this in when she was accosted by a complete stranger, who shook a hand she hadn't offered and babbled about what a pleasure it was to meet her. She was about to complain when she noticed her assailant was a rather handsome young man, and decided to indulge him. How shallow, she told herself, basing your actions towards someone on their appearance. But, said the part of her brain currently flooded with interesting hormones, he is a particularly fine specimen: good teeth, a charming grin and a floppy fringe of dark hair that gave him an air of boyish enthusiasm. She shook her head, trying to dislodge thoughts of a distinctly unladylike nature. She'd always heard that these academic conferences were essentially just an excuse for . . . He had been speaking to her all this time, and he'd just asked her a question.

'I'm sorry,' she told him, 'could you repeat that?'

'Certainly. Sorry about that, I was babbling a bit. I'm Gerald Makhno, a representative of the MarsCon committee. I presume you're registering for our event, Professor Summerfield.'

'Oh yes,' said Benny, carried away by his enthusiasm. 'In fact, I'm one of the speakers. And please call me Benny.'

'Benny,' he repeated, and she suddenly wished for a less masculine nickname. 'Unusual, but it suits you.' He gave her a sly, and unambiguously flirtatious, grin.

Oh God, thought Benny. And a good decade younger than her, too. Professor Summerfield, sexual predator of the lecture circuit. This could be the start of something severely dodgy. With any luck.

Professor Scoblow, somewhat piqued by her handsome sub-ordinate's interest in an academic rival, raged silently behind the reception desk, blowing contemptuous smoke in the direction of two young human maintenance types who were giggling too loudly for her liking.

Once the skinny human archaeologist – didn't Makhno appreciate a real woman when he saw her? – had disappeared into the elevator, Makhno following behind with her bags, Scoblow proceeded to spit verbal bile at her non-human underlings. She grabbed the shortest one by the trouser leg.

'What do you see in human women?' she squeaked.

'Er . . .'

'They're furless, bony things.'

'Well, yeah.'

'And they've only got two nipples, haven't they? What's the point of that?'

She stormed off before the lad could answer.

To Benny's acute relief, The Hotel did have an elevator. Actually, it was less an elevator and more a 'spiraller', moving as it did around tracks on the inside of the hotel's helix structure. The effect was not unlike being on a helter-skelter with ideas above its social station, an odd sensation of not quite moving in the right direction. There were few experiences that required travelling in such an odd manner.

The inside of the lift was teak-panelled, with a small brass-framed window allowing a view of the slopes and terraces of Olympus. There was a particularly good view of the plaza. Below, Benny could see the monorail dropping off a party of native Martians. They seemed somewhat the worse for alcohol – probably celebrating one of their team's many rugby victories. As they piled out on to the platform one tripped, falling head-first against the side of the carriage. His friends picked him up and they all moved off into the night in search of further entertainment. Just another Friday evening. The monorail train slid away from the platform, a football-sized dent in its chrome side the only evidence of any accident.

As the elevator completed its graceful ascent to the forty-fourth floor, Benny turned her attention to Makhno, who had spent most of the journey in polite silence. She could feel he was aware of her, that he had the urge to stare but was resisting only through a tremendous effort of will and deeply inbred etiquette. She found this obvious internal conflict somewhat endearing.

'Excuse me,' she asked. 'Why are you treating me like Pope Priscilla the Second, returned as per prophecy? I'm not used to people being starstruck around me.'

'Sorry, but don't you get this from everyone?' blurted Makhno. 'I mean, everyone in our field.' He blushed. 'Archaeology as the new rock and roll, and all that.'

He gently put her bags down outside room B34, and offered her the keys. She nodded for him to open it, and retrieved her luggage.

'Run that past me again,' Benny asked, tossing the bags into a corner of the spacious room and collapsing on to the huge bed. She bounced a good foot up into the air before settling, the result of powerful bedsprings and weak gravity. 'Archaeology as the new what? What the gibbering frig has this got to do with me?'

' "Archaeology as the new rock and roll",' Makhno repeated, disbelievingly. 'Oh come on, surely you read the student journals. I mean, a lot of people seem to think archaeology's a waste of time, just some old rocks. But to those of us who take the subject seriously, you're a legend.' He sat down on the edge of the bed, then rapidly and rather self-consciously stood up again. 'You just make it seem so cool.'

He reeled off a list of her recent exploits. Some bits seemed to have been exaggerated; the Polar Express never seemed that interesting at the time. Other details, such as that business with the Bane Corporation, had actually been toned down for the sake of plausibility. Benny was unused to having the details of her life processed via the rumour mill. The sensation was less than pleasant. Were there really dozens of wannabe Bennys out there in the campuses, reading about her exploits every month? Weird.

She had to admit to herself that the events of the last few months had been pretty intense, though, hearing them recounted back to her like that. Perhaps, she suddenly realized, not everyone spent their lives being threatened by megalomaniacs and avoiding certain death in the jaws of hideous crab monsters. Some people could probably go a full week without discovering an ancient artefact of immense power that threatened all mankind. She found herself wondering what they did with themselves instead.

Makhno suddenly slapped a hand over his mouth, stifling a gasp and breaking Benny's daydream of everyday tedium.

He was pacing the room, checking behind the curtains, not quite daring to open the wardrobe.

'What now?' she demanded. 'Don't tell me; you just remembered a holo they made of my legendary sexual exploits using a hidden camera. I should be so lucky. My recent efforts would be hard pushed to fill a three-minute comedy sketch.'

He whirled to face her. 'I bet you woke up hung over.' He paused. 'I bet that porter robot of yours, er –'

'Joseph,' Benny supplied wearily.

'That's it. I bet Joseph woke you up, brought you your breakfast and told you in that disapproving way he has that there was one of your young male students outside. That young man has a secret crush on you, and you quite like him, but before either of you could do anything he was murdered and the trail led here . . . Am I right?'

'Thanks to the generosity of my department when booking my ticket to Mars, I woke up in the cargo hold of an automated hyperspace freighter surrounded by crates of bananas,' Benny corrected. 'Alone. I had bananas for breakfast for the third day running. Joseph is, as far as I know, right where I left him.'

'My Goddess, even so, it's the perfect scenario.'

'What?' she demanded, increasingly irate.

Makhno ignored her, shaking his head earnestly. 'Don't you realize? It's the classic set-up. Professor Bernice Summerfield arrives intending to have a quiet couple of days in which she can finally do some academic work, and she finds herself in a luxurious and glamorous setting.'

He paused, staring right at her. 'The question is . . . who's going to be the first guest to get murdered?'

That nice young man Makhno had disappeared upstairs with the Summerfield woman and no doubt he wouldn't be down until she had sated her lust. Just thinking about it made Scoblow's fur tingle. It wasn't natural.

Professor Scoblow required stress relief, and for someone to remind her that she was still desirable. So, she left a subordinate in charge of guest liaisons and nipped into the elevator. She punched in the code for the top floor, and felt girlishly excited as she made her spiralling ascent. When she reached the top she unlocked the door to the Presidential suite with another code sequence, and tiptoed in.

The lights in the suite were off, the vast floor space crowded with the shadows of ornate furniture. It smelt of lemon tea and ginger, as it always did. The centrepiece of the room was a mahogany desk with an active computer system set out on it. The computer's vidscreen was alight, casting multi-coloured shadows as fractals crawled across it, the room's only illumination. No one sat in the chair before it.

'Are you here, darling?' Scoblow whispered, delighting in the conspiratorial atmosphere, even though the suite was soundproofed. Anyone who could afford this suite had enough money to cut themselves off from the laws and customs of the wider world. It was an unfamiliar power that Scoblow had never realized was attainable until the last week. Not that she could afford such a lofty position, but the sensation had rubbed off on her through spending time with the suite's current occupant. He had the air of a man who could not be touched by any mortal force.

She nudged open the white double doors, the ones with the peacocks on that led into the bedroom.

'Come to me, my delight,' she whispered, creeping forward, trying not to be unnerved by the silence. She ought to have changed into her kimono by now, but instead she slipped off her jacket and undid a couple of buttons of her blouse. As her eyes adjusted to the darkness, she noticed that the room was in a state of disarray, a chair flung into a far corner, vidtapes and papers scattered across the floor.

'Darling?' Scoblow asked, slightly louder now. Before she could turn round, someone was running up behind her, strong arms grabbing her around the waist. She squealed in panic, terribly aware that no one could hear her.

Her assailant chuckled darkly, and bit her neck. She gasped.

'You naughty, naughty boy,' she admonished, her fear dissipating as her lover swept her off her feet and carried her over to the low bed.

Bernice moaned, her face in her hands. She took her hands away, and stared at the tasteful marbled walls.

'My Goddess,' she whined. 'Don't you think it's a bit unhealthy, obsessing about someone else's life like this? Don't you have anything better to read about?'

'I'm just glad this isn't one of your digs,' said Makhno, getting into his subject to the extent that he wasn't listening to a word Benny said. 'We could really do without sub-Lovecraftian evils slipping their ancient chains and trashing the place, or one of those weird reality-bending devices. The tourists are bad enough.' He paused, suddenly thoughtful. 'What type of jaunt do you reckon this is going to be, then?'

'Well, I don't bloody know!' wailed Bernice. 'It's not like I go looking for this sort of thing.'

'Really?' asked Makhno, genuinely surprised. 'I always presumed you had some kind of agenda, and just claimed to wander into these things accidentally out of modesty. I mean, there must be some purpose to all your heroics.'

'Nope.' Benny exhaled loudly. 'No purpose, no crusade, no agenda. People only invent these ideas – crusading heroes, redemption through adversity, et cetera – to try and prove there's some higher purpose to all the suffering and bullshit people go through. Well, I've wandered in eternity a bit in my time and I can tell you that's just not how it is. Shit happens. People deal with it. That's all. They do the best they can, and rarely does it make them better people or teach them valuable moral lessons. They just end up rather more battered and jumpy than they were before. End of sermon.'

'That's very cynical,' replied Makhno, somewhat shell-shocked. Benny almost felt guilty for shattering his childlike faith in her role in the universe. Almost.

'Realistic,' said Benny gently. 'The only beautiful ideal I believe exists out there is the ideal pint of beer, and I still haven't found that. Not for want of trying, I should add.'

With an operatic sigh of pleasure, Scoblow collapsed forward, burying her face in her lover's chest.

'Oh, you're the best,' she enthused, her tail curling around his leg.

'You're not so bad yourself,' he replied in mock disinterest, his rapid breathing telling another story. She tweaked his cheek, gave it a little scratch, as if in reproach. It was a game they played, but Scoblow could never quite tell how much he ever meant anything. There was something dangerous in his eyes, something that made her wonder how much she could trust him. It was both frightening and exciting, as all the best pleasures are. She let these worries drift away as she lay there, feeling the rise and fall of his chest beneath her head, listening to the beat of his heart settle back into its normal rhythm.

'Is she here yet?' he asked quietly, barely audible. There was a strange anticipation in his voice, the echo of some other, as yet unrevealed, emotion.

'Yes,' she replied bluntly, surprised at the regret she heard in her own voice. She felt him tense slightly, then rather self-consciously relax.

'She isn't going to be a problem, is she?' Scoblow asked. She propped her head up, trying to see his eyes in the darkness, to divine the feelings beneath. 'Is there anything I can do?'

'Oh no,' he said without noticeable emotion. 'I will deal with Professor Summerfield myself.'

* * *

Makhno had left Benny alone, returning to his duties.

She should really have busied herself unpacking, or fired up the room's little computer to do some work on her paper. But instead she just lay in the darkness, admiring the view from her window. She was on the side of the building facing away from the Central Plaza, giving her a view of a part of Jackson City she had yet to travel through. It was an urban landscape of surprising simplicity, lacking the chaos and confusion of most similar places. The founders of Mars had thought through their building programmes, trying to create a new world for their descendants, a world that carried forward the best of Earth into a new environment. Neither a utopia nor a dystopia, but a place of hopeful calm. As night had settled the buildings of Mars had lit up, web-like trails of neon illuminating their smooth, albeit tarnished, metal surfaces. The monorail lines and canals seemed alike, silvery strands criss-crossing the crimson landscape. Many of the older, pre-war buildings looked fresher and cleaner than those that had been new a decade ago, but had rapidly succumbed to the advancing lichen. The nutrients seeded in the air by the atmosphere processors had resulted in a thick green moss that now crawled over many of the structures, although some of the more important or expensive buildings had been coated in a moss-resistant liquid which stopped any spores from taking a hold.

Benny decided that lying around admiring the scenery wasn't going to get her anywhere. She rolled off the bed and ordered the lights to fade up. A pile of magazines sat on the dressing table. She grabbed the top one and examined the cover. It was a glossy brochure for an academic convention entitled *Ancient Evils and Apocalyptic Wars: Shared Myths of Armageddon*. She flicked through the pages, which were brightly illustrated with various images of the end times, drawn from a number of different cultures, human and alien. Interesting. Unfortunately, it was the brochure for a conference that had just ended rather than the one she was lumbered with. Tossing the brochure into the bin, she reluctantly reached for the registration pack Makhno had given her. Sliding off the elastic band, she noted the poor quality of the paper compared to the brochure for the Apocalypse conference. She was obviously in the wrong field.

She skimmed the list of scheduled lectures. Professor Scoblow was presenting a paper intriguingly titled *The Ritual of Tuba: The Significance of Martial Brass Band Music in Human–Martian Relations*. Benny's own contribution was listed simply as *Untitled*, although a more apt title would have been *Unwritten*. She really had to do some work on that, she thought, mentally slapping her own wrist. She was just about to reach for her notes when she spotted an entry on the events listing. It said simply 'Friday, 7p.m.: informal meeting for drinks in hotel bar'.

Benny looked at her watch. Twenty minutes to have a wash and change into her best frock. With a sudden burst of enthusiasm she headed for the shower, whistling an old show tune as she went.

3

ON THE INTERNAL DYNAMICS OF PARTIES

It was as if the workers in a skimmer factory had fallen into their machines and had emerged with odd bits of vehicle welded on to them. Benny had never seen so many weird bionic attachments in her life, especially considering the age of the humans saddled with them; all the men and women pushing very close to their first century of life. Their prostheses were varied: pneumatic arms, plastic knee joints, steel jaws, brass vidlinks. As Benny entered the bar they turned to look at her, then, realizing she was a bodily intact thirty-something and therefore of minimal interest, went back to their conversations and drinks.

Benny was baffled. These were not academics; there were no tweed jackets with leather patches on the arms, all beards were neatly trimmed and the conversation was bawdily macho rather than shriekingly bitchy. As she waded into the decrepit mêlée, she looked around her for a flash of corduroy, a hint of brogue in the elderly throng. The hotel bar was large but low slung, with the precise shabbiness that comes of trying to deliberately give your hostelry a 'lived in' feeling. Benny suspected it had been refurbished within the last six months. Squatter-chic was all the rage in the home Solar System, if the vacuous free magazine she had flicked through on the train was anything to go by. Next year this place could be a techno-feudal alehouse or a pseudo-Mugwumpian Jizztav.

Whatever brought the bright young things in. Or the slightly faded old things, by the look of the current crowd.

The noise of chattering pensioners shouting into each other's hearing aid was overwhelming. As she nudged her way through the crowd as politely as possible, a man nearby accidentally spilt beer into the rusty socket of his artificial eye. The lens popped out in a shower of sparks, much to the amusement of the man and his drinking cronies.

Benny couldn't help but smile. She hoped she would have that much life in her under similar circumstances.

Makhno spotted Bernice pushing her way through the crowd, and made a beeline for her. To his surprise, he found himself manhandled into a seat, a pint glass of ale forced into his hand.

'There you go, Gerry mate,' chirped Seez Westfield.

'Er, thanks,' replied Makhno, suspiciously examining the two figures who had diverted him. 'What's this for?' he asked, holding the pint aloft.

'Payday, innit?' replied Sotherton Ashley, more often known simply as Soaz. 'Share and share alike, innit?'

As the only person of similar age at The Hotel, Makhno had found himself subject to the social advances of Seez and Soaz, The Hotel's casually employed freelance odd-job men. Although they were charming enough, Makhno found the two lads slightly alarming; their job descriptions were worryingly vague, their lines of work suspect.

The two youths were polar opposites, yet strangely compatible. Seez was lanky, relaxed, with multi-coloured dreads and beard, and the baggy clothes to match. Soaz was short, shaven-headed and frenetic, dressed in figure-hugging holo-fabrics.

'Coming out later?' asked Seez casually, snorting some odd-looking powder off the back of his hand.

'I can't,' replied Makhno. 'I have to hang around if the guests need me.'

'Downer,' said Soaz. He bounced on his stool excitedly. 'It's gonna be a good 'un, y'know?'

Makhno nodded. Personally he found Seez and Soaz's idea of a good night to be exactly the sort of thing which produced week-long hangovers and excessive credit loss. He took a hefty swig of his beer, and scanned the crowds. Benny was nowhere to be seen.

'Who you after?' asked Soaz, eyes gleaming with interest.

'No one.' Makhno shrugged, as casual as he could manage.

'Ah,' said Seez sagely. 'A lass.'

Benny found the Pakhar Professor Scoblow at the bar, sitting on a high stool with her little legs dangling aimlessly. She had a drink, her pipe and an air of casual contempt for the world in general.

'May I?' asked Benny, indicating an empty stool. Scoblow nodded and Benny sat. She ordered a double shot of RedStar with ice, and sipped it tentatively. The sensation left her lips numb and her throat sore. She winced.

'Martian vodka,' said Scoblow, indicating her own glass, in which the RedStar had wisely been diluted a little. 'Nothing quite like it.'

'Potent,' replied Benny, and extended a hand. 'Professor Bernice Summerfield.'

Scoblow shook the offered hand politely, but with little warmth. 'Professor Megali Scoblow. But then we already know each other, by reputation if not in person.'

'Indeed,' acknowledged Benny. 'I certainly read your article on early Martian religion with interest.'

'And?'

Benny took a deep breath. 'Well, I find your assertion that academic perceptions of Martian religion are coloured by sentimentalism and cultural myopia on the part of a number of human writers rather patronizing.'

Scoblow squeaked happily. 'A predictable response from a member of the anthropomorphist school of thinking. Can't you acknowledge the way that human thinkers, with their narrow vision of what constitutes "culture", have invented most Martian rituals in an effort to make their subjects easier for humans to relate to?'

'No!' exclaimed Benny. 'The evidence for a secondary caste system has long been established and –'

'Personally, I find both your views to be too extreme,' said

Professor Trinity, who had managed to get behind them without their noticing. 'Well, I do think the role of religion in Martian culture has been exaggerated by our early scholars: the Martian culture has always been primarily martial, if you will excuse the pun. They have always fought, either against the elements or more sentient enemies. There has never been much time for contemplation in the Martian mentality.'

Scoblow looked smug, but Trinity turned her steely gaze to the little Pakhar.

'However, your reaction is too extreme. Undoubtedly, faith and ritual have always been significant in the Martian way of life. It is simply the context, the nature of the expression of this faith, that is due for more thorough scrutiny.'

'And you are?' Scoblow asked, her academic ego clearly smarting. The old woman stared straight back at her, and Benny could feel Scoblow wither. It was the gaze of a headmistress, someone who was frustrated by the lesser intellects around her, someone consistently pained by their failure to keep up.

'Professor Scoblow,' said Benny. 'Allow me to introduce Professor Trinity, author of the divine *The Decline and Fall of the Martian Empire*, the less divine *History of Mars*, and one of the few people I am happy to lose a debate to.'

'Professor Trinity!' exclaimed Scoblow, suddenly understanding how Makhno had felt earlier. 'Professor Elizabeth Trinity? Well, I of course defer to you on this too. Your work has been an inspiration to me for years. I must say it is a pleasure to see you here, Professor Trinity. We didn't know whether to expect you or not.'

Trinity smiled politely. 'I was in fact due to make a rather lucrative, but boring, academic tour of the rim planets, but the galactic transport links aren't what they were, what with all these mergers and what have you lately. With my lectures inaccessible, I chose to take up your invitation instead.' She leant forward, a hitherto unseen glint of mischief in her eyes. 'To be frank, I prefer events like this anyway, although my accountant might disagree. I'll take Mars over money any day, but, alas, he doesn't have these finer feelings and keeps my career chugging along the path of maximum profit.'

A nearby group of elderly amputees were watching a drinking contest between two of their own. The crowd cheered loudly as glass after glass was downed, each drink raising greater and greater shouts. Trinity raised an eyebrow.

'At least I'm among my own generation,' said Trinity drily. 'I presume this lot aren't here for our event, Professor Scoblow?'

'Oh, no,' replied Scoblow. 'This lot are a veterans convention, celebrating the anniversary of the Battle of Mars.'

Trinity pointed to a great holobanner that had been hanging over the bar all this time without Benny even noticing it.

YORKCORP WELCOMES THE 191ST LEGION

'Commemorating, not celebrating,' Trinity said quietly. She turned to Benny. 'In spite of my criticisms, Professor Summerfield, I have to admit to finding your work refreshing. Where do you find those wonderful sources? They seem almost first-hand.'

Benny downed her RedStar in one gulp.

'Sorry, mate,' said Seez as he accidentally bumped someone's elbow. He and Soaz were trying to negotiate their way out of the bar, but the clientele were getting in the way.

'I'm not your mate,' indignantly snapped the man who Seez had knocked, spinning around to face the lanky youth. He was in his early hundreds, but with muscles like a steroid-pumped twenty-something. He wore his silver hair cropped short, and a green sleeveless vest over his tattooed torso. His face looked as if it had suffered a few solid blows from a hefty spade.

'Hey, he said sorry,' said Soaz, butting in as usual.

'I heard that, boy!' barked the tattooed elder, turning on Soaz with such vigour that the younger man jumped back in alarm, ironically knocking the collective elbows of another group of patrons. They turned to complain, but were stared down by the tattooed man, who seemed to assert some authority over the elderly crowd.

The tattooed man turned back to Soaz. 'I heard him, but that doesn't make this hairy, multi-coloured hippy asswipe my "mate".' He swung around back towards Seez, who didn't flinch. 'You see these, boy?' He tapped a finger against a series of horizontal scars on his upper right arm. They seemed to have been deliberately burnt into his flesh with a laser. 'These are my rank stripes, asshole. These make me a general. So that means you don't call me "mate", you call me SIR!'

'Right,' replied Seez drily. There were a fair few people like this on Mars: people who were still going on about the War. He'd be getting nostalgic in a moment and talk about Siege Spirit.

'Right what?'

Seez paused, as if deep in thought about the required response. 'Right, sir?' he enquired tentatively.

The general seemed about to reply to this blatant insolence, but one of his friends shouted at him from across the bar: 'Hey, Keele. Stop playing around with that kid and get back here.'

'General Keele?' asked Soaz enthusiastically, and much to Seez's confusion. '*The* General Keele?'

General Keele seemed pacified by this fannish enthusiasm. 'Listen to your friend, boy,' he drawled, tweaking Seez's goatee. 'He knows the score.' Then he returned to his friends, leaving Seez's mouth open in shock. As the two young men made their way out via a 'Staff Only' door, Seez turned on his friend.

'So what's so important about that guy?' he demanded impertinently.

'What, General Keele?' replied Soaz. 'He's the guy who liberated Mars, you ignorant wankstain. Saved this place after whatchimacallit cocked up. Big-time hero, man.'

'Shit,' said Seez, impressed. 'And where did an uneducated little crukwit like you learn stuff like that?'

Soaz winked. 'Young Martian Defence Force. Four years my dad had me in there, boy and adolescent.' He did a little three-fingered salute.

'Cool,' replied Seez. 'Got any good badges?'

'Home Security badge,' said Soaz proudly. 'They taught me how to pick locks and deactivate burglar alarms. Useful, eh?'

There was a twinkle in Seez's eye.

Makhno had barely escaped from Seez and Soaz when he almost crashed into Scoblow, staggering out of the ladies' loo in a haze of mild intoxication. She gazed up at him with those little black eyes, and jabbed an accusing finger into his stomach.

'I saw you,' she said, glassy eyes narrowed. 'Talking to those rough young sailor types.'

Makhno didn't feel inclined to listen to this drivel, and he wasn't too keen that Scoblow's face was level with his crotch.

'Not the sort of people you should be associating yourself with, no no no,' continued Scoblow. 'Let me look after you, Gerry. I'll keep you on the straight and narrow. Well, relatively –'

'Look, there's Tuburr the Mighty!' exclaimed Makhno, pointing over her shoulder.

'What?' said Scoblow, her head spinning round. As she looked away, Makhno lunged back into the mêlée, hoping to lose himself in the crowd.

Professor Trinity seemed to know absolutely everybody. She drifted between the groups of academics who were slowly filtering into the bar, Benny in tow. Hands were shaken with varying degrees of warmth, pleasantries and banalities were exchanged with all the precision of a long-practised ritual, one which had long ago lost any meaning. The galaxy was a big place, but for the academics who made a living from the interplanetary lecture circuit it was just one big commute.

They had met on the ice plains of Prashant to discuss Chelonian floral culture. They had debated economics in the shadows of the great spires of Denkam. They had even held a conference on 'The Influence of Machine Intelligences on Warfare' in the catacombs where once, long ago, just such a race of cybernetic creatures had slept their dreamless sleep.

Until meeting these people, and hearing their stories, Benny had never realized you could do so much, travel so far, without ever staying in anything less than five-star accommodation. It was a gravy train, the conference circuit, and the participants knew it.

Once, long ago, this kind of event had been strictly demarcated by disciplines. But different species had different visions on what constituted, say, theology, and so the lines had become more and more blurred as cross-culture academic exchanges had increased. Eventually the boundaries had collapsed beneath the tremendous desire of academics of all stripes to attend as many conferences as possible. So now historians, archaeologists, cultural commentators, poets, scientists, sociologists, linguists, economists and academics from any other area of study even vaguely applicable would turn up to any conference they could con their respective universities into paying for them to go to. They cribbed funding from all sorts of institutions and individuals, made extravagant public claims about the intellectual importance of the conference scene, all in the faint hope that one day they would find themselves forever on the circuit, never once having to return to teaching bloody students.

Benny actually quite liked most of her students, and enjoyed setting the red ants against the blue ants in her seminar groups. But, if push came to shove, she would prefer loafing around the conference circuit, picking up fat cheques along the way like a toddler following a trail of sweets.

Benny and Trinity had been pounced upon by Desmond de Montfort, an incredibly tiresome little tit of a man whose taste in clothing fabrics was tantamount to a violent assault on the eyeballs of others. Trinity was fielding his dull and obsequious questions with icy politeness, clearly scanning the room for an excuse to escape. Finally noticing Trinity's disinterest, de Montfort turned his attention to Benny, trying to engage her in an ancient and pointless debate about Martian gender politics.

'Ah!' exclaimed Trinity. 'Excuse us, Desmond. This is truly fascinating, but I really must introduce Professor Summerfield to our generous patrons.' She grabbed Benny by the wrist and dragged her away before de Montfort could protest.

'That de Montfort was boring everyone around him rigid back in the fifties when I was doing my doctorate,' Trinity muttered into Benny's ear.

'I can believe it,' replied Benny.

At the edge of the room they found a better class of socializing going on. These were the academic elite: heads of department wearing flashy suits they couldn't have afforded back when they were young enough to wear such things without looking ludicrous, grungy youngsters who had collected huge signature advances for the publication of their daring first theses, and those tweedy elders of the academic community who, like Trinity, had earned the respect of their peers by being consistently brilliant for decade after decade.

Benny, who was too old to be a prodigy, too young to be an elder, and whose dubious academic credentials and lack of administration skills put a place in the hierarchy out of the question, didn't know quite where she belonged in such esteemed company. She let Trinity guide her through this gathering of the academic great and good, who nodded politely and sipped their cocktails as they passed. In a discreet alcove they found Scoblow and a few others paying homage to a couple who were obviously sponsors of academia rather than active participants in it. They were rather ordinary, middle-aged people, but their confident manner and healthy tans set them apart from the pallid, twittery scholars around them. Their dress didn't suggest wealth, but the fawning manner of the bursary-hungry crowd around them did.

'Professor Summerfield,' said Trinity, the crowd deferentially making space for her. 'I would like you to meet the sponsors of this conference, Phillip and Christina York. Phillip, Christina; may I introduce Bernice Summerfield, a fellow attendee.'

To her surprise, Benny found that the trillionaire couple seemed genuinely pleased to meet her.

'Hi,' said Phillip York, squeezing her hand firmly. He was a rather chubby individual, the cut of his suit the only indication that he was anything more than a small-time businessman. He was virtually bald, his greying hair cut in a short, nondescript fashion at the back and sides. 'You do realize, Professor Summerfield, that your presence here has raised this hotel's insurance premiums by seven point two per cent?'

Benny's mouth hung open.

'My husband is joking, of course,' said Christina York, nudging her husband in the ribs. 'It is a pleasure to have you here.' Her immaculately applied make-up gave the initial impression that she was somewhat more young and glamorous than her husband, but underneath the cosmetics Benny imagined they were quite a good match.

'Phillip and Christina own –' Trinity began, but Benny cut her off.

'– YorkCorp. I guessed.' She waved her hotel keycard in the air, its holographic YorkCorp logo shimmering in the smoky half-light of the bar.

'Ah,' said Phillip, rather sheepishly. 'A little ostentatious, but our marketing people aren't happy unless we assert our corporate identity across our whole product range.'

'And this hotel is one of those "products"?' asked Benny, lightly. She was warming to the Yorks, and had a funny idea they weren't the sort of people to take offence easily. Christina's lilting laughter proved her right.

'Oh, The Hotel is far more than a product,' said Christina fondly. 'It is, we like to think, the home of YorkCorp. It was our first purchase, and we later built our head offices just down the road. That way, we can live here whenever we are on Mars.'

'We bought the place when it was run down, twenty-seven years ago,' recalled Phillip. 'We spent the last of Christina's inheritance turning the place around. It all started here, and we try never to forget that it was here on Mars that we got started. Which is why we help fund events like this. And, of course, for similar reasons we couldn't refuse the Veterans Association when they were looking for a place, even though it does make things a little cramped.'

'Oh, I'm sure we'll all get on just fine,' replied Trinity. Benny was watching Trinity as she spoke, and was pretty certain the old professor felt the exact opposite of what she said.

Around ten, Scoblow went hunting for fresh young academic talent. Makhno seemed entirely uninterested in discovering her charms, even though she had offered them to him without any strings. Her lover in his penthouse had asked not to be disturbed, so he could work on his current project in the solitude it demanded. That left her with a cold single bed to look forward to, an entirely unsatisfactory situation. She had seen some rather tasty young human doctoral students talking to Summerfield earlier, and decided to track them down. Why should that Bernice woman have all the fun?

'Well, you're a furry little bugger,' boomed a deep voice from nearby. 'Would you like to warm an old man's bed for him tonight? You'd make a nice substitute for a hot-water bottle, cuddly little thing like you.'

Scoblow turned to lay her most withering gaze upon the overweight, white-haired human who had addressed her. Slumped into a chair, he was leering at her over a table full of empty glasses. His beard was flecked with beer foam, his eyes rheumy with old age. He seemed not to have noticed the distaste in her eyes, but that could just have been because he was too old to see properly.

'All my mates have given up and gone to bed, the rats,' he rambled, regardless of her contempt. 'No offence, mind, you being a rodent and all that. They – my mates, that is – are getting too old for this sort of thing, or so they tell me. Too bloody soft, that's what I tell them.'

Although he didn't have any false limbs or obvious scars, Scoblow gathered from his uncouth smell and pseudo-military dress sense that he was with the veterans convention.

'Your mates from the War?' she asked, her interest perked. As a historian specializing in Mars, she made a habit of collecting war stories about the planet. Her libido was cast aside in favour of more cerebral desires.

'From the time of the defence, yeah,' said the old man, a little defensively. 'Why do you want to know?'

Scoblow pulled up a stool, and cleared some elbow space

47

on the table. 'I'm Professor Scoblow. I'm a historian, and I'm always interested to hear about the old days, if you don't mind.'

The man seemed hesitant.

'I'll buy you a drink,' added Scoblow, twitching her nose suggestively. She might warm the old man's bed after all; he seemed in fairly good condition.

'A drink? Make it a double and I'll give you enough stories to fill your next dissertation.' He leant across the table, wrapping his huge hand around Scoblow's tiny paw, shaking it with surprising tenderness. The skin of his hands seemed surprisingly smooth and unscarred for an old soldier.

'My name's Isaac Denikin,' he began. 'And back when the invaders came, I was just a young man . . .'

Phillip York approached General Keele cautiously. Phillip found Keele's legendary reputation and fierce manner more than a little intimidating. Keele had, in a popular myth the man had made no attempt to deny, reached into one of the enemy's damaged battle armour, grasped the creature within and crushed the life out of it with one mighty squeeze. Phillip didn't know quite whether to believe that story or not, but the idea of what such a man, even decades older, could do to a mere human he didn't dare think.

'General,' he said, in what he hoped was a businesslike and masculine manner. Keele was what was known in popular colloquialism as a 'spartan': a vigorously homosexual soldier who deplored effeminacy or weakness in either gender. To Keele and his military ilk there were two types of people: those who fought their way through life, either literally or figuratively, and those weak scum who let others make their decisions for them. Phillip wanted to convince Keele that he was the former, a Samurai of the boardroom. Standing next to the man, Phillip realized how foolish that ambition had been.

'York,' acknowledged Keele. He was propped up at the bar, the latest in a long series of shot glasses in his hand. 'Don't like the ass on that barman of yours. Far too flabby; guy needs to get down the gym.'

Phillip coughed. 'Well, my staff's buttocks aside, I hope your people are enjoying the facilities here.'

To Phillip's colossal relief, Keele's granite face cracked into a broad grin. 'We certainly are, York. Fine place you've got here. No ass to buy, these days –'

Phillip gulped, hoping a request wasn't in the offing.

'– but then you can't have everything. Besides, most of my people are past that sort of thing these days. Otherwise, I'm just glad people like you still remember us. It's way too kind of you, putting us up so cheaply.'

Phillip smiled, a smugly charitable glow within. 'Well, it was the least we could do, General. After what you people did, all of us owe you for life.'

Keele shook his head with uncoordinated vigour, and Phillip realized that, in spite of his apparent coherency, the old man was absolutely smashed. Phillip's nerves started playing up again, knowing the former killing machine wasn't in full control. He'd heard stories about veterans' implants suddenly becoming active again after decades, as their self-repair systems overrode the disarmament codes.

'We just did what we had to do to survive,' Keele was saying. 'Of course, we should never have needed to, if we hadn't been betrayed so bad. Sure taught us not to trust civilians. No offence intended, York.'

'None taken,' Phillip replied quietly. The old man was clearly paying him little attention, lost as he was in the past.

'Yeah, we were shafted good and proper,' muttered Keele. As the old general stared into the distance, into his own past, Phillip mumbled some platitude and backed away. The old man made dismissive noises.

As Phillip walked away, he heard Keele mutter a name, undiluted hatred seeping into every syllable. It was a name Phillip, like every other resident of Mars, knew well.

'Tellassar,' snarled Keele, digging his fingernails into the bar's varnished surface.

4

WAKE UP, SWEET BENNY

Soaz knew he should never have mentioned the lock-picking thing to Seez. Although outwardly laid back to the point of catatonia, his friend could become annoyingly obsessive once he got an idea in his head. As they wandered out of The Hotel and into the cool Martian night, Seez had become fixated on one single idea for an evening's entertainment.

'Let's swipe a skimmer,' said Seez enthusiastically. 'Let's swipe one now.'

'No way,' snapped Soaz emphatically. 'Later, maybe. Now, no way. This gig's too sweet for us to go messing it up by swiping one of the guests' skimmers.'

'S'pose,' acknowledged Seez reluctantly. 'What do we do instead, then?'

'Down to Club Obiwan for a dose of the top stuff. No prescription shite, but the real deal.'

Seez perked up at this suggestion. 'Yeah,' he enthused. 'We got the cash. We owe ourselves some top-quality brain-meltage. Let's go.'

The night was drawing to a close. Academics and veterans alike were drifting out of the bar, retiring to their rooms, or the rooms of compliant others. Not the time of night you expect further introductions to be made.

Benny was sitting alone, staring at a RedStar cocktail charmingly named A Red Under the Bed and wondering how she was going to finish it without being violently ill, when a shrill voice brought her back into the real world.

'Professor Summerfield,' snapped Scoblow, rousing Benny from her drink-and-spacelag-induced haze. 'I would like you to meet Isaac Denikin.'

He was in his seventies, with a doleful expression that was entirely cancelled out by bright blue eyes. Like the other veterans, Isaac had grown out of any dress sense that he might have once possessed. Unlike most of the other veterans, Isaac still had all his own limbs.

'Hello, Isaac Denikin,' said Benny, shaking the old man's hand. 'I don't know who the hell you are, but feel free to call me Benny nonetheless. Any friend of Professor Scoblow's is, if not a friend of mine, at least someone I'll give the benefit of the doubt before stabbing in the lungs.' Benny paused for breath, and frowned. 'I'm babbling, aren't I?' Scoblow and Isaac nodded solemnly, in an indulgent parental manner. 'Never mind; sit down, and ignore most of what I say.'

Scoblow and Isaac did as they were told, looking at Benny over the stacks of empty glasses between them. 'Now, what can I do for you?' asked Benny.

'Professor Scoblow thought you might like to know about my experiences with Martians,' said Isaac. 'She thought you might find it useful.'

Scoblow held up the leaflet that listed all the papers that were to be given at the Conference. '*Untitled*, by Professor B. S. Summerfield,' added Scoblow drily.

'It has a title now,' Benny informed them confidently, trying to think of it. '*The Martians*.'

Scoblow smiled, her incisors poking out of her lips. 'Do you think that you're the first person to arrive at an academic conference with a vague title and no idea about what you're going to say? I think it's in the interests of this conference for me to give you as much help to . . .' She paused meaningfully. 'As much help to finish your paper as possible.' With that, she nodded politely to Isaac, made her excuses and left.

'How very conscientious of her,' said Benny, glaring daggers in her direction. 'So, Isaac, what would you like me to do in exchange for your time? I'm sure you didn't come here just to be interrogated by a second-rate academic.'

Isaac leant forward, an expression of profound concern etched into his lined features. 'You are right, of course, Benny. I do wish for a little something in return. I have been away from Mars for a long time. I have travelled through, and occasionally settled on, many different worlds and systems, some of which I have for a while considered my home. One place I spent a good few of my middle years on was a planet now in serious trouble: Tyler's Folly. Reports are vague, and I have not been there for decades. I believe you went there a few months ago, Benny. Anything you could tell me would be most gratefully accepted.'

There was something about this rather old-fashioned man with his old-fashioned way of speaking that quite appealed to Benny.

She bit her lip. 'Well, I don't think anything I could tell you would give you hope. The place was in a dire mess even then. But I'll tell you what I know.'

Isaac smiled warmly. 'Thank you, Professor. After you have told me of matters on my old home, I will tell you about life here, the place I spent my youth. A fair exchange, wouldn't you say?'

There is no easier burden to carry than a loaded moneycard in the top pocket, especially when one is out and about of an evening, intent on spending the cash on whatever pleasures are available. Seez and Soaz felt buoyant, both due to their heightened financial state and the prospect of what transient delights they might invest their wages in. They positively floated through the streets and alleys, chatting about nothing, admiring attractive passers-by. There was no poverty or violent crime on Mars; such people were shipped off to less affluent planets as soon as they arrived, or had their work permits and visas rescinded the moment they stepped out of line. The two men were young, on a natural high (albeit soon to be increased by chemical means), and in no danger of bumping into any of the horrors that might puncture their youthful idyll. Life was fine.

Upon reaching one of the cheaper commercial districts, they skirted around a row of small shops and nipped into a back alley. There they joined a discreet queue of a dozen or so bright young things from various species. None were tourists or members of the Martian elite. All were barely out of adolescence, dressed in clothes which were vaguely fashionable, and hellbent on attaining a good time. Mars was hardly the coolest planet you could live on; in fact, with its ageing population and cosy values, it was considered something of a backwater. A good eighty per cent of the population were on fixed incomes. That had kept inflation low for hundreds of years, and made Mars one of the cheapest places to live in the galaxy. As a result, the young people who manned the tills, cleaned the rooms and fixed the plumbing of the wealthy had substantial disposable incomes for their age, and could party as furiously as their equivalents on ultra-fashionable Io.

Seez rocked back on his heels. 'Queue,' he said simply. 'Downer.'

Soaz shook his head in the manner of one who has seen everything. 'I remember when we could get straight into the Obiwan. It was a much more exclusive crowd back then. These days, this place is just too popular.'

'Can't keep a good thing to ourselves,' said Seez philosophically. 'Gotta share the joy.'

Soaz shrugged in reluctant agreement.

At the front of the queue were the usual bouncers, two monosyllabic native Martians. Recognizing Seez and Soaz of old, they used a card-scanner to relieve the young men of a couple of sovs each and let them in.

Inside the club, a vertiginous spiral of thin concrete steps led to a large, sparsely furnished room. The lighting was a harsh, icy blue, rendering the exotic collection of species present in sharp monochrome. At one end of the room was a bar serving stylish, potent and crushingly expensive drinks. At the other end, a DJ mixed an eclectic blend of pre-logged tracks, spontaneously generated rhythms and snatches of signals downloaded live from the audionet. The genre of choice was nu-acoustic, a reaction to the repetitive, harshly mechanical electronica that was de rigueur for the generation who defended Mars during the siege. Intergalactic travel had slowed the pace of fashion, but generations still rebelled against their parents' and grandparents' aesthetic tastes.

The mood of the club was calm yet sharp, slightly on edge. The main floor area was packed to bursting point with humans and aliens dancing around each other in slow, pulsing movements, sipping on drinks chilled to freezing point, whispering secrets into each other's ears. Around the edge of the room were darkened alcoves where people sat, conversed, and engaged in more intimate pursuits.

Seez and Soaz worked the room, nodding acknowledgement to their favourite regulars, smiling warmly at attractive newcomers in delightfully sparse clothing. They danced the same slow dance as everyone else, Seez with a natural rolling rhythm and Soaz with a frenetic jerkiness. They spent extortionate amounts on Red Perils, and gulped them down with unwise haste.

Something else was required. In search of that little something extra they pushed their way through the crowds towards the darkest alcove in the club. There they found a three-metre-tall insect with flickering mandibles and a hard green exoskeleton. The insect's fierce appearance was somewhat undercut by the fact that it was drinking a banana daiquiri.

A banana daiquiri with an umbrella in it.

'Wa!cho#r,' chittered the insect.

'Don't mind if we do,' replied Seez, accepting the offer to sit down. By long agreement he always led the negotiations in these matters, Soaz being of too hasty and nervous a nature for the subtleties of bartering. Instead, the little man sat next to Seez and kept quiet.

'What you got?' asked Seez.

'Prak'nak duo'sh puu !X,' replied the insect, waving a spiny foreleg expansively, as if to indicate an Aladdin's cave of delights.

Seez shrugged nonchalantly. 'All good stuff, I'm sure, but we're after something a bit special tonight.'

'Qu'ok pah n!Xsk?'

'Now you're talking my language,' said Seez. 'How much for a dose each?'

The insect named his price. Tough but fair.

Seez whistled. 'Pricey, but I'll trust you on it.' He and Soaz dropped their moneycards on the table. With a magician's sleight of hand, the insect swept a foreleg over the table. In the place of the cards sat a couple of small blue capsules.

'Cool,' said Soaz.

'Down the old hatch,' agreed Seez. They took a capsule each, cracking them between their teeth. They both shuddered as the viscous substance within made contact with the membrane of their throats. Already well on their way to a heightened state, they downed their Red Perils to get rid of the taste.

'Most refreshing,' enthused Seez, standing up rather shakily. 'A pleasure doing business with you.'

'*Ch'o kkke'!X*,' replied the insect politely. He swept their moneycards through a card-scanner, then returned them. '*Pallachembro.*'

'Thank you,' said Seez, bowing. 'And the same to you and your good lady wife.'

By one in the morning the staff had tidied up the rest of the bar, and were threatening physical expulsion if Benny and Isaac didn't clear out and let them lock up. Reluctantly, and not a little apologetically, the professor and the veteran staggered out of the bar.

She'd told him her life story, he'd told her about life on Mars during the siege. There was a large amount of alcohol sloshing around her bloodstream which made her wonder how much she'd remember of his story in the morning. She was more worried about what she'd said to him. She knew that she'd used the word 'clitoris' at some point, and only wished that she could remember the context.

The lights in the lobby were dim, the night porter's reading light shining out like a beacon from behind the reception desk. Benny could see the lines of concentration etched into his youthful features as he read a lurid-looking paperback. The title was picked out in holographic pink text, which floated a good two centimetres in front of the book itself.

Benny was in no state to read the letters.

Benny realized Isaac had asked her which room she was in. 'B34,' she said absently. That book was the same one that the old woman had pressed into her hands at the spaceport.

Isaac laughed more than Benny thought strictly necessary. The night porter looked up from his book, his deep brown eyes offering to help out without him uttering a word. Benny shook her head, gesturing for him to keep on reading.

'Next door to my good self,' exclaimed Isaac. The elevator doors opened with a gentle whirr, and Isaac bowed deeply. 'May I offer you a lift home?'

Playing the game, Benny curtsied her acceptance, took his arm, and together they stepped into the elevator. As the doors closed Isaac broke away from her, slumping against the window, his head resting against the glass.

'Beautiful, isn't it?' he said, clearly unaware that his posture blocked Benny's view. His voice seemed to crack with the re-emergence of some long-buried emotion. 'So beautiful, but back during the siege it looked like it might all be lost, all destroyed. All because of one bad decision. But, look; they rebuilt it. They remade it all. It all came all right, in the end.'

Benny didn't know what to say, and suspected Isaac didn't expect her to say a word. So she put a hand on his shoulder and stayed quiet, until the silence was broken by the lift doors opening. Isaac pulled himself away from the window in one swift movement, like a soldier snapping to attention. Benny knew he had been a soldier, once, a veteran. But she couldn't see him as the military type. Then again, she had been fed through the military machine, been the daughter of an admiral, no less. She doubted people could see that background reflected in her present self.

Isaac put his hand on her arm, the palm cool against her bare skin. She could feel the tiny hairs on her forearm standing up in response to a not unpleasant sensation.

They stumbled out of the lift, and faced each other while leaning against the wall between their respective room doors. The lights in the corridor were also on night levels, dimmed so as to render Isaac in a warm, soft-focus glow.

He looked at her with an intense, watery gaze. 'Bernice, I don't suppose . . .'

She shook her head gently. 'No, Isaac, don't suppose. I'm sorry but, you know, since my divorce . . .'

She trailed off, and rested her head against the wall, her eyes squeezed shut as if to contain the chaos she felt within herself, as if she were worried it would burst out, destroying the face she put out to the world and leading her into a life of impulse and madness. God, she was drunk.

'Ah,' said Isaac quietly. 'I understand.' He squeezed her arm softly, then took his hand away. 'After you've been hurt it can all seem too much, can't it? No matter how much you feel the need to get close to someone, you just can't face the risks involved.'

She felt his hand stroke her bare shoulder in a paternal, friendly manner. 'Just don't chain yourself up for too long. You might one day find you don't believe all the excuses you told yourself. Then you won't forgive your younger self for all those missed opportunities.'

He was as drunk as she was. His hand stayed comfortably on her shoulder for a minute or so. Benny didn't open her eyes as it withdrew.

A moment later, Benny heard the gentle click of a lock sliding into place. She opened her eyes to find that Isaac had gone.

Soaz could feel himself being slowly dragged away from his normal sensual world. It felt as if the space behind his eyeballs was slowly filling with liquid. The rhythms and chatter of the club seemed oddly muted, as if he was on the other side of a thick wall. He watched the crowd. Bipeds, tripeds and quadrupeds were dancing frenetically, tentacles, pseudopods, arms and other limbs flailing about like a squid in a blender. Each movement left silvery trails in Soaz's vision. A pulsing white glow blurred the edges of his sight.

Everything around him seemed to twist and shift. The exotic species of aliens, the mutated and augmented humans, they all disappeared into a white glow. Soaz blinked, and his sight returned. In the distinct fuzzy slo-mo of a major hallucination, he was somewhere else.

The white glow remained. Gleaming, beige plastic tables were being wiped spotlessly clean by humans in red and yellow livery. The strip lights above glared down. The room was filled with humans, eating and drinking. Most wore suits of black or grey, occasionally augmented with a brightly coloured neck tie. Others wore brightly coloured plastic coats, and had items of luggage strapped to their backs.

They all sat around the beige tables, eating from cardboard boxes, drinking from cardboard cups fitted with little plastic drinking tubes. Music of astonishing banality tinkled out from hidden speakers.

'Wow!' exclaimed Soaz. 'This is unreal!' And almost as soon as he had spoken, the vision was gone. He was back in the club with a motley collection of aliens and humans, back on bloody Mars.

'Bollocks,' said Soaz, with real feeling.

Benny stumbled through her darkened room, not even bothering to turn the lights on. She kicked off her shoes along the way, and flicked a catch on the side of her dress. She felt the built-in straps release their figure-shaping grip. She slumped in the luxuriously padded chair in the corner of the room.

Benny rubbed her eyes. She couldn't go to sleep; there was too much to do. Her mouth tasted like the shavings from the floor of a Pakhar's nest-room. Running the tip of her tongue across her front teeth, she found them coated and sticky. Yuck. She really needed to try some of that swish Maalrii toothpaste she had seen in the bathroom. She needed to get out of her evening wear, corset loosened or not. She needed to start work on her paper.

With all these urgent matters jostling in her mind, Benny passed out in the armchair. Her head lolled to one side, a cricked neck in the making.

Soaz never regained the odd vision he had experienced. While his mood was pushed into an artificial sense of exhilaration, his senses heightened, he never reached that state of total immersion again.

He and Seez left the club in the early hours of the morning. The streets were bathed in a dull half-light. Soaz wasn't sure whether the glow around them was real or not, but it was decidedly soothing.

Seez clapped his hands together. Not having shared Soaz's strange vision, he was still in a 'good time at all costs' mood, hell-bent on happiness. 'Let's do it,' he barked.

'What?' replied Soaz. 'Do what? What the hell are you talking about?'

'Steal a skimmer,' said Seez in his slow, permanently stoned manner. 'Steal a skimmer, remember?'

'Oh, that,' said Soaz resignedly. He felt strangely different to earlier in the evening, and couldn't be bothered to assert himself. 'Yeah, all right then.'

'Cool,' sighed Seez, stretching out the vowel sound.

Soaz looked around the parked skimmers lining the streets, tutting to himself. 'This one,' he said suddenly, pointing to a rather bland, but expensive, Mundano saloon.

'Does it have to be this bit of yuppy crap?' complained Seez.

'Yes,' said Soaz firmly, stepping back from the skimmer. He took a running jump, landing arse-first on the bonnet with a hefty thud. The skimmer shuddered as he hit it, all the doors popping open.

'Impact release,' explained Soaz, sliding off the bonnet, then dragging his aching body around to the boot. 'Works every time with these safety-conscious buggers.'

'If I knew it was that easy,' said Seez, opening the passenger door, 'I wouldn't have bothered being impressed by your supposed "special knowledge".'

'That was just the easy bit,' said Soaz defensively.

'I still don't get it, though,' said Seez, lounging in the passenger seat while Soaz rooted around in the boot. 'Lots of skimmers have that safety feature. Why this one in particular? It's just a standard Mundano. It's even that boring grey colour.'

'Yeah,' replied Soaz. 'A rep car. Look at the magazine on the dash.'

Seez picked up the publication and squinted at it through a

drug-addled haze. '*New Salesman*,' he read. ' "The weekly journal of the League of Salesmen." So what?'

Soaz sighed, and hopped into the driver's seat. He had a small bag in his hands. 'These skimmers are fitted with breath-testers, right? To check you're registered to drive it, and you're not so pissed you're going to plough through a line of school kids.'

'Right,' said Seez, with an expression of anything but comprehension.

'The owner of this car is a salesman,' said Soaz, very slowly and carefully. 'A door-to-door salesman, flogging atmosphere filters or some such crap. That means we should be able to fool the breath-tester using this.' He pulled a small canister from the bag and threw it to Seez.

'Urgh,' said Seez, examining the canister. 'Really cheap and nasty breath freshener. Minty.'

'Precisely,' said Soaz smugly. 'All those wankers use it. Give it here.'

Soaz took the canister and sprayed a little on to a small panel in the dashboard. There was a brief humming, during which the two men held their breath in anticipation. Then the dashboard lights flicked on, and the engine roared into life.

'Cool,' enthused Seez.

Soaz started out at a sensible pace, getting comfortable with the skimmer's handling. Besides, they were still in a fairly dense area, and the lines of skimmers parked up against the pavements, moving or static, made manoeuvring difficult. Once they were out into the estates, with their wide streets and thrillingly sharp turns, Soaz began to pick up speed. There were few other vehicles around this late at night, so soon they were racing down the unobstructed streets, flying past blocks of retirement flats and ranks of cute little bungalows.

'Whoa,' said Seez, things getting a little too hectic for him.

'Regretting this?' asked Soaz evilly. They were now back in a more built-up area, heading towards The Hotel. But Soaz, now firmly in his element, showed no sign of slowing down. He entered The Hotel's skimmer park with a handbrake turn that left Seez green. Because The Hotel was so full, suspension fields were being used to effectively pile skimmers on top of each other, three to each parking space. These towers made for great sport, a maze for Soaz to practise his skills. In spite of his initial reluctance, he was really beginning to enjoy himself. The drugs and the speed were making his blood pump faster, his adrenalin levels going through the roof.

Seez, on the other hand, looked increasingly queasy. He stared out of the window.

'Oh FUCK!' screamed Seez. Soaz looked in the direction Seez was staring. He briefly glimpsed a large, human-sized lizard crawling down the side of The Hotel, using its talons to swing from one metal beam to another. In a matter of seconds it had leapt from the first floor on to a pile of suspended skimmers, then down on to the ground in front of them.

'Yoiks!' shouted Soaz, dragging the wheel to the left, desperately swerving to avoid the thing. For one split second, it turned, and he was looking straight into its eyes.

Red, hooded eyes, burning like phosphorous. Dark green mottled skin, scaled and leathery. A bright yellow crest on the head. Claws and teeth shiny as steel.

Soaz's manoeuvre worked, and they missed the creature by half a metre. Unfortunately, they ploughed straight into one of the piles of skimmers. The suspension field was broken by their intervention, and three skimmers crashed on to them. Soaz's neck whiplashed forward, his head nearly hitting the dashboard. Seez was not so lucky, his head meeting the control panel with a firm crunch. They were both lucky to be jerked down, as the top skimmer had slid off the pile, causing the roof of their skimmer to buckle.

'Arse,' snapped Soaz. He heard Seez groan unintelligibly. As the skimmer stabilized, Soaz heard the emergency releases click into place, the locks releasing. He reached across, unbuckling Seez's safety belt and rolling out of the passenger door. His friend yelped as he hit the ground. Soaz slid out of his side and stared around. There was no lizard to be seen.

'A Xlanthi,' he said to himself, barely noticing the hysteria in his own voice. 'Didn't you see that? I was sure it was a Xlanthi. Well, that's what I heard they looked like, anyway.'

'Nah,' murmured Seez, staggering over. 'Why would dudes as big-time as the Xlanthi be running around a skimmer park like low-grade grifters?'

'Goddess knows,' snapped Soaz. 'She probably cares, too. I don't, as long as that thing is a very long way from here. Which is where we should go before someone nabs us.'

Seez frowned. Blood trickled from his nostrils, his nose clearly having suffered a nasty blow in the crash. 'I don't hear any alarms, mate.'

'You wouldn't, dipshit,' barked Soaz, grabbing Seez's arm. 'They're remotes, aren't they? They'll be waking the owners up right now.'

Seez looked at the pile of four wrecked skimmers. The top one looked in fairly good nick, bobbing up and down. The other three, including the one they had stolen, were twisted in a steaming metallic embrace, and looked less than road-worthy.

'Good idea,' Seez said. 'This is one sculpture I really don't want to pay for.'

As he spoke, a light shone out from The Hotel. A silver-haired woman had stuck her head out of a window on the first floor and was staring at the wreckage, then at Seez and Soaz. Her cheeks seemed strangely flushed, her grey hair all over the place.

'You killed my skimmer!' she screamed, her voice more frightening than a legion of Xlanthi. 'You bastards!'

Seez and Soaz ran for it.

Bad news doesn't always travel fast – we just like to think it does. We want to believe that the misfortunes of others pass through our lives like a shockwave, throwing everything into turmoil. We want to be shaken by sudden death. We cannot accept the fact that we can live so close to such things without them touching us.

In reality, most bad news travels like any other news – casually, as a footnote in a letter, or an 'Oh, by the way . . .' in conversation.

News of death is usually like this, a note of sadness among the ordinary gossip of the day. Unless we are very close to the deceased, or the circumstances are exceptionally shocking, news of death rarely disrupts our daily routine.

It was like this when Professor Bernice Summerfield found out that Isaac Denikin had died. She didn't hear screams and reach him just-too-late. The messenger who came to her room was neither ashen-faced nor trembling with shock.

Benny was woken by a knocking on her door. She got out of her chair awkwardly, mainly because the cricked neck she had developed during a night sleeping in the chair meant she had to keep her head at an odd angle or suffer excruciating pain.

'Who is it?' she moaned.

'Inspector Alekseev. I'm with the police,' said a male voice, surprisingly politely. 'Could I speak to you, please?'

'What time do you call this?' she grumbled as she staggered towards the door. She hated dawn busts. She pulled the door open.

'Eleven thirty in the morning,' said Alekseev drily.

Benny looked at her watch. 'Good grief, you're right. What can I do for you?' She staggered over to the drinks synthesizer, and pushed a couple of option buttons. 'Coffee?' she asked.

'No, thank you,' said Alekseev, stepping into the room and closing the door behind him. He seemed an odd mixture of nervousness and confidence, surface uncertainty belying a deeper sense of self-belief. He was in his early forties, with receding brown hair, and what could only be described as a pleasant, open face with slightly defensive eyes. 'I'm afraid I have some bad news. The elderly gentleman in the room next door has died.'

'Isaac?' she asked sadly.

'I'm afraid so,' confirmed Alekseev gently. 'You knew him, then?'

Benny sighed. 'Briefly. We met last night.'

'Perhaps you can help us, then,' said Alekseev, a note of authority slipping into his voice. 'There are some matters concerning the death which remain unexplained.'

'What like?' asked Benny.

'I'm afraid I can't answer that,' replied Alekseev sternly. 'Please sit down, Professor Summerfield.' He perched on the edge of the bed, and indicated for Benny to return to the chair she had slept in. Just to be difficult, she jumped on to the top of a short cupboard instead, her legs dangling. Alekseev gave her a despairing look, but made no further comment. She sipped her red-hot coffee gingerly, and gazed down at him.

'So, what can I help you with?' she asked, taking another sip.

'Firstly,' said Alekseev bluntly, 'did you have sexual relations with Mr Denikin last night?'

Benny inadvertently spat black coffee on the plush carpet. 'What?' she demanded.

'A simple enough question, Professor Summerfield. Did you have sex with Isaac Denikin? Somebody did, and the night porter saw you two come up here together.' There was a strange intensity in Alekseev's eyes, a determination Benny was all too familiar with, having been stitched up for a variety of crimes – usually murders – in the past.

'No, I bloody well did not,' she snapped.

'Are you sure?'

'Women know these things, Inspector, trust me. I liked Isaac, but not that much. Besides, he's old enough to be my dad. Hell, he even has my dad's na–'

Alekseev stopped her rant with a gesture. 'I'll take that as a simple no. So, if you didn't sleep with him, have you any idea who did?'

'Nope,' said Benny, then proceeded to outline her talk with Isaac in the corridor.

'So,' said Alekseev. 'He didn't seem to be on a promise when you last saw him, or he wouldn't have tried it on with you. And did you hear anything later? Any voices?'

Benny made an indignant noise. 'Look at me.' She indicated the cocktail dress she was still wearing, which was now somewhat crumpled. 'If I was awake for anything more than thirty seconds after I got in, don't you think I would have changed for bed? I didn't even write my diary. I can't remember the last time I was so incapacitated that I couldn't whip off a quick diary entry.' She hopped off the cupboard and put her face close to his. 'Is this the breath of someone other than a person who passed out straight away?' She breathed in his face and he winced.

'Lovely,' Alekseev said, standing up. 'Is there anything else you could tell me that might help?'

Benny shook her head. 'Nothing, I'm afraid. I hardly knew the guy.'

Alekseev made a strange clicking noise with his tongue, as if thinking something over. Then he strolled over to the door. 'Thank you for your time, Professor Summerfield, you've been most helpful. I think we can close the book on this one.'

Benny was open-mouthed with shock. She was used to more severe and thorough interrogations. Where were the threats, the invisible bruises, the dogged determination to find a culprit?

'You're closing the case?' she said, aghast. 'But what about all those unresolved questions?'

Alekseev shrugged. 'Probably nothing important. He was an old man, Professor. Old men are generally close to death. We'll arrange with the veterans, see if they want a memorial service. Would you care to attend if they do?'

Benny nodded mutely.

'OK, then,' said Alekseev. 'I'll tell them you want an invite. Thank you again, Professor. It's good to get a quick result like this; far better for all involved. Good day.'

With that, he was gone. Benny looked at her watch. He had only been there a few minutes. Was that what an old man's life was worth now, an investigation that took less time than the *Chronicle* crossword? What about those unresolved questions? And why question her at all, if there weren't any mysterious circumstances to his death?

Benny realized she hadn't even been told how Isaac had died.

She slumped back into her chair, closed her eyes and massaged her temples with her fingertips. The whole business stank something rancid. She had liked Isaac. He deserved someone's interest in his death, for someone to make the effort to get answers.

Benny sighed. She supposed that 'someone' would have to be her.

5

THE PAST CATCHES UP

Benny left The Hotel at one o'clock, knowing that although they said they'd closed the case, the police would probably be watching her movements. They'd probably have someone tailing her. She spotted a man in a black cloak in the lobby, and marked him down as a likely suspect.

There were two things she needed to do: write her paper and find out something, *anything*, about Isaac without tipping off the police that she was interested in the case. While she'd been in The Hotel's restaurant eating her specially negotiated late breakfast, it struck her that there was one place she ought to be able to combine both activities: the Martian War Museum. She'd dialled up the address on her table's stick-on datascreen. Like most places in Jackson City the museum was within walking distance – it was visible from her room – but there was a moving pavement that went straight there just outside The Hotel.

On her way to the lobby, Benny unfolded the leaflet that detailed her expenses account while on Mars. She'd found it in her delegate's pack. Breakfast was automatically charged to her expense account, as were 'all reasonable expenses while on Mars'. An interesting choice of phrase, the exact meaning of which she would have to check later. She tucked the leaflet into her jacket pocket, for use as evidence later at her trial for moneycard fraud, and stepped out into the cold Martian morning.

The last time she'd been on Mars she'd been twenty-four

and in love with a bloke called Tim, so her memories of the planet were fairly rose-tinted. Most of her time had been spent at the archaeological digs at Mare Sirenum, uncovering the tombs of the Martian Lords and sharing a sleeping bag. The contrast with her current luxurious, sex-free surroundings could hardly be greater. But back then she'd learnt that two items should always be part of a Martian survival kit: good thermal underwear and a pot of lip balm. She was wearing both now. Her hat kept the bright sun and Martian sand out of her eyes, but the coat was hardly adequate, designed as it was with the perpetual Dellahan autumn in mind, not the desiccated Martian winter. She wasn't wearing gloves, either. Despite that, the air was refreshing rather than freezing, and there wasn't a breeze blowing. Benny slipped her sunglasses on.

She spotted the moving pavement and crossed Central Plaza to join it. There would be a network of these in the city centre. Again, not a feature you'd find in more modern cities, but there were still a few of them to be found around the core worlds. Benny knew the drill. There were three lanes, each travelling about twice as fast as the previous one. You stepped on to the one travelling at walking pace, got used to it, stepped on to the one that moved you along as though you were on a brisk jog, then on to the one about as fast as an Olympic runner. You could tell the tourists by the way they hesitated between lanes. The citizens of Jackson, even the infirm ones, simply hopped straight across from the first to the third lane. Benny took her time, but was in the fast lane before she'd left the Plaza. She stood, legs apart enough for her to stay balanced, dusty cold air blowing at her face.

By express pavement, the War Museum was seven or eight minutes away from The Hotel. It loomed into view a couple of minutes before she arrived at the door. It was a vast, imposing dome. Originally it had probably been a military pressure shed or hangar, but rebuilding and restyling over the centuries had obscured the original building like barnacles obscure a rock. There were terrace restaurants and balconies now, and holographic signs advertising the current exhibitions. There was a long moving pavement to the entrance towards which Benny made her way. The route was lined with ancient human war machines, all perfectly preserved in the dry Martian atmosphere.

Benny wasn't a military historian, but she recognized enough of the exhibits: a jet helicopter, which would find flying in the thin Martian atmosphere rather tricky; a twenty-second-century VTOL fighter; the casing of a groundbreaker missile; a squared-off robot tank. Military technology had its own aesthetics, barely touched by fashion. Other visitors to the museum were cooing their appreciation, or reeling off trivia about them to their companions. Benny could understand why some people got off on this sort of thing: the hard, clean lines and the knowledge that any of these devices could level a city block in moments. She only hoped that the people who felt a thrill seeing these weapons could understand her own discomfort. As she passed the latest Saab Royce MechInf wardroid ('the four point fourteen,' a young boy behind her shouted out excitedly), she could only wonder how many people it, and machines like it, had killed in its time.

She had reached the end of the pavement. She stepped from it, taking a moment to adjust to a world which she didn't move through unless she made an effort. The entrance to the museum was a long, wide, informal space leading to a vast airy atrium. Actual-size spacecraft and aircraft hung from the ceiling in antigravity fields. It would have been far cheaper to use holograms, of course, but people wouldn't cross the city just to look at holograms. They wanted the real thing, even if they couldn't touch it or tell it apart from the fake.

There was a huge interactive map in the centre of the entrance hall, and the visitors were all queuing to mill around it. Even from this distance, Benny could work out roughly what the layout was. Five halls. One for each of the Martian Wars, one dedicated to the native Martians, the last one a more general history of human warfare in the space age from the skirmishes on Earth dealt with by the United Nations in the 1970s to the Galactic Wars themselves.

As humanity spread out into the galaxy colonizing world

after world, it had encountered dozens, hundreds, of alien races. Remarkably, for the first few centuries this contact had been mostly rather peaceful, leading to nothing but cultural exchanges and trading links. There were a number of reasons for this, and every student of galactic history had written at least one essay or answered an exam question on the topic. There had been exceptions, of course. A few alien races had tried their tentacles at invasion, only to be swiftly beaten back. There had been one exception. The Solar System had been invaded in 2157, with both Earth and Mars occupied for a decade by –

'Excuse me, are you Bernice Summerfield?'

It was a young couple. Benny knew enough about her students' fashions to tell that they were both girls. They had their arms around each other's waist, and both shared expressions that indicated that they'd probably just been snorting something they shouldn't have been.

'That's right,' she said.

'Kicker!' the shorter of the two exclaimed happily.

'We love you,' the other one singsonged, cocking her head to one side. With that said, they drifted away and didn't even glance back.

'Er . . . good. I mean, thanks,' Benny called after them.

Where was she? Oh yes, the Galactic Wars. 'The War', as everyone still called it, as everyone would call it until a bigger one came along. Those two girls would have been born just after it ended. They'd have been taught that victory had been magnificent, a triumph of the human over the monstrous. There was truth in that, of course. Had humanity lost, then it would have been utterly exterminated, the Solar System and the colonies stripped clean far faster and harder than even the most ruthless human mining corporation could manage. But so much had been lost. Three generations of young people had been soldiers instead of poets and explorers. They'd died in their billions, far too young. All that potential and beauty lost.

But because the human race had been the last race standing at the end of the Galactic Wars, everyone called it a victory. The display in this museum would be the same as the displays in museums throughout the galaxy: triumphalist, oversimplistic, and there would be no place for talk of human atrocities or human loss.

The trustees of this museum felt that the Battle of Mars deserved a full hall to itself, separate from the hall dedicated to the Galactic Wars as a whole. Benny stepped that way. The Battle of Mars had been early in the Galactic Wars, and the humans had won. That was pretty much all that Benny knew about it. That was not the sort of thing that she would admit in public here. She certainly wouldn't be telling the veterans filling up the rooms in The Hotel that their fight was strictly local history.

This room was busier than the others seemed to be. It was obvious why, when she thought of it: the veterans were coming here to pay their respects, and with the anniversary looming there would be renewed interest from the general public.

The archway into the hall was guarded by two huge exoskeletal warsuits. They were empty now, but back in 2545 they would have had a young soldier in them, like the chaps she'd got drunk with last night. Guys with wetware interfaces in their brains and cybernetic implants all over their bodies. She walked past the holographic imaging chamber – if she'd wanted to watch a hologram display she'd have stayed at home. There were various exhibits and displays running along the walls of the hall. Benny picked up an Expositor from the rack by the entrance and popped one into her ear.

The first display showed a claustrophobic control room of some space station or other. Two waxworks were looking frantically at their display screens. 'June 2545,' a calm male voice began. 'Monitoring stations in the Oort cloud surrounding the Solar System register massive disturbances in hyperspace.'

The screens began pulsing and oscillating like the surface of a pond full of piranhas.

'There were three hundred battlesaucers, all on a heading for the Solar Planets.'

Benny didn't really want all the gory details, so she wandered past the next couple of tableaux. She worked out that the enemy skipped the outer planets, emerging from hyperspace inside the asteroid belt, on a heading for Earth via Mars.

She stopped at a giant model of Mars.

'The inner planets were ready for them. They had been expecting an attack for some while and had plenty of time to prepare.'

Points of light appeared under the Martian seas.

'Photon missiles equipped with FTL drives were shipped to Mars, and concealed in undersea bases.'

The next display along showed one of these. It looked as if it had been constructed from bits of old drainpipe. Benny wondered whether this was poor modelwork or whether it was meant to look like that.

'The plan was that the Minister of Defence, Tellassar, would order the launch of the missiles. Tellassar oversaw the construction of the seabases in person. Tellassar knew every detail. Only Tellassar could launch the missiles.'

True to form, the next display was an old 2D screen, showing what looked like an arms manufacturer's sales video. The sleek missiles burst out from under the sea and launched into the Martian sky. Once clear of the atmosphere, the FTL drives fired. There was a rainbow burst of light and the missiles darted out into space, seeking out the enemy saucers and obliterating them. Death had never been so beautiful, so clean. It was like some beautiful choreographic display. A dance number, with missiles. Benny watched as each parabola ended in a burst of light and a shower of sparkles.

It hadn't happened that way, she knew that much.

'Deep within Missile Control on Mars, the contact signal was received. Tellassar was summoned from the Government Bunker.'

The next display showed Missile Control, and it looked pretty much the way that Benny had expected. Emergency lighting, a large holographic map in the middle of the room with uniformed men and women standing around it.

Benny peered at the picture. 'Is this a genuine picture of Missile Control?'

'It is,' the Expositor confirmed.

'Source?' The military were not in the habit of having publicity photos taken during interplanetary attacks.

'This image was taken during a test missile run, three days before the arrival of the invaders.'

So, not a picture of the actual scene itself, but near as dammit. She looked at them all. Soldiers, of various ranks. Space Fleet personnel, like her father had been. Sidearms. They had various medals and insignia that she'd be able to check up on. She was pretty sure that there would be name badges, but at this scale it wasn't possible to read them and there weren't any zoom facilities.

She'd been staring at the picture for a little while, and she'd formed a small bottleneck. There were a dozen or so people waiting patiently for her to move on.

One last look, and a brainwave.

'Identify Isaac Denikin.'

'Isaac Denikin is the third from the left.'

Benny bent in for a better look. It was him. Five decades younger, a beautiful young man. Now, if *he'd* been around last night and invited Benny back to his room, then her answer might have been very different.

It had been him, of course. That fresh-faced youngster was now dead, in some police mortuary.

Benny moved on.

'Tellassar betrayed us,' the voice said, displaying its first sign of emotion. 'The enemy ships arrived. The records from Missile Control survive. There is no doubt that Tellassar knew that the enemy were at the gate. The automatic targeting systems of the command centre's battle computer locked on to the enemy. Three hundred firing solutions were calculated. There were more than three times that number of missiles at Tellassar's command. But the missiles were never launched.'

Benny stepped over to the next display. A large question mark. Benny glanced ahead, to see how much more of the story there was. A small party of veterans were all comforting one another. A sad bit coming up, she noted.

'Why?' The Expositor, so calm at the beginning of its

speech, seemed to be on the verge of tears. 'Why were the missiles not launched? We were betrayed. Mars was betrayed by Tellassar. Only Tellassar had the codes to launch the missiles. They were not used.'

There was a deathly hush. The veterans began to drift to the next display, obviously emotionally unprepared to deal with Tellassar's failure to launch the missiles. Old grudges die hard.

'But the missiles were detected by the enemy. Their fleet changed course.'

Benny moved on. Now, on a dozen holographic screens, the actual footage of the battlesaucers arriving on Mars was being replayed and replayed in endless loops. Every surviving image, from space monitoring stations to eyewitnesses with eyecams. All showing the same thing – a relentless wave of smooth metal discs the size of cathedrals slicing into the thin Martian atmosphere, shedding cargoes of bombs, missiles and one-man fighter units. It was an old B-movie image come to life.

There were pictures after pictures of the surface of the sea boiling and surging up in a great spout of water.

'They targeted the seabases first, destroying all but one. Only Tellassar's Missile Control survived.'

Another pause.

'The conclusion is inevitable,' the voice announced.

Nothing in history is ever inevitable, a part of Benny's brain warned. It was a standard warning given to history students throughout the ages, at least in the ages and parts of the universe where such things were believed. Trying to impose a narrative on events was an essential part of understanding history, but there were so many pitfalls. If you had a strong belief, you tended to see everything as a glorious confirmation of that belief. Marxists saw everything as the triumph of Marxism, capitalists saw everything as leading to progress and the imposition of liberal democracy.

She tapped the Expositor, pausing its monologue, and stared at the question mark.

The name 'Tellassar' did seem to feature really rather heavily in every reason that Benny could come up with to explain why the missiles hadn't been fired. So *why* hadn't he fired the missiles? That must be the question, surely.

She tapped the Expositor again and the answer was handed to her.

'Tellassar was in league with the enemy. Tellassar betrayed us.'

There was an explosion three metres to her right. Not a recording, a real explosion.

Benny's lifestyle was such that she instinctively knew both that the initial explosion wasn't large enough or near enough to hurt her, and also that there could be a second or a third.

Klaxons were ringing, security teams must know about the situation.

It was three of the veterans. Two of them were holding down the third.

'Traitor!' he was shouting. 'Traitor!'

They had been looking at a portrait of Tellassar. It was the next display along, or rather it had been. Now there was a large scorched patch of wall. The veteran must still have some obscure weapons system grafted on to his body, one that had been active for fifty years. It took both the other veterans to hold him down, and judging by the hissing hydraulics, he was stretching the capacity of their exoskeletons to their limits.

Benny looked at the charred wreck. She was staying in a hotel full of these people.

They calmed him down a bit and let him get up just as the first security team arrived. The guards carried stun batons, and were at least forty years younger than the veterans, but it was pretty clear that they weren't going to pick a fight.

One veteran stayed with his colleague as he was led away to answer some questions. The other remained. Benny recognized him from the previous night.

'Are you OK?' she asked.

He was almost embarrassed. 'I'm fine. Sorry about that, it must have been pretty alarming.'

He looked around. Just about everyone else had cleared the gallery.

'You're not the nervous type, are you?' he asked.

She shook her head. 'I've been in worse places than this museum.'

He nodded.

'Were you there?' she asked.

'I was at Ransom, strapped into a carrier with five hundred troops. The plan was that we'd get up into space once the missiles had done their work, we'd get out there and finish them all off. It didn't go to plan.'

'No.' Benny glanced back at the images of the saucers arriving. 'The spaceports must have been prime targets.'

'They hit us right after they hit the seabases,' he said. 'They dropped firestorm bombs on us. We never worked out how they worked, but they were a cross between nukes and napalm. Melted everything in their path.'

He tapped his face. 'I was very lucky. Escaped with radiation burns that my suit was able to cure. I was close to the shield generator. Only thirty survived more than an hour.'

Fifty years on, this was a story he'd told to his grand-children. At the time . . . Benny winced.

'Once they'd destroyed the missile bases and command centres, the saucers began to land. One to each major city; they either torched or ignored the smaller settlements.'

Benny rubbed her collarbone. 'I don't understand why they didn't wipe out the planet from orbit. That was their standard tactic.'

'They knew that humans were governed by emotions. They knew that Earth wouldn't launch missiles at Mars while there was a significant human population. So they used us.'

'A human shield.'

'Yeah. It worked, of course. The Senate voted not to wipe out the invaders by nuking Mars. By a majority of three.'

'There are eighty-five billion people on Earth,' Benny said. 'Barely three billion on Mars.'

'And most of them were pensioners at the end of their life anyway,' he said softly. 'Mars was lucky they won the vote at all.'

'So Earth sent in the troops?'

'No. Mars rose up against the invaders. The surviving

troops regrouped under General Keele; we got a few lucky breaks. Look –'

They walked over to the relevant display. Photographs and artist impressions of the resistance.

'Mars liberated itself?'

'Well, there were a few offworlders.' He pointed at one picture and the fuzzy image of an old man and a girl in her late teens appeared. He had thin white hair and an aquiline face and was wearing a stylish blue business suit. She was plump, with a mass of curly black hair. 'I remember them. They downed a saucer at the Argyre Dam and helped coordinate the final attack.' He scanned the other pictures. 'There I am, look.'

He was. Fifty years younger, but Benny would probably have been able to identify him even if he hadn't pointed himself out.

'Mars was liberated. Earth was bombed with bioweapons, but saved from the total destruction the enemy would have caused. Tellassar vanished.'

'Why didn't the missiles launch?'

'Tellassar.'

'Simple as that?'

'Simple as that.'

'Thanks.'

There was very little else to the display, just details of the rebuilding and a map of Earthspace with each sighting of Tellassar marked out . . . less than a dozen in fifty years.

Benny drifted into the gift shop.

A teenage girl was stacking the shelf, a robot was at the till. Benny tried her luck with the girl.

'Hi, I'm looking for a copy of the picture of the war room. The same one on display in there.'

The girl nodded, knowing which one Benny had meant. 'There's one in the Anniversary Book.'

She waved her hand towards a table. There was a stack of heavy, hardback books.

'I was looking for something a bit more portable,' Benny said. It wasn't the hundred-sov pricetag (after all, she could buy it on expenses), it was the fact she'd have to lug it all the way home.

The girl bit her lip. 'Not sure that there's a print of it.'

Benny moved over to check the rack, and after a couple of minutes rifling through them she managed to find the image she was looking for. Small, but any decent analytical software would be able to blow it up to the required size. She didn't understand the technology involved, but knew that photographs from surveillance cameras all used fractal imagery these days, precisely so that you could go back and check the minutest of details.

She bought the print at the till, saving herself, or rather the York Corporation, ninety-nine sovs.

And as she'd saved all that money, she didn't feel too guilty about taking her moneycard to the shopping arcades to flex its muscles. As she stepped on to the moving pavement that led to the Guest Arcade, she wondered where her conscience would draw the line. A nice warm coat – that was a 'reasonable expense'. A pair of gloves. Perfectly 'reasonable'. Unreasonable was somewhere between 'nice shoes' and 'more earrings', she concluded.

Mars was famous for its shops. Well, all the rich old people had to spend their money somewhere. They couldn't take it with them, and – try as they might – they couldn't spend it all on bingo and booze. So the Martian economy had seen the evolution of a vast number of methods of prising cash from pensioners. The historic parts of Jackson City had been converted into elegant shopping arcades. The old plastic domes, brick halls and subterranean chambers had been man's first settlements on the red planet, and this history was emphasized in the remodelling and renaming. There were two big arcades, named after the first two men on Mars. The Grosvenor was the more exclusive – Benny quickly discovered that it was too exclusive for anything more than window shopping and she felt a vague sense that she would never earn enough money to be at home there. The Guest was the downer of the two markets, but it was still posh enough to make a thirty-five-year-old professor with a Home Counties accent look and feel very scruffy indeed.

The Guest Arcade had been built on the side of Olympus

Mons, looking out east over the city and as far as Ascraeus. One side of the building was a vast perspex sheet, carefully supported by steel girders. Back in the early days of the terraforming, one gunshot to that would have caused explosive decompression. If that were to happen now then all the clonefur coats, fountain pen sets, wigs, leather handbags, golfing equipment, perfumes, cardigans, sensible shoes, hats, precooked meals, luggage and costume jewellery would have gone flying off into the violet sky. But the Martian air was thicker now, and the worst that would happen was that there would be a stiff breeze.

Benny stepped up to the map of the arcade, trying to take in the hundreds of shops on dozens of floors. A real labyrinth. The map was interactive, so she asked it to show her where she could buy a coat. She wasn't prepared for a whole array of adverts for shops popping up and hollering for attention. The colour and clamour had exactly the opposite effect to that which had been intended: she turned away from the map, deciding to search for herself.

Looking down this level of the arcade, something caught her eye. The man in the black cloak that she'd seen outside the hotel was standing outside a picture framer's, pretending to be fascinated by the exclusive prints of furry animals and fake native Martian art. The cloak was very distinctive, and that set a warning off in Benny's head. Plain-clothes policemen wore . . . plain clothes. The whole point was that they didn't stand out. She toyed with the idea that it was all some cunning double bluff, and that perhaps the police wanted her to know that she was being followed, but she rejected that after a few moments' consideration. She'd had a lot of contact with a lot of policemen on a lot of planets, and if they wanted you to know something they'd have a word in your ear and tell you straight.

She hadn't seen him at the museum. Perhaps he was just out shopping. It turned the situation from something out of a spy movie to a man staying at a hotel out shopping. Benny decided to work with that hypothesis for the moment, but to keep the situation under review.

Benny walked into the nearest shop and found herself

looking at a rack of beige coats. Cashmere, very heavy and rather expensive. But beige.

'Exquisite tailoring, madam,' the drone assistant gargled.

'Er, yes. Not really my size. Do you have anything a little more ectomorphic?'

'We can make them to measure, madam.'

She felt the material. It really was rather luxurious. 'Gosh. Is that extra?'

'No, madam.' There was already a whirring noise from inside the machine's torso. Benny could almost feel it sizing her up.

'I'm quite long in the leg.'

'I noticed that, madam.'

'How much?'

Benny opted to wear her new coat, which rather disappointed the folding robot by the till. It was warm, comfortable and rather stylish. It was cut to emphasize her rather meagre curves, and reached down to her knees. It was quite an old-fashioned coat, but rather an elegant one. *Retro*, she decided. Wearing beige at such a young age was clearly a postmodern, ironic action. It really did fit her like a glove, as well. Which reminded her: the next reasonable expense was a nice pair of gloves.

Black Cloak was ten metres away, and this time he definitely turned away from her to avoid making eye contact.

Benny's first instinct was to confront him, to ask him who the hell he was. But she fought it down. He could be one of the veterans, with all that weaponry still built into him. She remembered the smoking portrait of Tellassar in the museum. She remembered Isaac, the flimsiness of Alekseev's explanation for Isaac's death. There might be a killer loose on Mars, someone capable of killing an old man in cold blood. In the circumstances, confronting strangers didn't strike her as the most terrific idea that she'd ever had.

She was fairly sure that he was following her, but she needed to prove it. She zigzagged through the crowd away from him, nipping down an escalator. She had a quick examination of some amber necklaces and Black Cloak appeared again, nonchalantly loitering at the other end of the stall. His face was hidden behind the cowl of the cloak.

Benny nipped up three floors, popped into a shop, quickly decided to leave, stood in front of a window looking at domestic service drones, nipped across to a stall and bought herself a pair of synthleather gloves. He followed her every step of the way, but he'd become the hunted now. Benny was checking the rest of the crowd, making sure that he was alone. This was a coward, she reminded herself. This was a man that waited until you were alone. Isaac died alone. Black Cloak wouldn't make his move until she'd broken off from the crowd for a moment's solitude.

Benny's chance to do just that came sooner than she'd expected. A woman about her height, with about her hairstyle – a few more flecks of grey – and wearing a beige coat not unlike her camel one walked past. This woman was fifty if she was a day, but from ten metres away Black Cloak would be hard-pressed to tell them apart. Benny began tailing the woman, keeping close. Her moment came when they passed behind an ice cream stall. Black Cloak couldn't see either of them, but he'd seen Benny heading in this direction.

Benny shrugged off her coat, folding it over her arm with the lining facing out to disguise it as best she could. She waited for the woman to get away, to see who Black Cloak would follow.

She was rather shocked when he walked past Benny, not even registering her. He'd seen a tall woman in a camel coat, and assumed it was her. Now he was following the older woman just as intently as he'd been following Benny. Benny trailed him, keeping close enough not to lose him.

He followed the woman to a gift shop, where he watched her buy a couple of cards. He followed her to a creditpoint, where she transferred some money over into medical bonds.

After that, she went to the ladies' loo.

He stopped in his tracks, waiting for her.

After a second, he started moving towards the door.

Benny's eyes were suddenly wide. The woman was on her own in there, near enough. My God, that was what he hesitated for: making sure no one else was coming in or going out. She'd set the woman up, led her to her death.

Black Cloak walked through the door. Benny watched it swing shut, unsure what to do. Call the police . . . no time. Confront him . . . a psychopath who'd been following her.

She'd led the woman to her death. Dammit.

Benny strode over to the door and slammed it open.

Black Cloak was in the middle of the room, staring at the door of the only occupied cubicle.

'Looking for someone?' Benny asked, her voice echoing from the aquamarine tiles.

He jumped, startled, and turned to face her. She was already inches from him.

She kneed him in the groin, and he sagged. As he slumped, she reached into the cowl and grabbed his hair.

'Benny,' he muttered.

'How do you know my name?' she demanded, tugging at his hair, quite prepared to pull it out by the roots. 'Why are you following me?'

'It's me,' he said feebly.

She reached over with her other hand and pulled back the cowl. It was her ex-husband. It was Jason Kane.

Benny felt the same wave of relaxation and faint horror she always felt when she saw him, her top and lower halves taking the news in entirely different ways. Her brain was telling her very firmly what she should do, what the sensible course of action was. This was a man that she'd married too quickly; this was a man who thought that monogamy was the posh name for colour-blindness; this was the least reliable entity in the entire universe. Not only this universe, but all the parallel universes, alternate timelines and microuniverses, too, even the stupid surreal parallel universes where they had custard instead of gravity and woodland creatures played card games. This was a man that had hurt her. Leave him well alone, her brain said. Whatever he's doing here, why ever he's following you, just ignore him. Leave. Go now.

Various other bits of Benny were telling her brain that it was entitled to its opinion but could it just fuck off for twenty minutes or so. She let Jason stand up, and watched the look of relief melting over his face.

She kneed him in the balls again.

6

INTERLEWD

Jason lay on the floor, spluttering for breath.

'Jesus Christ, woman,' he gasped, 'do you treat all your exes this badly?'

'Just the ones who follow me around for hours, including into the ladies',' snapped Benny. Don't dare confess how few exes there are, she thought. Don't put yourself at any disadvantage. Just remember who's in the wrong room here.

'Well, fortunately for you I'm the forgiving type.' Jason struggled to his knees. 'Shall we go?'

Benny floundered. How dare he? Bastard. But then, his grin so wide and guileless, and the memory of the dry warmth of his hand in hers, hit her like a wave. Her sense of moral outrage struggled for an instant with her sense of style: then style won. How cool would it look to walk out of the ladies' room, flushed with exertion, with an undeniably sexy man on her arm?

'Come on then,' she said, and pulled him up. She deliberately didn't think about the touch of his skin against hers, and the strange little twist she felt around her heart.

'A beige coat?' he asked.

'Beige is the new black,' she answered automatically.

He wandered over to the mirror and ran his fingers through his hair, frowning at his reflection. 'Benny, do I look better with my hair smoothed down, or tousled?'

Smoothed down, as it had been on their wedding day? Or tousled and rumpled, the way it was on the wedding night? Is

84

there any force on earth more powerful than nostalgia? Benny watched his fingers teasing out a strand of hair from behind her ear, and thought for a moment about the shape of his fingers in her mouth. She wanted to rub her face against his hand. Did he feel the same? Was he watching her in the mirror, pulses racing with the excitement of remembering? As far as she could see, he was totally concentrated on getting his hairstyle just perfect.

All right then, you bastard. I'll be ice-cold. Just good friends. *Civilized*.

Just then, she caught sight of a frightened, elderly face peering round the door of a cubicle. The skin was heavily powdered with a biscuit-coloured base, the lipstick a shade of red just too dark for the hair that fluffed out to cover the head. The hand clutching the door was knotted and wrinkled, with ropes of veins standing out against the brown skin. Framing the wrist was the well-cut sleeve of a beige wool coat.

'Are you all right?' quavered the woman in the voice that went with a face like that.

Benny decided it was time to take charge. 'It's all right,' she said. 'This is my husband. We were just leaving.' Jason tucked her hand under his arm and they marched out of the ladies' room together, heads held high.

Halfway across the arcade, Benny suddenly remembered that she was angry. She wrenched her arm away and slapped him hard around the face. He stared at her, the picture of outraged innocence.

'And what were you doing following me?' she demanded. Jason looked hurt.

'I thought it was you, but I wasn't sure,' he said. 'I wanted to make sure before I started chatting up the wrong woman. You never used to hit me all the time.'

'That was when we were married. What do you mean "chat me up"? Isn't it a bit late for that?' Was it true? Did he still want her? Memories of warmth and darkness . . . Her mind had begun to forget what he looked like, but her body still remembered the rest.

'Just an expression.'

Damn.

'Shall we go and get a drink? I'm staying at The Hotel.'

'Me too!' she gasped.

'I know that. How do you think I found you? Come on. I need some alcohol to cushion the pain.'

Benny found to her annoyance that she was smiling warmly back at him, unable to resist.

There's nothing going on here. He's just being friendly. You're the screwed-up one out of the two of you. Hopelessly devoted to a marriage that's over . . . He's probably had sex with every sentient being that couldn't run fast enough since you broke up.

Still she felt a languorous warmth spread through her as he took her hand to help her on to the gondola.

The waiters bustled round deferentially. They brought the drinks on a special silver tray (Benny knew it was special because the words 'Priority Gold-Club Guest' were etched on it) and polished the table before Jason and Benny sat down. They even brought a fresh bowl of nuts. Benny was surprised, wondering what had happened to the you-can-pay-double-because-you're-an-insurance-hazard routine. It took her a moment to realize that the bustle was directed at Jason.

'How did you con your way into a place like this?' she asked accusingly. 'What sort of story did you spin them to get that sort of service?'

'No bullshit, I promise.' He took a long swallow of iced vodka, sucking an ice-cube into his mouth, gazing into her eyes all the while. Benny wondered if he was flirting with her. Or had she just erased all memory of his table manners? She wished her libido had more taste . . . Benny pressed her long legs together, trying to get control. I will not do this to myself. I will not act like a horny schoolgirl. What was he saying? Can't walk and chew gum at the same time, that's my trouble . . .

'I've – erm – I've taken up a new line of work. Gone legit.' He seemed nervous suddenly, playing with the lace doily their drinks had arrived on, rolling it up with the fingers of his left hand without looking at it. 'Would you like to come and have a look?'

'Where is it?'

'Um, in my suite. The penthouse.'

'The penthouse.' Benny knew she was breathing faster, almost shivering with excitement. She hoped he hadn't noticed. 'You can actually afford all this? Without any criminal activity?'

'Yep,' said Jason happily. 'Come on, and I'll show you how.'

He stood, helping her up just like the etiquette textbooks said a gentleman should.

The ride in the lift was almost unbearable. Benny stood next to him, feeling his warmth even across the inches that separated them. She ached to reach across to him and pull him against her, shred off his clothes and rub every inch of herself against him. She visualized it beneath her lowered eyelids, listening to the slow, steady pace of his breathing . . .

She stole a glance at him, and he noticed and smiled at her, and the distant friendliness of his expression hurt her heart. She was thinking these forbidden thoughts, unpicking the locks behind which she had secured her feelings for Jason, driving herself over the edge with longing, but from his expression he might simply be wondering if Room Service had cleared up after last night's Bundle-Bunny. Could he be indifferent to her? Or was he just hiding his feelings better than she was? She would count to five, and then she would do it. She would kiss him in four, three, two, one . . .

The doors dilated open on to the penthouse floor, flooding the lift with light and holographic birdsong. Jason held the door and Benny stamped crossly out, hating herself for wanting him. She felt cross and scratchy and rejected, although not a word had been said by either of them. But it was all in that look he gave her, the infuriating understanding smile she had felt on her own face when talking to Gerald Makhno. So it was to be just friendship.

'It's in the bedroom,' he told her.

She wanted more than anything not to be walking down this light, airy corridor that smelt and sounded like a spring afternoon in Surrey, towards the bed of the man who didn't want her. She wanted to be alone with her thoughts in her own room, lying in her bath, sipping bourbon and watching the dirty movie.

Is any of this showing on my face? Does he know? The ultimate humiliation.

'This is it,' he said nonchalantly, flinging open huge white doors with peacocks painted on them. His face was alight with some emotion – hope? A need for approval? – that Benny was too preoccupied to analyse.

'Oh my goodness,' said Benny, impressed in spite of her scratchiness. 'This is . . . it's just . . .' She gazed around her, taking in the off-white silk that lined the walls, the low white bed, the matching couch, the paper screens that divided off the bathroom. The exquisitely manicured miniature trees that filled the balcony. The peacock-blue rug spread at the foot of the bed. 'Do you really like this?'

'Have I finally got some taste, you mean?' said Jason wryly. Benny was too busy gazing to notice.

'It's fabulous.' She stroked the walls reverently. 'You hardly dare touch anything in case you get it dirty. Should I take off my shoes?'

'If you really want to do the thing properly, you should change into a kimono.' Jason flung her an armful of the softest white silk. 'You're supposed to wear one at all times. Although I'm sure they won't turf me out if they catch you still in real clothes.'

'Kimonos, the whole time? Where do you get dressed?'

'Still worrying about the proprieties. Actually I get changed in the lift.' He laughed at her expression. 'You're so sweet when you look shocked.'

'It's a glass lift.'

If he only knew what I'd been thinking all the way up here, Benny thought. I shocked myself. How could I let myself think those thoughts about a man I know is so bad for me? Why can't I feel this way about nice, constructive, reliable men? Does he really get changed in the lift?

'I tell you what,' said Jason, and now there was a hint of challenge in his eyes. 'Let's both put them on.'

She raised an eyebrow, reminding them both not to take anything for granted.

He held out his hand conciliatorily. 'You put it on in here, I'll get changed in the bathroom. I'll give you five minutes alone with my work. And then you can tell me what you think.'

She nodded.

He dropped a padded envelope on the bed, and scooped up another mound of gloriously soft white silk. 'See you in five minutes, Benny.' Then he grinned. 'Or maybe I should make it fifteen.'

He disappeared into the bathroom.

Benny undressed quickly and slipped into the kimono. The silk brushed sensuously against her nipples, making them tingle. She caught a glance of her reflection in the mirror and was amazed at what she saw. Her pale skin was flushed a delicate rose. Her eyes were bright. The clinging silk made the most of her long, lean figure. She tousled up her hair from its normally sensible crop. She could almost fancy herself like this . . . She stroked the softness of her neck, slipped her hand beneath the soft folds of her kimono for a moment, pretending she didn't know what she was doing. Pretending it was all unconscious and she was still sensible Professor Bernice Summerfield, fully dressed and tightly buttoned up, instead of this almost-naked, hopelessly aroused woman in an anonymous white kimono.

What was Jason's new job? She lay down on the creamy couch and slid her finger along the top of the envelope, debonding it. There was a book inside. She tipped the envelope upside-down, letting the contents plop out.

Pink lettering proclaimed that this was *Nights of the Perfumed Tentacle* by Jason Kane. The cover showed a hairy leg in a fishnet stocking with tentacles wrapped around it, tastefully photographed in black and white. She tapped the nanolectern at the base of the spine, so that she could lie still with her hands tucked behind her head while it hovered at eye level. She flicked through a few pages, and gasped.

. . . all I wanted was tentacle. Long, flaccid, marvellous tentacle. Tentacle! Tentacle! Tentacle! Tentacle! The rubbery grip of tentacle. The wonderful, pink-fleshed suction pads of tentacle. Tentacle's moist embrace. I couldn't get enough.

As I luxuriated in the dark green smell of freshly pleasured Earth Reptile, I realized that one partner was no longer enough to satisfy me. I was a man. A virile man. I had needs. Needs which only the denizens of Alexander 3 could satisfy. Denizens who knew every trick, every technique which could satisfy a man. A virile man with needs such as mine.

'Down on your knees and suck my reptilian pseudopod,' barked the Elder. He didn't have to ask twice.

I dropped to my knees and reverently took his blunt khaki protuberance between my . . .

Benny closed the book down hastily, shocked at herself – although not at Jason, she had to admit. If you were supposed to write about what you knew, then he was certainly more than qualified to produce this – stuff – by the gigabyte. It was the perfect lifestyle for Jason, she thought wryly – writing porn to fund expensive suites in plush hotels, no doubt to impress as many beautiful girls as possible . . .

. . . softened flesh spread like custard on the pie of my face. As I greedily sucked on the voluminous cloaca before me, I felt a strange co-mingling of shame and enjoyment.

I realized in that moment, as the taste of milk and honey filled my mouth, that society's conventions, that the law, that the other zookeepers, could all be damned. This felt so right, so natural. Suddenly liberated, I shifted, allowing her to reciprocate the favour. Her flippers brushing against me, she marvelled at my body hair as I marvelled at her smooth, smooth flesh. As her plump fronds unfurled, releasing their sweet nectar, her husbands responded, swimming joyously towards . . .

Benny glanced over towards the bathroom. The silhouette behind the white screen grew nearer and sharper. Then Jason was back in the room with her.

'So what's the verdict?' he asked. 'Do you like it?'

Benny wriggled on her seat, feeling the rub of raw silk against her calves. Stop it. Sit still.

> . . . She moaned with pleasure, stinging me again, because she could, because I was hers to command. I looked down at the weals on my chest, unable to believe that pain could be so sweet.
>
> 'We eat our mates,' she gurgled.
>
> She wanted to hurt me, she wanted control. But by demanding mastery, it came to me, my mistress had become my servant. I knew what she wanted, and now I could withhold it. And I had power over her. She knew it, too. I saw it in some of her eyes.
>
> She gasped, millennia-old conventions swept away in moments. Without another word, she rolled over on to her thorax, volunteering her wrists. I needed no further encouragement – I took the golden binders that so recently had marked me out as her slave, I slipped them on to her, held her carapace down as I . . .

'This is going legit?' Benny asked, to cover her discomfort.

'It's legal. Christ, it's almost mainstream. Twelve million copies sold so far. My royalties are a Standard Currency Unit a copy. The publishers want me to write a sequel.'

'I'm sure they do,' Benny said through gritted teeth. Her book was a seminal text in the world of archaeology, it was the product of a decade of meticulous research. It had rave reviews. Until now, she'd thought it had sold quite well, and as each meagre royalty cheque had arrived she comforted herself with the thought that people didn't really read any more.

'They like me. I'm the only one of their authors who writes under his own name. It means I can do signing tours and vid-interviews. It's semi-autobiographical.'

Benny's eyes widened. '*I'm* not in this, am I?' Her entire sex life with Jason flashed before her. Twelve million people had already read this book. She reached for it.

'Nope,' Jason said, a hint of regret in his voice. 'I sent it in as my autobiography, wondering if they'd be interested. The publishers edited out all the references to you and marketed it as porn.'

Benny cocked her head to one side. 'I'm not sure whether to be flattered or insulted.' But she definitely wanted to see those unpublished chapters at some point.

'It's the xeno aspect that they're interested in. It's a gap in the market. Everyone's *thought* about what it must be like making it with an alien.' Jason saw the note of disapproval on her face. 'Well, everyone but you, obviously. Not many people have actually done it.' He sat next to her on the couch. 'So you didn't like it?'

She tried not to notice the way the silk outlined his – his – Benny fervently searched for a non-sexist, acceptable word, and tried even harder not to stare. She could smell the peppermint of toothpaste on his breath.

'I didn't say that,' she answered, trying to sound cool and in control. It was hard to sound like anything with just two layers of whisper-thin silk separating them.

'So you *did* like it.' He moved closer. Now their thighs were touching. She found herself pressing against him.

'I – I think it is – very you,' she managed. His right hand touched the back of her neck. His left hand stroked her face, and then slid downwards, into her kimono.

'It's just that, for me, the description of sex on the printed page has never really done it for me, so –'

She could feel his index finger circling her nipple, swirling, swirling. Her insides were dissolving. She struggled to control herself.

'Very me,' he said, a hint of self-mockery in his voice. 'You mean hot, exciting and sexy?' His lips covered hers and she felt the dart of his tongue.

'Yes,' she gasped, leaning forward. 'And bad for you, so very bad for you, but something you can't resist . . . I can really see you making your mark in the – in the –'

His hand stopped its delicious circling motion.

'Yes?' he said, and his voice was suddenly like iron. 'In the what? Come on, Benny, say the word.'

She opened her eyes and looked at him, the word frozen on her tongue.

What had she done wrong?

'You mean the Sex Industry,' he answered for her. His hand fell away from her breast and lay in her lap like a stone. How could it feel so alien when a moment ago it had been an extension of herself? 'You still can't get your silly, transformed, twenty-sixth-century head around the fact that I once had a job working as –'

She put her hand over his mouth to stop him, tears welling in her eyes.

'A prostitute,' he continued, snatching her hand away and dropping it instantly. 'You just can't see past that, can you? You're never going to forget that, are you?'

'I didn't mean –'

'I'm still just a bit of rough with a complex to you, aren't I?' he shouted. 'I need *sorting out*. I need *therapy*. I need to exorcize all those demons and get them out of my system. All that screwing screwed me up. It never occurs to you that there might, just might, be a bit more to me than that, does it? That was *years* ago, it was over years before I even knew you.'

Benny, rejected and furious, felt a righteous wave of anger swelling over her. She took a deep breath and then let herself drown in it.

'Well, fuck you,' she screamed, tucking in her kimono. 'Just because I don't like the thought of other people . . . because I worry about what it did to you, all those men and women getting pleasure from you . . . It should be part of love, Jason, part of a loving relationship – not something that you buy and sell . . . How dare you get angry with me when I lay beside you all those nights and thought about the other people you'd been with, who'd abused you – and just for *money*? If you'd loved them, if you'd been in love a thousand times, or even just fancied them, just *fancied* them, Jason, but for them to touch you for *money* –' She started to sob.

'Well, at least they were honest about it!' he shouted.

Benny peered through her fingers. 'What do you mean?'

'At least,' said Jason slowly, 'they didn't sit there primly on the sofa, wanting me to get into them, but not daring to ask. *You* were treating me like your whore, do you know that? Like your *whore*. That's all you've ever wanted from me, isn't it? Someone who'll make the first move, so you don't have to take the risk.'

'How dare you –'

'You know it's true. You didn't marry me because you loved me, did you, Benny? You married me because you wanted to shag me. And you knew I wanted to shag you. And you knew I'd always ask first. If I hadn't made the first move, would you ever have grabbed me and said, "Come on, let's go"? Or would you just have gone back down to your room like a good little girl? I was just a tart with a heart of gold to you. You liked it, but it was a distraction. I had to fight for your attention and you always thought I was bad for you. Not what you do. It never once occurred to you that what we had was good, did it? Or that just the fact that I want you and you want me is enough to make a worthwhile afternoon? Well, I'm afraid I can't cope with that. Sorry.'

She wiped the tears off his face with the silk of her sleeve. 'Jason, I never meant you to think that –'

He touched her face gently, his anger suddenly spent.

'But *you* thought that, didn't you? I was faithful to you, Benny. I still am – but I bet you don't believe that, do you?'

'I'd better go,' Benny heard herself saying. And, no, she didn't believe him.

She stalked out of the suite, still wearing her kimono.

In the lift on the way down, she frantically reviewed what Jason had said. Was it true? Is that why she had married him? Had she treated him no better than all the people who had paid him by the hour, and double time for an overnight stay? She had loved him, she thought fiercely. She had loved him. It was Jason who had messed up. He was so unreliable, so frivolous

but that doesn't mean he didn't love you

and so absolutely bad for her in every way

like chocolate and afternoon sex and ice-cold bourbon and all those other things you thought got in the way of your work, you never thought love could be like that did you how could he doubt that she had loved him when she had married him in spite of all of that?

and how could he think you loved him when you let him know, all the time, that he was a diversion, a distraction, something you knew you shouldn't have but you wanted anyway

and how could she not go back up to his suite? She had to explain. She couldn't let his challenge to her go unmet.

Just for once you're going to be honest about what you want.

She pushed the button for the top floor.

He was lying on the bed when she came back to the bedroom, staring at the ceiling, still wrapped in his white kimono. He sat up on his elbows when she came in.

'I want –' She hesitated.

'You want to explain,' he said quietly. 'That's what you're going to say. You want to rationalize, intellectualize. You want to talk about it.'

'No,' she said. 'No, that's not what I want.'

She took off her kimono and stretched sensuously, stroking her body. Jason caught his breath, staring at her as she stepped towards him.

'I want you,' she told him. 'I wanted you as soon as I knew it was you. I thought about making love to you in the lift on the way up here. I don't just want a fuck, I want to fuck *you*. That's all I want. Isn't that enough?'

She climbed on to the bed beside him and pushed herself against the white silk that wrapped his body. He lay still, saying nothing. Unable to wait, before they'd even kissed, she unfastened his kimono and unwrapped him. He was golden-brown all over now, from exotic holidays and signing tours, she guessed, all his new-found fame and wealth. He was so beautiful, so beautiful, and she pressed her skin against his, rubbing herself against him.

Still he lay without moving. He wasn't going to cut her any slack, she realized. She was going to have to make all the running. Well, fine. He had been right. In the past, while always enjoying it, she'd treated their lovemaking as a distraction, something faintly beneath her that she had to be talked into, every time. She would make up for that. This time she would seduce him . . .

Jason moaned as her tongue trailed the length of his body.

. . . She wouldn't lie to herself, she'd concede at last that this was exactly what she needed and wanted, something she might have taken from every one of the men with no name who had crossed her path over the months since she and Jason had been separated. Something that now, by some twist of fate, she would take from her own husband . . .

For once, she and Jason were equal, both of them panting, unable to stop. For once she would take with pleasure the pleasure he offered her. Not romance, not companionship. Pleasure.

Why was she still *thinking*?

. . . Straddling him, Benny squeezed her eyes shut, thrilled at having what she had been thinking about for the last two hours. She opened her eyes again, rocked against him, totally devoted to her own need, utterly abandoned, as even Jason, looking up now to see her face, had never seen her . . .

'Oh, Benny,' he groaned, helpless as the moment overtook him, a little faster than either of them had expected. 'Oh, Benny, my darling. I love you so much. I've always loved you. I've missed you so much, so much. Will you marry me again?'

But Benny, lost on her own pinnacle of pleasure, didn't hear a word.

7

DRUNK IN CHARGE OF AN IMBECILE

Benny tried not to look too smug as she stepped into the lift and pressed for the tenth floor. Instead she tried to concentrate on the work at hand: the keynote address from the local bigwigs, the Yorks. The thought that she'd left a spent Jason sleeping in his room didn't cross her mind once. Not once did she remember him rolling her on to her back. Not once. More than once.

Concentrate.

Benny had a notepad and pen – hotel stationery – with her. She ran the risk of appearing to be a girly swot, but she wouldn't be taking notes of the speech. She had to give her own paper this time tomorrow, and at the moment it was at the 'just typing it up' stage that her students were so fond of. It was nearly finished. Only the words needed doing.

Actually, no. Before this paper was finished, she needed to have even the vaguest idea about its subject. That greying Pakhar Scoblow was right: she'd chosen the title for her paper, *The Martians*, because it could be about absolutely anything at all.

And that was the problem, wasn't it? If she'd called her paper *Shipping Forecasts and the Areopapacy 2418 to 2419* or *The Ethics of Martian Terraforming* or *Metatextuality in the Campus Novel and Space Opera of the Late Twentieth Century* then this would be easy. She'd just plonk herself in front of a terminal knowing exactly which sources to look up, she'd get her words down and then she'd read them out.

By choosing such a stupidly open-ended title she'd made it impossible to write the paper, while making everyone think she had some seminal work ready prepared.

Dammit, she liked her new coat, she liked silk kimonos and expenses-paid living in luxury hotels, she liked eating meals prepared by some of the greatest chefs in the galaxy, she liked them to be brought to her by smartly dressed young chaps who looked up for it, she liked having fantastic sex in penthouse suites with millionaires. Benny had nothing against the academic life, and the galaxy's universities were providing a very useful service, but she had always hoped that one day she'd live like this. She'd also hoped that she'd live like this for more than just the one day. And now she was in the process of blowing it, failing the audition.

The lift *binged* and the doors dilated. She'd arrived at the conference.

Gerald Makhno and Professor Scoblow were standing in wait for the elevator. Makhno, at least, smiled at her. He was handing out badges and leaflets. The Pakhar was waiting for the lift.

'I like the coat, Professor Summerfield,' Makhno said, clipping a badge to its lapel.

'Is beige really you?' Scoblow asked cuttingly, sniffing in a way that made Benny feel distinctly uncomfortable.

'It's not beige, it's camel,' Benny replied automatically, wondering what she'd done to offend the elderly gerbiloid.

Scoblow stepped into the lift, her snout still twitching.

'Not listening to the keynote address?' Benny asked.

The door closed before the Pakhar could reply.

'We've heard the rehearsal,' Makhno answered on her behalf.

'You're staying, though, aren't you?' Benny replied.

'Oh yeah.'

The Yorks were at the far end of the hall, checking that their autocues were working. The hall was filling up with people now – mostly academics, but with a good mix of veterans and other pensioners. It was nice to think that what they were doing here was being welcomed by the wider community.

Benny and Makhno drifted over to their seats. Bernice was dimly aware that the real purpose of this sort of gathering was to make polite conversation with other academics, find out their field of interest and divine the latest trends in one's chosen field. That, and also to find out where, exactly, it was possible to find funding these days, and who here was shagging who.

Benny heard herself make a pleasant sighing noise.

She would be sitting two rows from the front. She negotiated her way past a curly-haired man, his blonde companion and their robot dog, and took her seat next to Elizabeth Trinity. Makhno sat on her other side.

The Yorks were dressed in almost identical business tabards, although both had been made to measure. Christina's face was a mask of expertly applied cosmetics, quite a work of art. It must cost a thousand sovs a day to look like that. She was undeniably very beautiful – she suited the retro-Dynasty look – but little did Christina realize that every woman in the room would secretly be wondering what she must look like first thing in the morning. Phillip York must wake up next to a monster every day, all greasy skin and bedraggled hair. Like most businessmen – hell, like most men – he had just grown old. He'd left the cosmetic surgery and facial exercises to his wife.

Benny thought of an excellent first line for her paper. It was what she had been thinking as her shuttle arrived in Martian orbit: *five hundred years is a long time*. Without further ado, Benny scratched it into her notebook. Good start.

The Yorks moved up to their positions on stage, and a hushed silence fell without any prompting. Now, that was classy.

'My lords, ladies and gentlemen,' Phillip began. 'Five hundred years is a long time.'

Benny scribbled out the only seven words she had written.

Christina continued, seamlessly, 'It is five hundred years since the foundation of the University of Mars. In the beginning, Mars was a centre of excellence. Passage to Mars was expensive: the equivalent of something like fifty years of an

99

average graduate salary. But the graduates, the scientists and the engineers came, they came in their millions. They saw that Mars was the future, that mankind's destiny was in the stars.

'They were the best of the best,' Christina said. 'For the first couple of generations, anything was possible on Mars. There was a revolution in all spheres of human activity.'

Benny tuned out a little at this point. It was always dangerous when the words 'destiny' and 'revolution' turned up. This wasn't history, this was propaganda, and the same old story that every schoolchild was taught. Yeah, it had been expensive to send people to Mars at first, and yeah, anyone who wanted to come here had to pass exams and fitness tests. But a generation later, Earth was sending its population overspill here in its tens of millions. It wasn't the crème de la crème any more, it was all those people that couldn't get a job on Earth, all the bitter and twisted middle managers and friendless entrepreneurs who spotted a quick sov selling shitty products and services to a captive market. It was natural selection. The introduction of what used to be called market forces to Mars had seen the extinction of the utopians and the academics and the dreamers in the wild. Now they only lived in the reservations: the campuses, the vegetarian bookshops and coffee bars, the planning departments of computer firms.

Benny jotted all this down, and then realized that she'd not exactly endear herself to her hosts if she said it out loud. So, like everyone else in the room, she kept quiet while the corporate sponsors told her lies about the glorious past. The mighty warships powered away from the Martian shipyards, spreading the word and the light throughout the human galaxy. And when the aliens didn't like what they heard, then missiles built in Martian factories rained down on them. Humanity's position in the galaxy was forged, and Mars was at the heart of the foundry.

'As humanity spread out into the galaxy colonizing world after world, it had encountered dozens, hundreds, of alien races. Remarkably, for the first few centuries this contact had been mostly rather peaceful, leading to nothing but cultural exchanges and trading links.'

Benny was adding her own mental annotations. There were a number of reasons why Earth's contact with alien races had been so peaceful. There had been exceptions, of course. The Solar System had been invaded in the 2150s, and the homeworld had been occupied for a decade. The Martians were not the only species brought to the brink of extinction to clear the way for human settlements.

'In fact, as the human race spread, so did *humanity*. Many alien races found that our sports, our religion, our way of doing things, were the best ways.'

For a few hundred years this pattern continued: limited interplanetary conflicts, local threats to humanity that had to be overcome. But by the beginning of this century, the frontiers of Human Space had begun to encroach on the territory of some of the big galactic players. For the first half of the century, Earth Intelligence thought that the greatest threat was from the Dragons, reptilian humanoids with an empire slightly bigger – and a lot more established – than Earth's. The truth was that in the unexplored sectors beyond Dragon Space there were warlike races that had ruled their vast empires for thousands of years. The humans and Dragons were minnows swimming alongside whales and sharks.

The Galactic Wars.

A generation later, as the Yorks' speech demonstrated, the War was the stuff of legend. It was simple, black-and-white stuff. The good humans fighting the evil aliens, guided to inevitable victory by brilliant leadership and a sense of cosmic justice. Humanity was one of the sharks now, and that was a cause for celebration. But while the Yorks were talking about the glorious future, Benny was more worried about the damage done to the past.

This was something with which the Yorks agreed.

'During the War, the universities and libraries and archives were all prime targets. The computerized information networks that linked the colonies were infiltrated and corrupted. Books and their readers had been burnt, knowledge had been lost.

'The great universities that had survived like Mars, St Oscar's, Berkeley and Loughborough were now beacons of light in a galaxy that was threatened with a new dark age.

'And so, once again, Mars is important in the preservation and furtherance of human knowledge. It must never be allowed to fall to the darkness. Thank you.'

A polite round of applause, but not the rapture that they might have expected.

Benny came out of the opening ceremony not entirely sure of what she had just listened to.

She was almost totally absorbed in her paper, facts and theories spinning around in her head, slowly coalescing into a coherent argument. She allowed herself to be swept along in the between-lecture surge to the cafeteria, bar and so on. Barely aware of her surroundings, she drifted along, immersed in her own thought processes. Although the theory seemed to be shaping up nicely, she was sure there was something important she was neglecting . . . Oh yes, she thought. That whole 'mysterious death' business. Well, there was no way she had time to investigate. Someone else would have to do it. Unfortunately, there was only one 'someone else' available.

She turned on her heels and headed for the elevator. The coffee up in the penthouse would almost certainly be better, anyway.

The elevator reached the top floor and the door dilated. The security door was still closed, and the word 'bastard' had been scratched into it. Benny examined the damage; it had been clawed into the varnish. Odd. Well, anyway, she banged on the door.

'Yah!' screamed Jason as he flung the door open. He was semi-crouched in a fighting stance, and was wielding a chairleg padded with foam rubber, his favourite type of minimum-bruising-maximum-internal-damage weapon. He was unshaven, still wearing his kimono and to her great surprise was wearing cheap plastic reading glasses. With his receding hairline, and slight double chin, he seemed much older than the Jason she married. A scared old man, prematurely aged by too much fast living. Her hormones hadn't let her notice all that yesterday.

'Oh, it's you,' said Jason, gasping for breath. He tossed his makeshift club over his shoulder. 'Come in, come in. Change.'

He held out a kimono.

'I can't stay, Jason,' Benny said, trying to hit a combined note of firm authority and maternal sympathy. Changing the subject, she looked around. 'Who the hell have you pissed off now?'

'Oh, nobody,' he replied lightly. He slumped into a swivel chair in front of his terminal, and tapped a button so that the on-screen text disappeared before Benny could get a closer look.

'I've always thought that not having to dress up for work was one of the greatest boons of the creative life,' said Benny, collapsing on to the copious sofa which was bigger than the bed in her room. 'But, seeing the state of you today, I can now see the benefits of uniforms and dress codes. You look like shit.'

'Gee, thanks,' replied Jason, baring his teeth in a fierce smile.

Benny shrugged. 'I need you to do some detective work for me.'

Jason took off his glasses and rubbed his eyes. When he took his hand away he had Benny pinned down with an intense stare.

'What?' he asked. He seemed unable to comprehend what she was saying.

'I said, "I need you to do some detective work for me." *Comprendez*?'

Jason laughed; a short, bitter sound. 'Why? Is it a suicide mission, one of your dumb-ass crusades?'

Benny had heard quite enough. 'Look, you want me to trust you, and that's what I'm doing. You know how much I've always wanted to be a proper academic. This lecture I'm doing tomorrow is my big shot. You must realize how much this means to me. But there's something else that's come up. Just do this for me, Jason. I need you to do this.'

Jason rolled his head back and stared at the ceiling. When he tipped his head forward to look at her, there was an expression of resigned sadness in his eyes. 'You know I couldn't refuse you,' he said quietly. 'So, what do I need to detect?'

'Isaac Denikin. He died the other night, in the room next to mine. I want to know why.'

'Stay?' he asked.

'I want to, but I can't. I need to write this paper.' Benny leant forward, meeting Jason's stare. 'Thank you for doing this, Jason. It means a lot.' She stood up, kissed him gently on the cheek, then left without saying another word. As she walked back to the elevator she could feel tears pressing at the back of her eyes, but she refused to let them escape.

When Benny had left, Jason put his mind to the matter in hand. In other words, the business of detection, and how to do such business in a manner guaranteed to win back your ex-wife. And he was completely, utterly certain that was what he wanted. Screw the dead guy; he was beyond help. What mattered was getting Jason's life, his marriage, back.

That moment yesterday when she came back for him. Seeing her in the doorway. The fluid movement of her kimono falling away. Her body was a work of art, so familiar, but so welcome. Her weight and her warmth and the taste of her skin and the smell of her hair.

Benny. Her presence made his work virtually impossible. How could he give a shit about the sordid business of screwing aliens – let alone writing about it – when she was there, the only sentient being he really wanted to be with? He remembered when they had first met, the only two humans on a distant alien world. The initial common experience of being from the same species was what brought them together, but as time went on Jason had felt a deeper empathy between them. They both knew the universe was full of pain and misery, which would sneak past your defences and screw up your life the second you let your guard down.

Jason knew he needed Benny, and that she needed him just as much. They needed each other, to cling to during the darkest part of the night.

He tried to suppress these thoughts. Moping wouldn't get

him anywhere. What was needed was action, and for that he needed a first-class, top-notch team on board to help him. He knew just the people.

Seez and Soaz may not have had their own skimmer, or at least one they had any right to possess, but they did have their very own dinghy. During the dead hours of the afternoon, when the canals were fairly free of traffic, they would paddle out into the plains, find a nice spot and chill out.

With wallets and heads aching from the previous night, that was how they had decided to spend this particular day. They had drifted to a secluded part of Tharsis and generally messed around, listening to music, lazing about and kicking the red stones so they sent trails of thick Martian dust into the air.

Seez lay on the dusty ground, his eyes closed and his head resting on the collapsed dinghy. He could hear the *plop* sound of Soaz skimming rocks on the canal's silvery surface. His fuzzy senses were feeling a lot more lucid than when he had woken that morning, and he had just about managed to shift the memory of the previous night. He suspected Soaz was having more trouble at this, as the skimming stones sounded increasingly clumsy and violent in their passage.

Seez's idyll was disturbed by the ringing of his mobile. Without opening his eyes, he plucked it from the hook on his belt, held it to his ear and flicked the talk switch.

'Seez,' he said simply.

'Kane here,' said Jason on the other end. 'You and your mate busy? Stuff going down, if you're interested.'

Seez hit the mute button, opened his eyes, and turned his head towards an expectantly hovering Soaz. 'It's the mullet man,' he explained. 'I think he's got a job for us. Are we up for it?'

'Christ, yes,' replied Soaz. 'Anything to pass the time.'

Seez tossed the dinghy to Soaz to inflate, and returned his attention to Jason. 'Ready to go, man. We'll meet you wherever you need us.'

By the time they had downed four pints each Jason was beginning to regret choosing The Printer's Devil as a meeting place. Usually, such a meagre skinful would barely have impaired his judgement. But this was Old Red Devil, a primate-modified version of an old Martian ale, and the liquid equivalent of being hit by a small car.

Trying not to panic about the fact that he could no longer feel his legs, Jason decided to bring matters to order. He interrupted Seez and Soaz's conversation about the relative acting merits of Shannon Tweed and Emma Thompson by slapping both palms against the table.

'Now, boys,' he said, once he had their attention. 'How do we go about this detecting business?'

Seez mused on this, melodramatically frowning. 'Evidence,' he eventually concluded. 'What we need is to gather some evidence.'

Jason sighed deeply. 'Great plan, Endeavour. Care to expand on this precious nugget of wisdom?'

'Certainly,' said Seez confidently. 'Evidence can be of various kinds. Testimony, which can be gathered through interviews. Then there's the physical evidence, to be recovered from the scene of the crime.'

'And how do we obtain this evidence, of either kind?' asked Soaz.

Seez looked smug. 'That's the simple part; Jason's missus found the police deeply unhelpful. However, they will doubtless have collected all the required evidence already. So, instead of getting our own evidence, we go and nick theirs.'

There was a momentary silence, as Soaz and Jason absorbed the implications of Seez's plan.

Jason shrugged. 'Seems a good enough plan to me. Let's do it.'

Seez gestured to his empty glass. 'One for the road first, though.'

Soaz should have known that Seez would find another terrible idea for the use of his lock-picking skills.

'Come on, lad,' said Jason encouragingly. 'You're the master of unlocking.'

'Bad grammar, that,' Seez chastened Jason.

'Will the both of you just shut up,' snarled Soaz, crouched

down before the lock on the police mobile incident room. He had wired together a Lucky Lotto random number generator and an infrared signal transmitter, the latter of which was taped to the locking mechanism. Theoretically, this type of lock worked by the transmission of a simple number string coded into a remote key transmitter. Chance alone dictated that they would hit the right number within a matter of minutes.

'Come on,' he coaxed the lash-up, fully aware that if they were caught he would be the prime prosecution target, while Jason and Seez would portray themselves as insensible accomplices. If anything, the three of them were equally insensible. Soaz had barely managed to assemble his amateur skeleton key without soldering a hole through his hand. Fortunately, the alley the mobile incident room was parked in was deserted, as was the incident room itself; the police were clearly working to a strict mid-morning-to-just-after-lunch regime.

'Gotcha,' hissed Soaz with satisfaction as the door clicked open. He indicated for Seez and Jason to follow him in, but carefully. Although the body of the mobile incident room was of a standard, production-line quality – in other words mediocre, with security to match – it was still nonetheless a police vehicle, and could have more sophisticated counter-measures within.

The interior was, in fact, sparse bordering on the pathetic. One end of the vehicle was dominated by an industrial refrigeration unit, presumably containing the remains of the unfortunate Mr Denikin. None of the three men opted to go and check the contents for themselves. Instead, they opted to congregate around the only other feature of the incident room: a large, wobbly wooden table, surrounded by a number of cheap plastic chairs of the kind found in schools and waiting rooms. Gingerly, they sat in a chair each, the uncomfortable seats squeaking and groaning, like ageing servants weary from decades of carrying their masters' weight.

'Right,' said Jason, indicating the items on the table. 'Let's go through this item by item, and try and leave it as it was before.'

'In other words, a bloody mess,' added Seez.

Soaz could only agree. The table was predominately covered in unwashed coffee cups, sandwich wrappers and associated detritus. Somewhere under all that lot, papers and folders could just be made out.

'OK, let's excavate,' said Seez. Jason glared at him, but said nothing. The three of them began to lift up cups and rubbish, sliding out the papers from beneath.

Soaz's first discovery was a post-mortem report. 'Cool,' he said, brushing biscuit crumbs off the cover. The first page was a précis of the report as a whole, dominated by a generic drawing of an adult male human on which the pathologist could illustrate the location of wounds, identifying marks, et cetera. Aside from an eyepatch and a twirly moustache, this diagram's noticeable addition was a huge, jagged shape in the centre of the chest, sketched on in red biro.

'Think I may have something here, guys,' he muttered, flicking forward to the section on the chest wound. When he found it, he skimmed the details in seconds. Heart removed . . . claw marks . . . colossal strength . . .

'Oh dear,' said Soaz. 'It's the Xlanthi!'

'What?' exclaimed Jason, plucking the report from Soaz's limp grip. He'd heard of the Xlanthi, of course. A race of cannibal lizards from the notorious star system of Castonier. But he didn't know very much about them.

'If it had been a Xlanthi then there wouldn't be very much of Mr Denikin left. Urgh,' he said, seeing the photographs of the wound.

'What?' echoed Seez.

'His heart was ripped out,' said Soaz numbly. 'By some huge animal. And we saw it; it was a Xlanthi. We were lucky it didn't shred us as well.'

'Oh yeah,' said Seez casually. 'The Xlanthi, I remember that.'

'Good for you, asshole!' snapped Soaz. 'And stop smirking, this isn't funny.'

'Oh man, the Xlanthi!' repeated Seez, giggling.

'Quit it!' shouted Soaz.

'Xlanthi, my hairy arse,' said Jason, tossing the report dismissively at Soaz. 'You two were just off your tits, as bloody usual. Serves me right for hiring a couple of bloody slacker wasters –'

'Hey!' interrupted Soaz. 'Who got you into this bloody place anyway?!'

'And who are you calling a slacker?' added Seez slothfully.

Soaz and Jason were on their feet now, glaring at each other over the table. Soaz could feel his anger increasing. 'Look, you balding git, we've put ourselves out for you and your bloody slapper –'

'You take that back, you –'

'Hey, guys –'

'You bast–'

'Ow!'

'Oi!'

Their impromptu brawl was interrupted by a cough from the doorway. Soaz loosened his grip on Jason's throat, and looked around to see a kind-faced gentleman looking on in interest.

'Hello,' said the newcomer, not unkindly. 'I'm Detective Alekseev. You three are all nicked.'

'Is that your wife, then?' Seez asked, peering over the desk. 'Don't think much of that.' In spite of the trying circumstances, and the punch-up that had landed them there, he couldn't resist having another go at baiting Jason.

'Yes,' Jason said glumly, ignoring the slight against his beloved. 'Or, to be more precise, no. It's my ex-wife.'

'I was expecting someone a lot rougher,' Soaz said. 'By your standards, she must be a hot ticket.'

'Those legs,' Seez breathed admiringly. 'Not bad for her age.'

'No wonder we didn't see you down in the bar last night. Must beat shagging that hamster.' Soaz hesitated. 'Mustn't it?'

'I mean,' Seez continued, 'she's too old for me, of course. Well, too old for me when I'm sober and have my contacts in, but I bet she goes like a –'

'Do you mind?' Jason asked.

Alekseev came over to them and handed back their work permits. 'You're free to go, subject to the bail conditions detailed there. Any further violation will automatically revoke your visas, and may lead to a prison sentence.'

All three of them stood, even Seez, knowing that this was a time for looking guilty and keeping a lid on the wisecracks. The biddies on the Martian Rotariat liked their planet to stay crime-free. If they withdrew your work permit, you were escorted to one of the ports, shoved in the first ship and then fired off the planet. At that point, you had to tell the captain that actually, no, you can't pay for the passage and that all your official papers have been impounded. So, no, that's right, you didn't really officially exist, and if he were to throw you out of his airlock no one would ever even notice. Fascist bastards, thought Seez petulantly.

Kane's wife didn't speak as they walked over to her, and she didn't need to. She looked like one of those cartoon characters with a scribble cloud hovering over its head to show it was angry. This hostility was aimed squarely at Kane.

They walked back over to the moving pavement in total silence, but there was some serious marital telepathy going on. Seez and Soaz left Benny and Jason to it. They had problems of their own. Previously their less legal activities had gone unpunished, deliriously exciting adventures with little consequence. Now that period of their development had come to an end, they were moving from reckless youth to adulthood, with all the responsibility that implied. It was an end of an era for them both. At least that's how it felt now that the alcohol had worked its way out of their systems.

'This has not been a good day,' mused Soaz. 'Not good at all.'

Seez merely grunted in agreement.

'We have tarred our previously pristine criminal records, bruised ourselves in physical combat with a supposed ally and failed to be even paid for our many troubles.'

Seez grunted again. 'He didn't even pay us.'

'Not a good day,' Soaz reiterated. 'Where to now?' he asked.

'Hotel,' said Seez, who reverted to his least talkative when irked by his troubles. 'Drink.'

'Good idea,' said Soaz, without that much enthusiasm. They walked the rest of the way in silence. As they crossed the Plaza, they were passed by a female Pakhar in decorator's overalls, carrying a dribbling can of pink paint and whistling to herself. She had clearly been doing some work at The Hotel.

Soaz shook his head after she had passed. 'Man,' he said wearily. 'They're even getting other people in to do our jobs.'

Seez only grunted in reply.

'I can't believe that an hour ago I was ready to marry you again,' Benny said, the first words since they'd got back to her room, or even since they'd left the police station.

'Were you?' Jason said, a tiny chink of hope appearing on his face.

'What the hell are you undoing your shirt for?'

'Y'know, I . . .'

The next word Benny said was 'Jason', but there was no doubt from her tone of voice about how she was defining the word. *Singular noun, be very careful what you do or say next if you value your life.*

Jason paused.

'I'm so terribly, terribly sorry,' he said.

'You're *always* sorry. I shouldn't have bailed you out,' she said softly. 'I should have let them throw you off the planet.'

Jason was rummaging in his cloak. 'Here, look.'

He handed her his moneycard.

'It's not the money. It's not the damn money,' she said, feeling the first tear in her eye.

He pressed the card into her hand. 'What's mine is yours. Richer or poorer.'

Benny snorted.

'I mean it. I'll do anything for you.' He leant towards her.

Benny smiled. 'Anything?'

'Yeah.' There was something very satisfying about the glimmer of hope on his face, particularly because she knew what she'd say next.

'Get out of my room. If I want to see you again I'll call you. Skip bail and, God help me, I'll have every DK in the galaxy on your case.'

Jason hesitated, and then realized that it was the best offer he was going to get. He scooped up his cloak and left.

Benny sat on the end of the bed, turning the goldcard over and over in her hand, trying to get that damn tear out of her eye. She'd wanted to trust him, she'd wanted to believe him and he'd let her down again. He might have made his millions, but he was still filth. She was intelligent, she was cunning, she could outsmart supervillains and monster over-lords with plans to conquer the galaxy. How could she be taken in every time by a little git who couldn't even organize his beard to grow beyond the 'scruffy stubble' stage?

Finally, she reached over and slotted the moneycard into the computer terminal and dialled up the balance. She could do all that without getting off the bed.

Two hundred Martian sovereigns.

About one more night in that penthouse suite of his, assuming he didn't want room service or watch a subscription vid. A week's wage or an evening's supply for his druggie mates.

Benny slumped, wondering if the Conference organizers would consider hiring a hitman to bump off an ex-husband to be a reasonable expense. Or if she could find someone willing to do the job for two hundred sovs.

He wasn't even rich.

Benny was crying again.

8

KANE UNABLE

It wasn't Jason's fault that Benny's paper wasn't progressing; that was the thing that annoyed her most. Truth be told, the half an hour it had taken to get down to the police station and bail them out was insignificant, and she'd actually been quite glad of the distraction.

Jason had managed to go a whole three hours without disturbing her, and she had used that time wisely. She'd made herself some coffee. She'd drunk it. She'd ordered some toast from room service and waited a couple of minutes for it to arrive. After eating the toast, she'd taken off her jeans and put them in the trouser press. She wasn't the sort of person who usually pressed her jeans, but what was the point of a luxury hotel room if you didn't use all the perks? She lay back on the bed in her knickers and shirt, flicking through the dictionary for inspiration. Was the word 'defilade' any use to her? No. 'Displacement activity' summed up pretty much what she was doing: finding something to fill the time that had no relevance to the activity at hand. She mulled over the definition for a little while, then her trouser press told her that her jeans were ready. She pulled them back on, marvelling at how smart her trousers looked now. She walked around in them for a bit.

Time for some serious work. She sat down at her terminal, booted it up, changed the screen saver, altered a few of the word processor defaults. She spent twenty minutes playing eleven-D Tetris and about that long again checking that she hadn't got any mail. Then she had another shower.

An hour in and she finally opened up her new document.

The cursor blinked at her for a couple of minutes until she remembered the print that she'd bought from the War Museum.

She found it in her coat pocket, scanned it into the terminal and played around with the image until the picture of Isaac filled the screen. She fed in a picture of Isaac from his immigration papers (easily found on MarsNet), taken a week ago. She got the computer to confirm that the two pictures were of the same person. The computer thought that it was 99 per cent probable that they were. Benny thought that the system always left a 1 per cent error factor just in case. There was no real doubt.

MarsNet confirmed that Isaac Denikin had been born on Mars, and he had always maintained a home here (a small flat in Gratacap). But for most of the last fifty years he'd travelled. No details as to where he'd been, or what he'd done out there, but there was nothing here that Isaac hadn't told her.

Fifty years is a lot of time to make enemies. Benny ought to know: in a mere decade of interstellar travel she'd rubbed the Droge of Gabrielides up the wrong way when she'd refused to marry him; inadvertently insulted the Master of the Fifth Galaxy; there was that business with the Lord Herring on Sqakker's World. Mostly, if her experience was anything to go by, these local warlords and potentates swore eternal vengeance on one, but never really followed up on it.

So, had someone followed Isaac here to Mars and caught him with his guard down? Why here, and why now? No. It was more likely to be a guest here. One of the veterans. Isaac had been on Tellassar's staff. Did that make him a collaborator?

What she needed to do was some serious hands-on research. Get down to a library or a military base and do some serious keybashing. She could find out exactly who Isaac was, draw up a list of suspects. It would take her an evening.

Time she didn't have. She needed to write this paper.

That was already going to take her slightly longer than she actually had. She didn't have time to do any of this. She needed to get someone else to do it.

But who?

'Wake up!' Benny barked, slapping Jason around the head. 'Wake up, you bastard.'

Jason groaned, and raised his arms over his head in self-defence.

'Wake up,' Benny repeated, punching him in the stomach.

'Ow!' moaned Jason. 'Enough with the domestic violence. I'm awake, for chrissakes.'

'Good,' said Benny, pulling him into a sitting position in the manner of a rather brisk and brutal nurse. 'You've got work to do.'

'Haven't I done enough?' Jason complained blearily.

'Well, I suppose you would have,' she mused. 'If you hadn't completely screwed it up.'

Jason winced. 'Fair play, I suppose. So what now?'

'Well,' said Benny, picking up a glossy leaflet from the dresser. 'Seeing as you've failed to make it as a detective, I've found you an easier role.' She passed him the leaflet. 'Can you manage being another moronic tourist, or aren't you man enough for the challenge of wandering around gawping at stuff?'

Jason looked at the leaflet. Tellasar's Historic Bunker was emblazoned across the leaflet in gothic script. 'Why do I get all the boring jobs?' he whined.

Benny tilted her head, as if thinking this one over.

'Because you're an arse,' she concluded decisively. 'And because I have to write a paper.'

Armed with a list of questions Benny wanted answered, Jason blearily set out to get into the Bunker before it closed for the night. Luckily for Jason, it was only a couple of blocks away, buried beneath New Government House on Ungersternberg Way. He just had time to stop at a grubby-looking van serving fast food and purchase a Sulph Shake.

By the time he reached Ungersternberg Way he had finished

the creamy shake, and the sulphates were reawakening parts of Jason's brain he had forgotten he possessed. New Government House, impressive as it was, struck Jason as being a truly horrible piece of architecture. A huge, almost featureless pyramid, it expressed an admiration and fixation with precision engineering, and an optimistic sense of dreamy-eyed futurism. Jason, who preferred his utopian visions a little scruffier, a little more human, considered New Government House to be the work of a raving fascist deviant.

As he circled the monstrous eyesore, in search of the Bunker entrance, Jason meditated on the day's events, which were beginning to become clearer as sulphates overcame his alcohol intake. He wasn't sure whether to be annoyed with Benny or himself. Her constantly dismissive attitude was irksome, especially when she wasn't the one taking all the risks. But, then again, Seez and Soaz's story was pretty wild; he had heard rumours of the Xlanthi in his time, and from what he had heard they seemed to be very dangerous, bigtime operators. They were the sort of race who destroyed whole planets just to see what colour explosion they would make when they went 'boom'. Not the sort of people who bumped off senior citizens, or wandered around car parks in the early hours of the morning. It was absurd, like catching Genghis Khan shoplifting.

There was also the fact that Jason didn't feel he could quite trust the two young men. There was something about Seez and Soaz he didn't like, something uncannily familiar. Their don't-give-a-shit attitude, their unreliability, their relentless, almost pathological self-interest. Yes, there was a lot about them that made Jason Kane deeply uneasy.

But their reliability was a matter of minor significance in Jason's priorities. Far more important was Benny, and getting back into her good books and her bed. Although it was bloody rich of her to complain about him drinking on the job, the amount he had seen her put away in her time, often at the most inconvenient times.

It was negative and unproductive thoughts such as these which were obsessively cycling around Jason Kane's mind as he approached the Bunker entrance, which was as far away from the majestic columns of New Government House's main entrance as was possible. Whether this was for sombre effect, or merely to stop tourists getting under the bureaucrats' feet, Jason couldn't be sure. Reluctantly parting with his cash, he stepped out of the sunlight and into the Bunker.

A very long spiral staircase – a basic security measure, but an effective one – took visitors down to the Bunker proper. During his descent, Jason examined the historic posters he passed on the way. One had a naively painted Martian and an equally simply portrayed human, back to back, blazing away at unknown enemies with anonymous, generic black firearms. Menacing plungers just edging into view. The slogan 'United for Mars' was present, and repeated across many of the other posters. There were posters for almost all propaganda purposes. Conical shadows falling across the Martian landscape, warning to be prepared for enemy strikes. Cartoon potatoes, telling of the urge to preserve food supplies. Normal people with black, sightless eyes, a reminder that the enemy had a tendency to use replicants and mind control, that the population needed to be vigilant at all times.

Most of the other visitors to the Bunker were of pensionable age, and many were clearly veterans, wearing an odd jumble of military regalia and garish casual wear. Several silver-haired men and women wore Hawaiian shirts with lines of medals pinned to the front. Jason paused as he stepped off the escalator, watching them totter about. The Siege of Mars must have caused many of the most traumatic events in these people's lives, but as they stepped back into a facsimile of that long-gone world, with all the carefully preserved paraphernalia of a time long gone, they seemed to gain an air of wistful nostalgia. They seemed at peace with the past, able to look back on it without remorse.

Jason hoped there would be a time when he could face up to his somewhat chaotic and painful past and appreciate it, or at least accept it, in some way. Perhaps it was only when you were really old, when your faculties failed and the old desires faded, that you could tear yourself away from the demands and desires of the present and assess the past properly. It certainly wasn't something Jason was capable of in his present state of mind; every time he looked back all he could see were mistakes made, opportunities missed, words unsaid and friends betrayed.

He saw the future. He was living with Benny in a big house on Dellah, looking after the kids while she went on adventures. He'd fund all her trips, let her write that book of hers without pressure from the university. A happy ending.

But that wouldn't happen unless he got back into her good books.

Thankfully, the curators of the Bunker had decided against turning it into a dreadful 'Bunker Experience', but had instead gone for the old school approach of labelled exhibits and accessible information. Jason approved, not because it was his idea of fun – he found the whole prospect deadly dull – but because it made his job a lot easier. While the other visitors drifted from room to room, examining the sparse living quarters and cramped kitchens, Jason consulted his map to find the one room he was interested in, then headed straight for it.

In terms of historical authenticity, the war room was probably the least accurately preserved chamber in the whole Bunker. Security issues had demanded the removal of all sensitive equipment, and militech patenting prohibited accurate reconstructions of the missing items. Instead, the curators had opted to re-create the atmosphere and tension of the war room through a clever use of lighting, and installed the archive in the place to fill the room out. Large wall displays allowed visitors to flick through interactive maps depicting key skirmishes during the war. A central table allowed visitors to examine a holographic battlefield.

Around the edge of the room were an impressive array of militaristic-looking terminals. On closer inspection, these revealed themselves to be information access points, there for the use of academics and other interested parties to browse through the war archive. It was to one of these terminals that Jason applied his attention, setting up a search program to find the information Benny had asked him for.

* * *

Benny had so deeply immersed herself in Trinity's *Decline and Fall* that, when the knocking came, she was jolted back to reality with a start.

Benny had changed her mind: Trinity might have been a bit of a traditionalist, but she was a fine academic as well as a skilled and evocative prose writer, drawing her readers into the very fabric of the past they were studying. Considering the piss-poor royalties for academic writers, it was unusual to find one putting so much effort into their work. If only more of her peers would treat their readers so well, Benny thought.

The knocking continued, and Benny reluctantly put the book down and walked to the door. Outside she found Jason, looking suspiciously perky and carrying a wad of printouts. She ushered him in and slumped back in her chair. It had been a long day.

'What have you got?' she asked wearily, leaning and closing her aching eyes.

'I accessed the wartime personnel records of the Bunker,' said Jason, perching on the edge of the dresser. 'And he isn't in there.'

'Who, Isaac?' asked Benny, her eyes snapping open. This was absurd.

'No, Tuburr the Mighty,' replied Jason acidly. 'Of course I'm talking about Isaac. I can remember a name, you know. He wasn't a soldier, he wasn't a guard, he wasn't even a caterer or cleaner. He quite simply isn't on any of the personnel records relating to the period we're looking at.'

'Impossible,' snapped Benny, shaking her head emphatically. 'I've got a picture of him there.' She quickly located the postcard and held it up.

'Well, he isn't listed on any of these fellas,' said Jason, tossing the sheaf of documents to Benny. 'Neither is he mentioned in the minutes of command meetings or strategy sessions. See for yourself.'

Benny flicked through the pages briefly, then gave up and threw them against the wall in exasperation. 'Shit,' she snapped. 'This gets us nowhere. Inaccurate lists, dubious stories of alien lizards . . . everything we – sorry, you – have dug up today has been totally useless crap.'

'Thanks,' said Jason drily. 'Good to know you appreciate my efforts.'

'Oh, you know what I mean,' barked Benny. She knew, in some part of her mind, that she was being terribly unfair, venting on Jason the anger she felt for not being able to go out there and deal with the situation herself. But that calm, sensible, rational part of her mind wasn't in charge. The irrational, angry part of her was calling the shots, and Jason made for a convenient punchbag.

'How are you getting on with your paper?' he asked.

Benny glared at him.

'Hey, *that* isn't my fault.'

'Maybe you don't know what I mean,' she added. 'I couldn't care less either way. Now go away before I do something you'll regret.'

'What?' demanded Jason, as she pulled him to his feet by the scruff of his neck. 'You're throwing me out? After all the effort I made? After this morning?'

'Exactly,' snapped Benny, opening the door and pushing him out. 'There's only so much exertion a girl can take, especially with a gruelling day's academia to look forward to. Sleep tight.'

She slammed the door on his protests.

After he had finished raging at Benny's room door, Jason was at a loss what to do. Something you're good at, he thought. Remind yourself that you're more of a success than your ex gives you credit for.

Yeah, thought Jason. I'll do some writing. Remind myself why I'm such a bestseller and she's just a loser, a loser with tossy academic sales and no widespread paperback distribution, no multimedia clause in her contract. That would do the trick, remind himself of his true worth.

With this in mind, he stormed into the lift and hit the button to take him to his suite. The sulphates were still buzzing around his system, making him feel like a king, a god. He could do anything with this sort of energy. He could be a speedway star or win a disco-dancing competition or invent and successfully market a new household cleaning product.

Knocking out a chapter of alien water sports shouldn't be a problem, especially if the word processor's thesaurus was operating. He paced the lift's small floor space, eager to get to work.

When he reached his floor Jason headed straight for his room. Ignoring the insult scratched into the varnish on his door he swept his key card over the lock and charged right in.

And fell flat on his face.

'Bum,' moaned Jason, face down on the floor. Luckily for his nose, his instincts had been honed by years of keeling over drunk, getting into brawls and generally rolling from one crisis to the next. As soon as he felt himself go, his instincts had kicked in, twisting him around so that he hit the ground with his shoulder rather than his face. It ached, but there would be no permanent damage. Jason moved his leg, felt the tripwire still coiled around his ankle. He slid his foot out from under it, and rolled on to his back. He felt something cold and wet fall on to his face with a *splat*.

The room was dark but, looking up, framed in the light from the open doorway, he could see the word 'arsehole' crudely painted on his ceiling in big, friendly, pink letters.

Gerald Makhno had been burning the daytime oil. He wasn't sure whether that was a sensible description of his day, but he felt it to be true enough. Supervising an academic convention was clearly some rare form of torture, and only worsened by having a boss who spent half the time shrieking hamsterly abuse at you, and the rest off doing some mysterious errands. Scoblow was clearly suffering from sexual frustration, and had insisted on destroying Makhno's fantasies by going on endlessly about Benny and her husband. Her *husband*, for Goddess' sake. Reconciled and everything. He had seen them wandering around The Hotel together, and although they didn't seem too reconciled, Scoblow had insisted.

In need of intoxication whatever the cost, Makhno had agreed to meet up with Seez and Soaz for a drink. He had found them earlier in the bar, hellbent on oblivion. It was an attitude he could appreciate. But, on his way to the hotel bar, he saw something in the lobby that stopped him in his tracks.

It was Jason Kane, storming across the lobby in a manner which suggested an extremely, extremely bad mood. By looking at him, Makhno suspected that the Kane–Summerfield reconciliation was not going as well as he had earlier feared. Jason had approached the reception desk, and was making some kind of complaint in a psychotically irate tone of voice.

Without letting himself think about it, Makhno changed course, moving away from the bar and towards the elevators. He walked straight into a waiting lift and hit the button for Benny's floor.

Kane was a moron, Makhno thought as the lift ascended. He would have to be, to screw things up with Professor Summerfield like that. He wasn't good enough for her, with his scruffy dress sense, paint-stained head and receding hairline. Right now he was down in the lobby, being an obnoxious little tit, doubtless over some complete triviality. He just wasn't worthy of her.

Makhno had lain alone the previous night with just his copy of *Down Among The Dead Men* for company, beneath his promotional poster for the original hardback publication. He'd thought then of the ways he might pleasure Benny. He knew how, and he'd read somewhere that they would both be at the height of their sexual powers.

As soon as the lift stopped Makhno was out of the door, heading towards Benny's room. He pulled himself to a halt outside her door, and raised a fist to knock.

And stopped. His hand hovered in mid-air, then lowered itself. He had seen Jason and Benny together earlier in the day. Although they had seemed to be bickering at each other, there had been a tangible link between the two. Something in their body language, the way they always walked a precise distance apart, belied their surface hostility and was indicative of some deeper connection. In some strange way, which they were probably unaware of themselves, they obviously belonged together.

They clearly had enough problems sorting out their tempestuous relationship without Makhno diving in and complicating

122

matters. The arrival of a new young buck on the scene would certainly make Jason Kane jealous. It might prevent Benny from finding happiness. His footsteps deadened by the soft carpet, Makhno silently, regretfully, returned to the lift. He felt a watery sensation in his eyes, but whether that was due to emotion or exhaustion he wasn't sure. He closed his aching eyes as the lift began its return trip to the lobby.

Benny lay on her bed, staring at the ceiling. She had tried to do some work, but as soon as she tried to access some of the other programs, the terminal had crashed. 'Address not found', whatever the hell that meant. With the wonders of modern technology unavailable, she was left with only Jason and Isaac to think about. Compared to analysing her marriage, dealing with a brutal murder seemed the more pleasant option.

No wonder the police had closed the damn case so quickly. An old man with no living friends or relatives; who wants to deal with a brutal and inexplicable murder if you can just sweep it under the carpet? After all, that sort of thing was hardly good for the tourist trade. With Benny the only person who gave a toss – and she was hardly the sort of person to whom the police snapped to attention – burying the whole business must have been the obvious option.

And how the hell do you investigate someone these days, anyway? The history and relics of whole civilizations had been wiped away by weapons of mass destruction during that last war, no traces remaining. What hope was there in compiling even a basic biography of one old man, a man who had crossed borders and solar systems, who had rarely had a fixed abode, and who had lived a whole period of his life in the shadows of military secrets?

Sometimes, in archaeology, the pieces just didn't fit. The artefacts uncovered proved to be of utterly incomprehensible purpose, or seemed to come from completely different types of civilizations. Artefacts carbon-dated as being absolutely contemporary, forged or kilned in the very same week as each other, pointed towards completely different interpretations of the site in question. Most disturbing of all, sometimes no matter how hard you examined the artefacts and evidence, individually or as a collection, you got no idea of the bigger picture, no overall view of what this jumble of objects added up to.

That was frustrating enough in archaeology, digging among the bones of the long dead, reconstructing events that had no direct impact on present activities. But this wasn't ancient history; Isaac had been dead for less than a day. Yet already his personal history was elusive, an enigma as impenetrable as the Cathedral on Vremnya, a set of fragments as contradictory as the Timani Scrolls.

These thoughts were getting her nowhere. Liberating a bottle of something potent from the minibar, Benny flicked on the vidscreen and pulled the bed covers over her. Alcohol and the YorkCorp Shopping Channel numbed her brain, deadening her capacity for anxiety. Gradually, boredom and exhaustion took their toll, and she drifted into an unquiet sleep.

9

WHIZZ KIDS AND GRATUITOUS NUDITY

Benny was pleased she didn't have to lie back on a big leather couch. Benny and her counsellor faced each other across a light, pot-plant-filled room, each sitting in a comfy swivel chair. The counsellor was a businesslike woman, who spoke in pleasant, but very mannered tones. She occasionally took notes, using archaic paper and pen.

'So,' said the counsellor briskly. 'Tell me about these dreams.'

Benny shrugged. 'Where do I begin?'

The counsellor smiled kindly. 'Begin with whatever you feel most comfortable discussing.'

'OK,' said Benny. 'A lot of the dreams are just plain surreal, outright madness. There's the one where I'm in Tokyo, and a giant chicken goes on the rampage, ripping apart buildings and so on.'

The counsellor raised an immaculately stencilled eyebrow. 'And?'

'And then there's the one with the bamboo tanks – you know, as in military tanks rather than fish tanks.' Benny was getting into her subject now. 'Then there's the one with the bearded villain who turns me into Lego –'

The counsellor coughed pointedly. 'What do you think these dreams signify?'

Benny shrugged again. 'Dunno. What do any dreams really

signify? Are they of any significance, important messages from the subconscious, perhaps? Or are they just the random flotsam bouncing around the inside of your average moderately disturbed psyche?'

The counsellor looked rather embarrassed and taken aback by the breadth and depth of this response. 'Good questions, I'm sure. But let's apply them. How would you interpret this one, for instance?'

Benny blinked. 'Pardon?'

'This dream. How would you interpret it? I mean, it's obviously not real. Even if you could afford a counsellor, you've always been too stingy to spend good beer money on sorting your life out. So, what do you think?'

Benny paused, weighing up possible responses to this rather cheeky aspect of her own unconscious mind. 'Well,' she said tentatively. 'Either I'm tiring of my own endless self-examination – diary writing, drunken self-pity, that sort of thing . . .'

The counsellor nodded vigorously. 'Good answer, good answer. Or?'

'Or . . . I really shouldn't go to sleep with the telly on. Like cheese, it gives you bad dreams.'

'Damn right,' agreed the counsellor, before turning into a cockroach made of ice cream.

Benny's alarm buzzed. As was the way with such things, Benny had already woken a minute or so beforehand.

Soaz woke up, and looked straight up into the fearsome eyes of a gun-toting Chelonian.

'Shite!' he exclaimed, suddenly wide awake. Then he rather ashamedly noticed that the Chelonian was, in fact, somewhat two dimensional. It was a one-and-a-half-metres-tall cardboard cut-out, some kind of window dressing, with the title 'One Bad Mother' emblazoned across its legs at knee level. Presumably the name of a holo or something.

Shaking the remains of last night's kebab off the duvet, Soaz rolled out of bed and picked up the flat-pack reptile. With difficulty, he manoeuvred it out of the narrow door and into the even narrower corridor. Seez's bedroom door was wide open, thereby depriving Soaz of the pleasure of kicking it in.

He brought the standee crashing down on the duvet-shrouded bundle of subhumanity on the bed.

Seez stuck his head out from beneath the covers, and gave Soaz a bleary, quizzical stare.

'Where the bollocks did this come from?' Soaz demanded, indicating the cardboard cut-out.

'Skip outside the vid store,' Seez replied. 'Don't you remember?'

'No,' snapped Soaz. 'I don't bloody remember. If I had, then the bastard thing wouldn't have scared me half to death. Not nice, waking up to see one of these ugly hermos staring down at you. I thought I'd pulled.'

Seez shrugged. 'Well, at least you wouldn't have to worry about having got it pregnant.' He fumbled under his bed, producing a slice of pizza. He sniffed at it tentatively, then took a bite. Satisfied it wasn't about to kill him, he continued. 'Besides, it's a good holo that. By the standards of straight-to-vid actioners, it's a minor classic. Great when you're smashed.'

'Good,' said Soaz, cutting off a stream of amateur film criticism. 'You keep the bloody thing, then. And get ready; we're on window duty today.'

'Goddess,' Seez said to the Chelonian. 'I never knew he was such a latent hermophobe.'

It didn't deign to reply.

Cleanliness can aid the sleep-fogged mind, thought Benny. She stepped out of the shower feeling ten times better than when she received her wake-up call ten minutes beforehand. Usually she would just have ignored it, spent the best part of the morning beneath the covers. But the clock was ticking, and she hadn't even begun to assemble a first draft of her lecture.

Wrapping herself in the kimono she'd pilfered from Jason's room, Benny wandered back into the bedroom. She grabbed an apple from the complimentary fruit basket and her sheaf of notes from the table, then collapsed on the bed to have a working, albeit relaxed, breakfast.

Twelve pages, three cups of coffee and a couple of pieces of complimentary fruit later, Benny was relatively heartened by her progress. The bare bones of her paper were there. The next stage required her to enter all these notes into a computer, then get it to collate, structure and check all the information. For that she required a working terminal. And to get hers up and running, she needed to find someone in The Hotel capable of such a task.

Benny stood up decisively and flicked the switch on the wall that turned the room into 'day' mode. The sheets began to fold themselves up and tuck themselves in. The curtains swished open, revealing a stunning view of sunrise over Tharsis. Pink light flooded in, and so the lamps switched themselves off. The cleaning robot trundled from its wall socket, picking up the towels and sweet wrappers it found on the floor. The cupboard opened up, displaying Benny's full wardrobe: jeans, black poloneck, a few days' worth of underwear, her party frock, her new coat, her new gloves. Benny shrugged off her kimono, hanging it up alongside the coat.

She closed the wardrobe and looked at herself in the full-length mirror mounted on the door. Mournfully, she put a hand on her stomach. Beer-bellied Benny. It just wouldn't do. She prodded her middle with a finger. Her tummy was becoming dangerously close to being 'cuddly'. Being around all these old people, she'd become sensitized to the signs of ageing. The first few wrinkles, the first grey hair, blue lines in her skin that hadn't been there before. With her build there wasn't much that gravity could do to her – she was reaching the age where having tiny breasts was an advantage for the first time – but if she put on just a few pounds it really showed. She shifted on her hip. She wasn't *that* old, but not for the first time in her life she wasn't young, either.

Benny turned away from the mirror.

And came face to face with Seez and Soaz, hanging outside her window, mouths agape and cleaning gear in hand.

*   *   *

128

As the window polarized to obscure their view, Seez and Soaz burst into hysterical laughter. Although not compulsive voyeurs, Seez and Soaz had the healthy interest in gratuitous nudity shared by all right-minded individuals, and were not averse to attractive ladies with an exhibitionist bent putting on a show for them as they did their rounds.

They still had to wipe Benny's window. They swung on their support ropes, secure in the knowledge that they wouldn't fall. Ropes and levers were the only way of working one's way around the outside of The Hotel, and were therefore the only way to do window cleaning duties. Seez and Soaz were virtually the only people sufficiently resistant to vertigo to do the job.

'So that's what the Mullet Man's piece looks like with her kit off,' said Soaz, when he finally stopped laughing. 'Don't think much of that. There's two types of women, Seez: those that look good in clothes, and those that look good out of them. Very few women are both.'

What a clichéd load of old bollocks, thought Seez. But he let the comment go without questioning where his friend had suddenly picked up all this half-baked sexual politics. Seez liked nothing more than maintaining a quiet life.

'Your skinny types,' Soaz continued, 'those favoured by the fashion industry, are – by definition – your clothes horses. Straight up and down, so that they don't mess up the lines of the designer's gear. Always a disappointment au naturel.'

'Ah,' Seez replied philosophically. 'But it could have been worse. There is of course the third type: those who are pig-ugly either way. Bear in mind that we could have got a flash of one of the oldsters applying the talcum.'

'Urgh,' said Soaz, grimacing. Then he perked up a little. 'You know who we need to tell about this choice viewing?'

'Not Jason?' asked Seez, aghast.

Soaz tutted. 'Of course not Jason. He would be less than pleased, and would definitely refrain from compensating us for yesterday's debacle. No, we need to tell young Mr Makhno.'

Seez cast his mind back to the previous night. Makhno had

been in an even more sullen mood than they had, and proceeded to regale them with a rant on the wonders of Bernice Summerfield: the depth of her academic genius, the brilliance of her smile, the sharpness of her wit, so on ad nauseam. Seez and Soaz had slowly become bored rigid, then abandoned Makhno to his stupor.

'Makhno,' Seez decided, 'will be well pissed off that we saw the object of his desire in a state of undress.'

'Yeah,' said Soaz, grinning evilly. 'Funny, isn't it?'

Jason Kane objected to the slow, torturous process of waking up. He especially disliked waking up alone, and spent much of his time trying to stop this disastrous set of circumstances from occurring.

As he stirred back into a state of consciousness, Jason felt a sensation akin to being underwater, like bobbing on the surface of a dead sea. He rolled around unimpeded in the centre of his vast bed, with not a single soul to cling on to or bump into. Layers of silk sheets and folds of soft duvet wrapped themselves around him as he slowly surfaced from sleep.

Lurking in the shadows of a darkened bedroom on one's own felt like a sordid experience to Jason, far worse than the rosy glow of waking among warm, friendly bodies. For morale purposes alone, he rolled out of bed and ordered the blinds to open. He checked his watch: the day was but young, so he could get a head start on whatever tasks may need to be performed.

Buoyed up by an unfamiliar sense of actually being about to get things done, Jason whistled an old pop song as he pressed the service button.

The hangover demons crawled all over Gerald Makhno as he answered guests' queries, checked on speakers and generally tried to keep the bits of the conference he was responsible for running as smoothly as possible. He could feel the little mites, their footsteps on his flesh making his skin crawl, their little pitchforks searching out delicate parts of his body and prodding them hard. Their voices tickled the sectors of his brain marked 'regret' and 'shame'.

130

He had possibly overdone the drinking the previous night.

On the plus side, Scoblow was in a shockingly pleasant mood that morning. Although still a pipe-sucking obnoxious little rat, the cloud she had been under the previous day seemed to have shifted. Whatever anger had been clogging up her tiny brain seemed to have been worked out of her system in some way. She was a new hamster altogether. He watched her drift around the courtesy suite, schmoozing the speakers as they nervously read over their papers. There were several important discussion panels going on already, so Makhno's workload was relatively light.

He stood in the corner of the courtesy suite, watching the goings-on in a half-interested way, sipping coffee when his giddy stomach felt up to it.

'Oi!' whispered a voice in his ear, a hand clamping on his shoulder. He spun around.

It was, of course, Benny Summerfield. Needles of longing shot through his soul, rendering him unable to speak. Why couldn't she just bugger off and let him get over her in peace?

She held a finger to her lips. 'Don't let Scoblow know I'm around, Gerald. She'll start asking difficult questions.' She nodded towards the fire exit, indicating for him to step outside with her.

With deep reservations, he followed.

'What do you know about computers?' asked Benny, almost as soon as they were out in the corridor.

Makhno shrugged. 'A bit, I suppose. Mine's a knock-off student job, so I have to know a few tricks just to stop it packing in.'

'Smart,' enthused Benny. 'You're coming with me, then.' She grasped his hand and started dragging him along.

'Up to your room?' Makhno asked, only slightly resistant.

'That's where my terminal is, of course. Without it, I can't get my paper finished. And it wouldn't do your conference any good to be one speaker short, would it?'

'I suppose,' said Makhno wearily, 'you're going to say that this is what I'm being paid for.'

* * *

Seez and Soaz had returned their attention to the job in hand. They used squirt guns to apply spots of liquid to Benny's windows: this liquid contained genetically modified, dirt-eating microbes, which spread out across the surface of the windows, clearing all the dirt and grease in their path. Their job complete, they returned to their little spots of liquid, ate them, and died.

Of course, Seez and Soaz couldn't see any of this; all they saw was the dirt and liquid disappear a couple of seconds after they sprayed. It was an easy job, and by extension one which was almost indescribably tedious to perform.

Benny's windows successfully cleaned, they could move on to the next room. Their safety harnesses were strapped around the torso, a single safety cable linking each man to the outer girders of The Hotel's ludicrously complex spiral structure. In unison, Seez and Soaz took their feet off Benny's window ledge, pushed the buttons on the central panel of their harnesses, and hung limply in mid-air as the traction-drones at the end of their safety lines slowly crawled another three metres up the spiral.

'Hey!' said Soaz, snapping his fingers as they were painstakingly dragged around. 'This next one must be the room that dude was killed in.'

Seez, who was hanging upside down for a bit of variety, grimaced. 'Urgh,' he said, staring at the passers-by crossing the Plaza several floors below. 'I hope they've cleaned the place up. Blood makes me nauseous.'

Soaz sighed. 'Well, watching you dangle about like a baboon's bits makes me feel like chucking, but you don't hear me complaining, do you?'

'Fine,' snapped Seez sulkily, spinning around on his rope so that he was the correct way up. 'Better?'

'Thank you,' said Soaz icily, as the traction-drones came to a halt. 'Don't look if you don't want to.' They balanced themselves in the correct position, feet braced against the window sills to keep their aim steady.

They both fired their spray-cans at the window, Soaz peering in to try to catch some gory details, Seez staring at his feet.

'Can't see bugger all,' complained Soaz, as the microbes cleared the window for him. 'They probably took all the sheets and that for evidence.'

'Oh, shit,' said Seez quietly. 'Oh, hell.'

'What?' asked Soaz, spinning around, losing his balance and flailing slightly as he swung from the rope. 'Don't tell me you're getting vertigo in your old age? Fine time to start.'

Seez didn't speak, but simply pointed. Soaz followed his gaze downwards, to where a series of scratch marks – no, claw marks – had been gouged into the very metal of The Hotel. Whatever had caused them must have used tremendous force to dig into the centuries-old metal, which dated back to the time when people really knew how to construct a solid building.

The claw marks traced pretty much the exact path they had seen the Xlanthi take, down the side of the building and towards the parking area.

Soaz couldn't better express the situation than Seez, so he simply reiterated his friend's feelings on the matter.

'Oh, shit,' he gasped.

By the time Jason had showered and dressed, room service had arrived in force. A pair of chefs jointly prepared him a delicious, and completely fresh, breakfast from only the finest genetically bred produce. While the cooking was going on, other lackeys cut his hair, shaved away his stubble and coated his newly manicured fingernails with a compound so hard it allowed him to cut glass by hand. No service drones here: genuine human servants to clean up after him.

Once they had gone, he sat down to eat. He unfolded a napkin and laid it across the lap of his immaculately pressed trousers. He tasted a forkful of perfectly seasoned omelette, and looked at himself in the mirror on the dressing table.

It had been expensive, but worth it. He now looked like a man of importance, as opposed to merely being one. His hair was cropped short at the back and sides – mullet man, indeed – and dyed with flecks of blond. The laser-shave and post-shave bio-wash would keep his face clean-shaven and spot-

133

free for a full month, guaranteed (or your money back!). The three-piece charcoal suit hanging up on its peg would make him look sturdy rather than bloated.

He looked the business. Benny would have great difficulty dismissing him as the same old Jason now.

Finishing his breakfast, he dabbed at his mouth with a silk napkin, and mused on what to do first. Priority was still sorting out this whole murder lark, especially after being thrown out by Benny due to lack of results the night before. Well, yesterday's Jason would have scurried around trying to dig dirt to solve the case. The new Jason, the smartly dressed, self-confident Jason, would do no such thing. He would go out and, as a distinguished and rich author, hobnob with Mars' elite until he found out what he wanted to know.

And tomorrow morning he'd wake up next to Benny again.

He stood up, and only then heard a crack of thunder. He walked over to the window and stared out glumly. The sky was a dismal mauve, and fat spots of rain whacked into the window pane at regular intervals.

Jason wasn't going to ruin his new outfit so soon by going out in that sort of weather. He would have to find another way. He looked around the room, and spotted the standard terminal on the desk.

What had he been thinking? This was almost the twenty-seventh century, for Goddess' sake. Why should he go out and find information, when he could sit in comfort and find things out using the wonders of technology. And he knew just the place to start. One of the few leads he had was Seez and Soaz's Xlanthi sighting. The first step would have to be to find out more about them, and if this murder was their sort of gig after all. Jason doubted it, but it wouldn't hurt to check.

Switching on the datanet browser, Jason typed in an address: gww.knowyourenemy.lies.com.ea.

'Oh dear,' said Makhno, in the manner of garage mechanics the universe over. 'Oh dear oh dear oh dear.'

Benny sighed. 'Let me guess,' she said. 'You can fix it, but you're going to have to get the parts in special, and it's going to cost me?'

They were in Benny's room; Makhno sat at the terminal, perching on a swivel chair, while Benny had dragged her comfy chair over. She needn't have bothered; the sight of Makhno clicking through screen after screen of numeric gibberish was hardly inspirational viewing. Benny spent most of the time staring blankly at the rain as it spattered against her voyeur-cleaned windows. She tried not to constantly think about Jason, only a few floors above.

She repeatedly failed, and repeatedly punished herself for caring.

'No specialist knowledge required,' said Makhno. 'It's neither an unusual or surprising fault; YorkCorp's systems are all pretty creaky, prone to systems crashes. It happens all the time. It's just a matter of getting your terminal to mail the central mainframe, and reboot it from there.' He tapped a couple of keys and the terminal whirred to itself. A white bar appeared on the screen, and slowly began to turn red.

Benny made a noncommittal noise, suggesting a contradictory mix of reluctant gratitude and utter contempt for computers and all those who could use them.

'Luddite,' said Makhno under his breath. Benny thumped him gently on the arm, and he grinned.

She grinned back, and a strange expression appeared on Makhno's face, one Benny couldn't quite read.

'No, what is surprising is the sheer level of corruption,' he said haltingly, clearly trying to provide a distraction from whatever was going through his head. 'It's a good job you're such a slacker,' he added, and she hit him again. 'Because if you'd had any data on here when it went down you would have lost it for sure.'

'Thank the Goddess for indolence,' said Benny drily.

The white bar turned completely red, then disappeared. A YorkCorp logo appeared in its place, rotating slowly in the centre of the screen.

'There you go,' said Makhno smugly. 'All back to normal, courtesy of the YorkCorp mainframe a couple of blocks away. You're lucky you're on Mars; try downloading that lot over an interplanetary line and it'd take hours.'

'Well, thank you, Gerald,' said Benny, getting to her feet and nudging his shoulder with her hand. 'Now, I think both you and I have work to be doing.' It wasn't a subtle hint, but she was too busy feeling the hours and minutes to her lecture draining away to worry about etiquette.

To Benny's surprise, Makhno shushed her. 'Wait, wait,' he said, clicking through the menus again. 'I want to see how far this has gone.'

Typical, thought Benny. Tongue-tied with you most of the time, then give them a new toy and you become an irrelevancy, an unwanted distraction.

Makhno accessed a couple of files. None seemed to make any sense. He leant back, rocking on the back wheels of his chair in a precarious manner. Benny tightened her grip on his shoulder, maternally protecting a youngster from hurting himself. He didn't seem to notice the contact, being too absorbed in his own digital world.

'All files irretrievable,' he said quietly. 'This is pretty heavy duty damage; not just corrupted, but reduced to complete chaos. Scorched Earth.'

'What?' asked Benny, who preferred to be the one baffling the lower orders these days.

'Scorched Earth,' repeated Makhno. 'Data devastation on a grand scale. This was no system failure; it was a deliberate attack.'

Benny frowned.

Knowyourenemy.lies.com was a typical net site, the product of nerds hanging around with too much time on their hands. Two guys in LA had put together a site packed with irreverent gossip and xenophobic ranting about the 'scariest alien species likely to bite your ass off in Earthspace'. It was the perfect place to go for the juice on grade 'A' bastards like the Xlanthi, especially considering such a site was unlikely to get sued due to the Paine amendment's protection of net-based freedom of speech. Even the foulest of star-crushing alien killers tended to have lawyers nowadays.

Jason tapped his complimentary pencil against his complimentary notepad and read what his datascreen had to say about the Xlanthi:

```
Serial 10Q
Subject: Xlanthi
Social Structure: Solitary
Physical description: Humanoid lizards with
crests and large claws on hands and feet.
History: The name Castonier is notorious
throughout the galaxy thanks to the
inhabitants of its first planet, Xlanthius.
The Xlanthi culture is based around the
violent and ritual murder of all rivals.
Xlanthi society is regulated by the Law, an
elaborate system that not even the Xlanthi
seem to understand or apply consistently
(ignorance of the Law is itself a serious
offence). All but the most minor
transgressions of the Law are punishable by
death, the corpse of the criminal being
chopped into bits, roasted and served to the
victim in a ritual feast. Fugitives from
justice and their descendants are pursued
relentlessly across the galaxy, and anyone
interfering with the Xlanthi authorities is
considered guilty of the original offence.
  The Xlanthi are superhumanly strong and
agile, with a fearsome set of natural
defences (teeth, claws, armoured hide). In
addition, even Xlanthi infants are experts in
a variety of unarmed combat techniques. The
Xlanthi are master weaponsmiths, and trade
their weapons for powerful one-man warships.
In appreciation of their assistance during
the Galactic Wars, the Earth Senate has
declared that the Xlanthi are legally
entitled to hunt fugitives in Earthspace
without recrimination from the authorities.
Indeed, law enforcement agencies on many
planets, for example Pakhar, often supply
assistance to the Xlanthi Court in return for
```

contract hits. Xlanthi often find it difficult to tell humans, or indeed mammals, apart but killing someone by mistake is acceptable under the Law.

Travel to Xlanthius is inadvisable, indeed contact with the Xlanthi should be avoided under any circumstances. Spacefarers should be aware that – amongst many other examples – the Xlanthi consider the following to be offences in violation of the Law and punishable by a brutal death: Looking At Me Funny; Knowing French; Wearing Shoes; Flattery; Making Jokes About the Irish; Showing Respect; Talking Shop; Liking Tennis; Gratuitous Nudity; Feeling Uneasy Around A Xlanthi; Discussing Things; Smoking (Active and Passive); Having Facial Hair; Spilling a Pint; Mispronouncing or Misspelling The Word 'Xlanthi'; Denying Having Spilt A Pint; Fancying Scully Out Of The X Files; Splitting Infinitives; Showing An Interest; Having Eaten Fruit; Irony, Sarcasm Or Litotes; Running Away From A Xlanthi; Begging For One's Life; Apologizing.

Under the Law, the correct response when you have offended a Xlanthi, if one has time, is to strip down to one's underpants and demand, in Old High Xlant, to exercise one's right to an honour duel, unarmed and to the death, with as many Xlanthi as think they are hard enough. This is not recommended.

Jason sucked the end of his pencil as he read the display a couple of times, picking out what he felt were the pertinent points. Finally he scratched his conclusion into the notebook.

'No way. I mean *no way* am I going to mess with these fuckers.'

'Mr Kane?'

He was about to reach for the table lamp, ready to use it as a makeshift club, when he registered that the voice was human.

'Oi, Jason!'

'Hey, Jase!'

Correction, voices. He looked around and spotted Seez and Soaz hanging outside the window, blocking his majestic view of the Martian landscape, or acting as a human shield, if one were feeling paranoid or expecting reprisals. They were hammering at the windows with their palms, eyes manic. With their windswept, bedraggled appearance and apparent defiance of gravity, they resembled nothing less than the vengeful spirits of all those dossers Jason had refused to give money to back when he was working King's Cross.

Yesterday's Jason would have invited them in for some strong booze to warm their rain-drenched carcasses, then sat around cobbling together a plan. New Jason had his own plans, and wasn't going to compromise them by messing around with some rancid youths.

'What do you two scopes want?' he demanded tersely, opening the window a mere crack. The rain had stopped, but he wasn't risking any backsplashes from these losers.

'Evidence,' said Soaz frenetically, droplets of water sliding off his cropped hair, gathering in every line of his face. 'We've got evidence.'

'About the Xlanthi,' added Seez, his voice muffled by the soaking clump of dreadlocks obscuring his face. He spoke the words as if conveying some ancient wisdom.

'We've seen its claw marks.'

'We've just looked them up on the datanet. Look!' They pressed a printout to the window, smearing the ink.

Bloody typical. You go to the trouble to learn your way around new technology, improve your ability to access information, and some sprog of a whizz kid has already got to the goodies. Well, Jason was going to do this his way. If he didn't listen to what they had to say, then he could get the information for himself, and claim it as his own work.

To Jason, this seemed a perfectly sane and rational plan.

On the other hand, the strategy of the youth of today seemed to be to shout the word 'Xlanthi' very loud while hanging in a very vulnerable, exposed position.

This seemed irrational, somehow, and not a scheme he felt comfortable to be involved with.

'Piss off, or I cut your ropes and let you go "splat",' he warned the two young men, slamming the window shut.

He heard the word 'wanker' being used several times over the next couple of minutes, and it was only when he ran towards the window with a large knife in hand that they deigned to accept his dismissal.

10

PENSIONER MUGGED BY LIZARD

'Well, Seez lad,' said Soaz, as they picked up their window cleaning wages from the hotel office. 'That looks like we're out of this detective business for good. The esteemed Mr Kane regards our services as being surplus to requirements.'

'Yeah,' grunted Seez. 'What a wanker.'

'Well,' said Soaz levelly. 'That's as may be, but we must respect his decision. The best way to do this, I feel, would be to forget about Jason Kane and his poxy murder and do something we're good at instead.'

'Get smashed and talk drivel?' suggested Seez.

'Seems the best course to me,' agreed Soaz.

The wage drone handed back their cards. Seez had often noticed a strange phenomenon about moneycards. There was no display on them, and so it was impossible to see how much credit remained without using a reader. They should look exactly the same if they had a million sovs on or minus one hundred. But somehow, Seez had an instinct: he knew that his card had just been powered up, ready for action. It sat in his pocket like a coiled spring.

'Who's going to provide the entertainment?' Soaz asked.

'A good question.' Seez considered the answer for a moment. 'Robotic Barry?'

They both shook their heads. 'Not after last time.'

'Dave the Venezulan?'

'Overpriced, indiscreet and poor personal hygiene.'

'True, true, very true.'

'Pirate?'

'A bit out of the way . . . possible, though.'

Soaz snapped his fingers. 'Norbridge.'

Seez smirked. 'Excellent choice, Mr Ashley.'

'Scorched Earth, eh?' said Benny meaningfully. She had started pacing a few minutes before, and Makhno found it extremely distracting.

'Could this have started elsewhere in the network?' asked Benny. 'Only, I can't imagine anyone going to such lengths to corrupt my files. Except perhaps the book critic of *Archaeology Today*.'

'Well,' said Makhno. 'The virus had to have come from somewhere. Most viruses have a limited lifespan, just to be on the safe side. Something this destructive might have been targeted at another part of the network, and just happened to get to your terminal before it died out. MarsNet's quite antiquated, the firewalling and –'

Benny clicked her fingers, cutting off the babble. 'Bet I know whose terminal it started with as well,' she said purposefully. 'Come on.'

'Why?' asked Makhno as she opened the door and gestured for him to follow. 'Where are we . . . Oh no, you must be kidding.'

'Don't be a big baby,' chided Benny, locking her door behind him and walking over to Isaac's room. 'It'll only be a bit of blood.'

'That's not the point,' blurted Makhno. 'Isn't interfering with a crime scene a bit on the illegal side?'

'Look,' said Benny firmly. 'If the police really didn't want people interfering with their crime scenes, don't you think they would make more effort to keep them out than a bit of sticky tape over the door?' To demonstrate, she pulled the yellow tape away from Isaac's door in one go. She turned the handle, and the door swung open.

Makhno frowned. 'Do you know, I've never thought of it quite like that before. I suppose they must be more keen on amateur detective types than I thought.'

'The police are just like the rest of us,' said Benny as they stepped in. 'Ever keen to let some other stupid sod do half the work.'

'Makes sense,' said Makhno, nervously glancing around him. The late Isaac Denikin's room was almost identical to Benny's, albeit slightly smaller and showing the wear and tear left by a brutal murder and the attentions of a police forensics team. There was surprisingly little blood and gore, much to Makhno's relief. If he hadn't known, he wouldn't have been able to guess there had been a murder here. Deep down, though, the suspicion remained that the murderer was still in here: hiding under the bed, perhaps, or in the cupboard.

'Right,' he said in an efficient manner, righting a tipped chair and sitting in front of the terminal. He switched it on, and found it in a similarly inactive state to Benny's.

'Knew it,' said Benny, leaning over Makhno's shoulder.

'Yeah, but it doesn't really get us anywhere,' said Makhno, typing in a complex command string. 'What we need to know is what caused the crashes in the first place, and when they occurred. Which is what I'm about to do.' He sat back smugly, as the phrase RUNNING POST MORTEM appeared on screen.

'*Qué*?' asked Benny, blinded, deafened and dumbed by science yet again.

'The central mainframe is checking through its records, and analysing the corrupted data on this terminal's hard drive,' Makhno said, speaking in the slow and patient tone of a primary school teacher. 'That way, we can get some idea of what exactly happened. I'm surprised the police were so lax as to not do it themselves.'

'Alekseev – the guy in charge – didn't seem too bothered about finding out,' Benny noted.

Makhno tutted. 'Public services aren't what they were. The Rotariat would rather keep down taxes. The more you spend on the police, the more crime they detect, everyone knows that. The best way to keep the crime figures down is not to have any police.'

A series of statistics appeared on screen. 'Ah, here we are.'

'What does it all mean?' asked Benny.

'It means this terminal has had a case of Kancer,' said Makhno.

143

'Cancer?' echoed Benny.

'No, Kancer,' repeated Makhno, using the correct Martian emphasis on the 'k'. 'It's a very powerful computer virus, short-lived but virulent. The code is self-deleting, the copy protection infallible, making it a very expensive weapon in the sphere of info-terrorism. Kancer was used to trash every single bit of data on this terminal. There wasn't much, so it managed to spread to yours before its life cycle came to an end.'

'I don't suppose, what with all this corruption, you can get any idea what they were after?' asked Benny hopefully.

'Actually, you're in luck,' said Makhno, tapping a couple of keys. 'The central mainframe keeps a record of transactions, so the guest can be billed for any special services used. It says here that the terminal was switched on at 2.31 hours.'

'Just around the time of Isaac's death,' said Benny.

'Exactly,' agreed Makhno. 'An external device was connected to the terminal at 2.33 hours. The final entry is for 2.36 hours; a data chip access, presumably to upload Kancer.'

Benny paced across to the window, staring blankly out over Jackson City. 'So,' she said slowly. 'No information was actually downloaded off the terminal. That pretty much rules out espionage. Whatever our killer was doing with that terminal, it took less than five minutes, so it can't have involved going through any records in great detail.'

'That's about as long as it takes to read a moneycard. Weird.' Makhno paused. 'What next?'

Benny looked at her watch. 'Next, you show me how to sort out my research on my terminal. This is too bloody complicated; it'll have to wait until after I've given my paper.'

Seez and Soaz liked the suburbs of Jackson City. Retirement flats, drop-in centres and residential homes stretched out for miles. Hearses and ambulances rolled by at regular intervals, attending to the troubles inherent in such a large elderly population. Here, a couple of young men could make a tidy packet doing odd jobs for those too infirm to do their own

144

chores. Besides, the old folk were at the very least well off, and often appallingly rich, and there was never anything people liked to spend their money on more than getting other human beings to do menial tasks a sewer drone would consider demeaning.

But that wasn't why Seez and Soaz had come to the suburbs on this particular day. They came not to earn, but to spend. Although the paltry sum they had earned cleaning The Hotel's windows would not stretch to any class A substances, it would cover a pocketful of prescription highs from someone with a well-stocked medicine cabinet. In the suburbs, there were always plenty of unscrupulous and greedy pensioners willing to illegally sell on their medication for a few sovs. Seez and Soaz knew just such a man, and were on their way to see him.

Jeremy Norbridge lived on Ulyanov Road, a pleasant, tree-lined street in one of the less spacious, cheaper neighbourhoods. One side of Ulyanov Road was dominated by Autumn Red Home for the elderly, while the opposite side was just one long block of retirement apartments, external lifts transporting people from the ground to the other couple of floors. Most of the residents were at a stage in their lives when stairs would represent a serious challenge.

Norbridge lived on the first floor, and Seez and Soaz waited for an octogenarian lady with an exoframe to step off before getting on to the lift platform. It carried them up to the first floor balcony, and they strolled along to number 37, chatting aimlessly as they did so.

Seez knocked on the door. It opened with the impact, and closer examination revealed that the lock had been torn out of the door.

Seez looked to Soaz, his uncertainty and fear counselling retreat. Soaz, who had some concern for their loyal supplier, indicated that they should proceed. Silently, carefully, they entered Norbridge's apartment.

The scene within was one of textbook carnage. Furniture was broken and scattered. The tacky, kitsch little ornaments that Norbridge had spent his ill-gotten gains on were in pieces everywhere, shattered porcelain dusting the carpets like talcum. His priceless collection of Wedgwood gibbons lay in ruins. Everything was quiet.

'Jeremy?' called Soaz. 'You in, Jez?'

A whimpering sound came from one corner of the room, from behind an overturned sofa. Seez and Soaz crept forward, then looked over the top of the toppled couch.

Jeremy Norbridge was cowering behind the sofa, clenching one of its legs. He looked up at them in brief terror, then relaxed when he realized who it was.

'You two,' he said, letting them help him painfully up. 'Thank the Goddess. I thought it was back.'

'What was back?' asked Seez, still twitching slightly.

The old man's eyes widened in fear. 'The Xlanthi,' he said, voice quivering. 'The Xlanthi came here, and stole all my gear!'

The main convention hall was a strangely subdued area of The Hotel. Bored-looking youngsters manned stalls selling war-related merchandise, or hawking membership to veterans' societies or funeral planning schemes. With virtually no seating available for the attendees, they hovered and circulated, octogenarians filling up the space between stalls.

Jason lurked around a table selling limited edition prints of war machines hovering over the Martian landscape, pretending to examine the overpriced wares while in fact observing the veterans' social behaviour.

'That generation,' said the young lady behind the table, with a tone of reproach unsuitable for her age. 'All they ever think about is sex. Sex and violence, that is.' She nodded towards an elderly couple who were blatantly flirting, he demonstrating how he brought down a spaceship with a rifle, she pretending to look impressed.

Jason turned to look at the girl. Short in height, ginger hair, large brown eyes and a strangely lopsided expression. Her dreamy gaze, flowery skirt and bunched hair suggested she preferred solstices and being vegan to sex and violence. Not that he was ruling her out entirely.

'Yeah,' said Jason, turning on his best smile. 'But they

must be quite interesting people. Bet they have some stories to tell.'

'Ooooh,' moaned the girl theatrically, feigning terror. 'I've heard them all. Repeatedly.'

'Who are the lucid ones?' asked Jason.

'That lot are good,' said the girl, pointing to a restrained and serious-looking cluster of veterans. 'They're from the Temperance Division, so they can at least be relied upon not to pass out on you in mid-conversation.'

'Thanks,' said Jason, frowning as he made his way towards the group.

One particularly grizzled veteran squinted at Jason as he approached the group. His cybernetic eye had a lens missing.

'You don't look old enough to be one of us. What are you wanting?' The old man's voice was half-strained through an electronic voice box.

Jason had his story all sussed. 'My name is Pip Kleener,' he said, tapping into his new-found talent for literary invention. 'I'm here to interview some people about the old days. Care to be interviewed?'

'Why certainly, young man,' he said. 'What do you want to know about?'

'I'm interested in the common soldiers' view of their commanders, especially those in the Bunker,' said Jason. 'More specifically, I'd like to hear anything you can tell me about Tellassar.'

The veteran clenched his fist.

Seez and Soaz left Norbridge's apartment in a state of mixed emotions. Whether they liked it or not, they were back on the case Jason had kicked them off. The whole Xlanthi thing was back on the scene, too, which, as neither Jason nor his ex-wife seemed to believe in their presence, meant Seez and Soaz were on their own until they got some more proof together.

After a nice cup of tea and a couple of calming slaps, Norbridge had wheeled out a fairly coherent account of what had happened to him. The same night Seez and Soaz had seen the Xlanthi climb down the wall of The Hotel, one of the reptilian fiends had crashed through Norbridge's door, then torn his apartment apart until it found his stash of painkillers. Then it had gone, leaving Norbridge in a state of extreme paranoia and hysteria ever since.

'What do you think?' Soaz asked Seez.

Seez shrugged. 'Even if he's barking, or taken too many of his own pills, there's no way he trashed that place on his own. Old geezer like that couldn't throw a frisbee, never mind throw furniture. Nah, something happened. And it corroborates our story, so why not?'

Soaz pulled a doubtful face. 'It's pretty odd though, isn't it? I never really thought of big leaguers like the Xlanthi as the medicine magpie type. Why bother?'

Seez shrugged again. 'Dunno. Perhaps it's fallen on hard times. Or maybe it just had a headache? Who knows. Maybe I should have become a xenobiologist like my mum said . . .'

'Yeah, and maybe Jason Kane should be the next Pope,' said Soaz. 'Either way, we need a witness who won't keel over of a coronary in the next two days; Jez is a gonner if his nerves keep up like that.'

'Too true,' agreed Seez mournfully. He pointed to the Autumn Red Home. 'Why not see if anyone in that place saw anything? They always have night staff on, I've seen them.'

Soaz nodded. 'Good idea. Besides, the birds who work there are quite tasty, aren't they?'

Seez looked wistfully into the middle distance. 'Aah,' he sighed. 'Nurses' uniforms!'

Jason felt exhausted. Listening to all this bile and hatred was really wearing him out. As his cover story had spread around the hall, more and more of the veterans had wanted 'Pip Kleener' to interview them about their feelings on Tellassar. Unfortunately, they all had pretty much the same story to tell, and none of them had anything useful to say. It was all 'great betrayal . . . blah blah blah, traitor to Mars . . . blah blah blah'; Jason was sick of it. One thing was certain: none of these people gave a toss about Tellassar's lieutenants. Tellassar was the one they hated, the buck stopped there, and no one else even got a look in. On Mars, Satan had been knocked off the top spot as a symbol for all that was wicked.

Eventually, Jason changed tack, and asked to speak to the most senior officer there, someone who might have actually known Tellassar, who might actually have some insight beyond received wisdom and propaganda. He had been directed to a side room, where General Keele was running through a speech for later in the day. The place was empty except for Keele, Jason, a few chairs and a coffee machine.

'Hi there, young man,' said Keele, standing up when he saw Jason enter. 'Good military haircut you got there,' he said, ruffling Jason's newly shorn locks with excessive affection. 'What can I do for you, Mr . . .?'

'Kane,' said Jason, unwilling to carry on all that nonsense. 'Jason Kane. I'm looking into the death of one of your veterans, Isaac Denikin.'

Keele nodded sadly, indicating for Jason to sit. Jason did so, and Keele pulled up another chair, sitting so close that their knees rubbed together.

'I didn't know Denikin at all,' said Keele. 'But it's always sad to see one of our generation go. There soon won't be many of us left.'

'Denikin was one of Tellassar's inner circle,' said Jason. 'He was in Missile Control during the war. I thought his death might have been something to do with that, perhaps?'

'I rarely went to the Bunker or Missile Control,' said Keele, his voice rising as he got into his subject. 'I was out there with my land troops. But, until the betrayal, I still took orders from Tellassar, and had to go to the Bunker to see her, attend strategy meetings, that sort of thing. Don't ever remember any "Denikin" guy being there though.'

'Yeah, well, it was fifty years ago.' Jason stopped. 'Sorry, but did you say "her"? Tellassar was a woman?'

Keele laughed humourlessly. 'Yeah, I guess most people forget that the likes of Tellassar are male or female, have friends and family. All they know is the reputation of someone less than human, a monster. But Tellassar was a normal human woman, albeit a brilliant one. That just makes what she did worse.'

Jason just nodded mutely.

'I kept this on me ever since,' said Keele, taking a holocard from his pocket and passing it to Jason. It showed a red-haired woman, sharp-featured and fierce, wearing a military uniform and staring proudly, defiantly into the camera lens. 'Every day, I look in the crowds for this woman. Karina Tellassar, Minister of Defence, polymath, genius and traitor. She was the best of us all, and we believed in her like a god.'

'She's quite a looker,' Jason noted.

'For a woman. For a war criminal.'

'Granted,' Jason said, angling the card to see if he could get a look down her top.

Keele took back the card and fixed Jason with a stare. 'We believed in her, and she sold us all out to the aliens.'

'Do you know what happened to her after the Siege?' Jason asked.

Keele shook his head. 'No one does. A lot of people died, and our enemy had a . . . forceful style of management. If their servants failed in the slightest degree, or if they had served their purpose –' He drew his finger across his neck.

'You think she died?'

Keele nodded. 'I wish that she hadn't. I wish that I could wring that pretty neck for myself. Tellassar is dead, though.'

'Oh, mama!' Soaz said under his breath as he and Seez walked into the entrance hall of the Autumn Red retirement home. The hall was a spacious, wood-panelled room. To one side, a group of aged women in dressing gowns and wheel-chairs stared catatonically at the soap opera on the vid. On the other side was the chrome reception desk, behind which sat the cause of Soaz's exclamation.

She was about their age, possibly even less. Slim, with dark hair and immaculate make-up. Her manicured fingers, with their turquoise metallic nail varnish, were turning the pages of a paperback. If Soaz was sufficiently interested, he would have seen that the author of said book was one Jason Kane. But Soaz was not in a state of rationality; he was transfixed by the way that this woman's uniform, a one-piece white dress as worn by careworkers and nurses for over five hundred years, slid up her tanned thighs as she uncrossed her legs . . .

'Ow!' Soaz's line of thought was broken by Seez slapping him hard around the back of the head. The receptionist looked up, and Seez was instantly at the desk.

'Excuse my friend,' he said, smiling broadly. 'He came to Mars for a cheap lobotomy, but they botched the operation. I wonder if you could help me –' he read the name-tag pinned just above one perfect breast '– Nancy?'

'What can I do for you, sir?' asked Nancy, a flirtatious smile breaking through the formality of her words.

'Well, my uncle lives just across the road, and I'm afraid someone seems to have broken into his apartment.'

'Oh no!' exclaimed Nancy, with what Soaz considered excessive sympathy. She took Seez's hand and gazed up into his heavily dilated pupils. 'That's terrible. How can I help?'

Soaz felt an attack of nausea coming on. Why was it that people . . . girls . . . instantly latched on to his colleague? It happened without fail. He'd nothing against Seez, of course, they were mates, but the guy had merely a casual relationship with detergent and related products, no charisma and beetly eyebrows that met in the middle.

'Have you seen anything unusual out there?' asked Seez.

'Well,' said Nancy hesitantly. 'There's this old lady across the street who urinates off her balcony.'

'That's not quite what I had in mind,' said Seez flatly. 'I meant more the potentially criminal type of unusual. Anything suspicious, particularly involving aliens. Late at night, perhaps?'

Nancy shook her head, batting her delicate eyelashes. 'I'm afraid we don't have anyone on this desk after midnight,' said Nancy. 'And I haven't heard of anything odd happening on any of the day shifts.' She sighed. 'We get so bored out here, we would be bound to discuss anything like that.'

Seez was clearly about to offer to show her a life of excitement, incident and cheap booze when a shrill voice broke into the conversation.

'We saw something!' exclaimed one of the old ladies, her wheelchair rolling across the lobby eagerly.

'Yes, we saw something you'll really want to hear,' chorused the other geriatric.

'Ignore them,' said Nancy quietly. 'They're nuts.'

'What?' demanded one old lady.

'Pardon?' squeaked the other.

Nancy leant over the desk, allowing Seez and Soaz a fleeting, hypnotic glance down the front of her dress. 'Now then, ladies,' she said in a tone appropriate to chastising children and foreigners. 'What have you been told about telling stories? Remember all that trouble when you told everybody Dr Bowman was the Pope's nephew?'

Soaz's heart sank. He and Seez looked at each other in despair.

'But this one's true,' complained one old lady.

'It's about Mr Cromwell at number 54,' added the other.

'He has a visitor.'

'An alien visitor, who calls all times of the day and night.'

'Very antisocial hours. We know.'

'We see him, when we're sitting here.'

'Late at night, when everyone's in bed.'

'A Xlanthi, it was. We saw one on the news, once.'

Soaz looked over at Seez. 'Call this an instinct, me old mucker, but I reckon this might be worth following up. Nancy, could you give us a picture of him?'

Benny was busy typing data into her terminal. She had the bare bones of her paper, now. She was at that stage where she realized that she hadn't given herself enough time to do it justice, and that she was going to have to wing great sections of it.

Like many clever people in a universe which valued cleverness, Benny had always liked to think that she'd be truly great if she only pulled up her socks, approached things in a disciplined way or did basic revision from time to time. If she buckled down to it, she'd have an unrivalled reputation. After all, she was so much wittier than most of her academic colleagues. If she worked hard, it would be so unfair on the rest of them.

Her terminal *binged*.

She would have missed the little message if the computer was just a little bit faster, or if she hadn't been staring straight at it for the split-second it was there.

TERMINAL ACTIVITY LOGGED

Someone had just scanned her computer, found out what she'd been doing on it.

Benny shivered, realizing that someone had been watching her.

Somehow, she doubted that this was an eager archaeology freak who couldn't wait until she delivered her paper that evening.

Cromwell's flat was only slightly further along than Norbridge's; if there was a Xlanthi holed up there, then Norbridge was probably a logical guy to raid for drug supplies. The question was: why?

Soaz finished fiddling with the lock, and the door clicked open. They had knocked, then decided to risk having a look around when no one was in. Of course, there might be a Xlanthi in the bathtub, but they would just have to risk it. Soaz in front, Seez following behind, they entered someone else's flat for the second time in less than an hour. Breaking and entering was becoming dangerously like an everyday activity.

Unlike Norbridge's flat, a cacophony of debris and junk, this room had been stripped clean. The hallway was empty, just a couple of bits of litter and paper on the carpeted floor. The first room they tried was a bedroom. The covers had been stripped from the bed, the wardrobes were open and empty. There was the smell of solvent in the air – their connoisseur noses noting that it was cleaning fluid of some kind.

'Someone's been covering their tracks,' Seez said.

'Given it the full wipedown,' Soaz agreed. Over the centuries, a certain class of person had become adept at removing every trace of their DNA from the places they had been.

'Look at this,' said Seez, holding up one of a pile of old *News of the World*s he had found in the corner. Soaz flicked through it. Someone had gone through, highlighting any

articles about assassinations, murders or particularly auda-
cious thefts. Soaz tossed the paper back to Seez, and picked
up another one from the pile. The same sort of stories were
highlighted.

'Looks like this is the place,' said Soaz. 'Either that, or our
Mr Cromwell has one serious murderer fixation.'

'Nothing unusual about that,' Seez said. 'The papers
wouldn't print the stories if people weren't interested.'

'There's "interested" and then there's "underlining key
phrases in red pen",' Soaz sniffed. 'I bet this guy has a Bible,
I bet the bookmark's in Revelations.'

'The bookshelves are empty,' said Seez bluntly. 'The guy's
obviously cleared out.'

Soaz looked again at the empty wardrobes, the stripped
bed, and nodded grimly. 'Yeah, we may be too late here.'

They proceeded to the next room, Seez in front.

He cannonballed back, slamming the door shut.

'It's in there!' hissed Seez.

Not hearing any noise from within, Soaz pushed past him
and gently inched the door open. 'What is?' he scowled.

A Xlanthi.

It was sitting stock still in the middle of the room. It
didn't register their presence, which suited Soaz down to the
ground. Its eyes were closed, and as they watched it –
fascination overriding what little common sense they would
normally be able to call upon – the Xlanthi didn't move even
a millimetre.

'Pass me something to prod it with,' Soaz asked.

'What?' replied Seez in an urgent whisper. 'Are you
insane?'

'Do it,' hissed Soaz through gritted teeth. 'I think it's
dead.'

Seez disappeared for a while, then returned holding a
broken pool cue.

Holding the cue in one hand, Soaz edged the door a little
further open. He stepped into the room, cue ahead of him.
Every muscle within his body was agonizingly primed, ready
for him to run like the devil if the creature stirred. Running
would do him about as much good as flinching would in the

154

face of a nuclear explosion. Despite the fact that he was either right or dead, he kept as far away from the Xlanthi as possible.

He reached forward with the cue and gave it a nudge.

The Xlanthi's head fell off, hitting the floor with such an almighty thud that Seez and Soaz nearly jumped out of their skins.

They screamed in unison, clutching each other like Scooby and Shaggy.

When their nerves had settled, they approached what was left.

'It's not even real!' complained Seez, looking down the Xlanthi's neck. He felt cheated.

From the inside he could see that this 'Xlanthi' was an exoframe body suit, of the kind used to give paralysed humans mobility. But this was a souped-up model, clearly incredibly strong and agile. On closer examination the metallic claws turned out to be just that: metal, some kind of high-strength steel, sharpened and tempered for combat or climbing. The fallen head contained complex sensory apparatus, a helmet allowing the wearer all the usual options such as thermal infra-red, UV exclusion, motion tracking and so on.

'Looks like our killer was human after all,' said Soaz. 'Unfortunately, he's long gone.'

'Why clear out the flat and leave this?' Seez asked.

They looked across at each other.

Then they bolted for the door. They reached it, and passed through it, just as the suit self-destructed, neatly taking Cromwell's apartment with it.

11

BENNY COMES TO AN INTERESTING
CONCLUSION

The rain lashed against the windows of The Hotel, and there would always be some locals amazed by the novelty of it, there would always be tourists delighted by something that happened every day at home. The restaurant was packed with people sitting by the windows, looking out at the sheets of water falling over Jackson. Benny came from Dellah, a planet whose climate was permanently autumnal. Every day was slightly damp, with the promise that the drizzle might clear up and the day might end crisp and still. It never did.

The Martian rainfall was all artificial, of course, part of the terraforming procedure. The rain watered the plants, washed away the dust and dirt, freshened up the air. It happened once a week, on Sundays, a cloud belt sweeping across the various terraformed settlements. It always hit Jackson City on Sunday evenings, and always lasted about an hour. Benny thought that the Martian rain clouds looked chunky, more angular than their natural equivalent, but was prepared to concede that it might just be her imagination.

Seez and Soaz were wolfing down their Martian croissants, presumably because they knew they didn't have to pay for them.

Benny wasn't paying attention to them or the weather, because Jason had just promised to show her the face of the man that killed Isaac Denikin.

There was something slightly different about her ex-husband's appearance, but she couldn't quite put her finger on what it was.

Oh, that was it, she thought. Everything. He was shaved, smart, alert.

'Seez and Soaz got it from the old people's home,' Jason explained as he handed over the photogram.

An old man, pale eyes, thick white moustache. He'd have made a good Santa if the Grosvenor Arcade couldn't find anyone else to fill their grotto this year.

'Elias Cromwell,' Seez said between mouthfuls. 'Off-worlder. No previous anything. Police never heard of him. Just an ordinary old bloke. Billions of them here.'

Not all of them dressed up as cannibal alien lizards and tore the heart out of an old man's chest, though. Benny looked at the kindly eyes, imagined him dictating a letter to his grandchildren as he was walking in the garden of his retirement home.

'I guess he's a veteran,' Soaz said. 'Bounty hunter, mercenary, that sort of thing. A lot of records got lost during the war, a lot of the colonies don't do proper censuses.'

'He's old enough to be a veteran,' Benny noted. 'Could he have known Isaac from back then?'

Seez grinned. 'One of the girls at the old people's home was very helpful, showed me his record. He'd never been to Mars until a month ago. His retirement permit was perfectly in order. During the war he worked as an administrator on Garaman. He was there from 2541 right through to 2547.'

'That's what his public file might say,' Jason said. 'A lot of those "administrators" were involved in black ops. Perhaps he came back to fight the invaders.'

Benny shook her head. Jason could be right about Cromwell's involvement in the shadier side of Earth's military activity, but Garaman was on the other side of the spiral arm, right on the edge of enemy space. During the war it had been a major space facility. It was months away; so far that the troops going there went in sleeper ships. Assuming that the records were accurate – and they had to assume that – it seemed extremely unlikely that Cromwell had been on

Mars during the Siege. He'd have been behind enemy lines, or working on some secret weapon project.

'Even if Cromwell didn't have a grudge against Denikin from then, he might have met him since,' Seez suggested. 'Denikin travelled. We've based everything on the theory that his murder is some sort of revenge for the Siege.'

Benny shook her head. 'It has to be: the first time Isaac's been on Mars for fifty years, in a hotel full of veterans. It's just too much of coincidence that some guy with a random grudge happened to meet him here. Isaac was part of Tellassar's team: that has to be important.'

'He wasn't,' Jason reminded her. 'He was there, but he wasn't part of the command staff. Perhaps someone just came across his name on the guest list. It was a professional hit. Cromwell might be an old guildsman, who came here because he knew that this is where he could find his target.'

'Members of the Assassin's Guild don't usually turn up on Mars,' Seez said.

'No, but by definition there are a lot of them out there in the galaxy,' Jason replied.

Benny and Seez stared blankly at him. Soaz was still busy eating.

'A lot of assassins,' Jason explained. 'Because otherwise there wouldn't be enough to fill a Guild.'

'No,' said Benny, finally seeing his line of logic. 'So we keep an eye out for Cromwell?'

Jason shook his head and nodded at Soaz. 'He hacked his way into the emigration database.'

'Perfectly legal to do that,' Soaz sniffed. 'Well, not *totally* perfectly legal, but the police don't mind people doing it. Cromwell left this morning. Hired a shuttle, hauled himself over to the Moon. After that he vanishes into the Earth traffic. He could be anywhere now.'

'Anywhere but Mars,' Seez added. 'We're not going to find him.'

Benny nodded. This wasn't a satisfactory ending. She wanted to confront the man, she wanted to find out why he'd done it. Everything she'd found out about Isaac during the investigation just made him more intriguing. It was like reading the obituary of a famous person, discovering all the interesting facts and background at just the point that the information became pointless. Who cared where Isaac had travelled to, or what he had done, now that he was gone? Already people seemed to have forgotten him, as if the universe had closed up around the space where he had been. Cromwell had his motivation, even if it was only money. Someone wanted him dead, for a reason.

'Is he Tellassar, do you think?' she asked.

The others looked at her blankly. 'No,' they all said, slightly out of synch.

'Well, he might be,' she said. 'It would explain a lot.'

'Tellassar was a woman,' Seez informed her. 'Elias Cromwell wasn't.'

Benny's world view skewed slightly to take account of this new information.

'Didn't you know Tellassar was a woman?' blurted Jason.

'I do now,' replied Benny levelly. This was a revelation, but now she'd had a few seconds to assimilate the information, she realized it wasn't a colossally helpful or relevant one.

Jason looked at her expectantly. She stared back at him blankly.

'If you expect me to be impressed by this, then you're mistaken,' she said drily. 'This doesn't exactly solve Isaac's murder. It just establishes the gender of his boss. The two things are somewhat disconnected.'

'You went to the museum,' Soaz pointed out. 'You walked around that big display. How could you have done that without finding out? I thought you were an expert on Martian history.'

'Never mind that,' Benny snapped irritably. 'About the murder: Cromwell has gone, but there must be leads.'

'The trail's cold, Benny,' Jason said. 'Cromwell was the only link, and he's gone. It's a professional job, there was nothing that we could have done.'

'Any evidence there was was atomized when his apartment blew up.'

She looked up from the picture of the old assassin, nodding, feeling that same dull sense of anticlimax she had when Alekseev had first told her about the death. 'Thanks, everyone. You did what you could.'

'Thanks for breakfast,' Soaz said, scattering some of it from his mouth.

Benny smiled wanly.

'How's the paper going?' Jason asked.

Benny smiled wanly again.

'That bad?'

'We could help you,' Seez suggested. 'What's it about?'

Benny held out her hands. 'Sorry, lads, I need to –'

'Go on, what's it called?' Soaz asked.

'*The Martians*,' she said.

'There you go,' Seez beamed. 'Me and Soaz *are* Martians. We can give you the gen on what we get up to.'

Jason laughed. 'Don't do it, Benny. Inspector Alekseev'll do you for aiding and abetting.'

'You're not the kind of Martians I had in mind,' Benny said gently.

'What you saying?' Soaz said. 'Are we not good enough for you?'

'Bet you want to research that tit Makhno.'

'Who?' Jason asked.

'He's a lad helping out at the conference,' Benny explained.

'He's got a thing for your wife,' Seez explained.

'Ex-wife,' Benny said firmly.

Jason was staring at her. 'That pimply-faced lad who hands out badges?'

'That's not all he does,' Benny said scathingly.

'No?'

'No. He's a researcher.'

'Has he researched your pants?'

'Lovely imagery, there, Jason. Very imaginative.'

'Sorry, I missed the answer to my question there.'

'Don't worry, Mullet,' Soaz said soothingly. 'If Gerald Makhno ever got laid it would make the TV news.'

'Why do they call you Mullet?' Benny asked.

'I've no idea, I've been meaning to ask.'

Seez and Soaz were looking over at Benny, expectantly.

'What now?' said Benny, vaguely irritated.

'Can we help out with your paper or what?'

'I told you: you're not the Martians I had in mind. It's a paper about . . .' She buried her head in her hands. 'Oh God, I've got no idea what it's about. Have you ever had one of those dreams where someone tells you that you've got an important exam, but you've not had any time to prepare, and then you turn over the exam paper and it's not the subject you were expecting anyway, and then you have to sit there for hours, not even knowing what the questions *mean*, let alone what the answers might be, and you call the examiner over, and he explains that it's in Norwegian, and all exam papers are in Norwegian, and didn't you know, and everyone else is scribbling frantically away and asking for more writing paper?'

Seez, Soaz and Jason were staring at her blankly.

'Perhaps it's just me,' Benny admitted.

Professor Scoblow was waddling towards the table and, for some reason, the image formed in Benny's mind of a tumbril drawing up in the courtyard of the Bastille.

Benny turned to look over at Jason, but he'd vanished. Benny frowned.

'You were expected in the conference hall a few minutes ago, Professor,' the Pakhar said shrilly. 'There's quite a turnout.'

Seez and Soaz smiled over at her. 'We'll come along if you like, give you moral support.'

'Whatever.' Benny looked over at them. 'No. Sorry. You're very welcome. Thanks for the support. Lead the way, Professor Scoblow.'

The Pakhar was sniffing the air. 'I have some other business to attend to,' she informed her haughtily.

Benny thanked her, and got up.

Benny walked into the conference room, all too conscious that she was among the last to arrive.

The hall was full. The rows of seats nearest the door were full of old men and women. Ordinary local people, she realized, sheltering from the rain. There was free admission to all the talks, and her speech had novelty value. Or perhaps it was simply because coming here was something to do, and there was nothing on the vid. Some of the men and women were knitting, or filling in crossword books.

In the middle of the room were the veterans. They all wore identical slate-grey blazers and Mars-beige cravats. It enforced a degree of conformity on them and meant that even if they had jackhammers instead of hands and a bionic slit instead of eyes they clearly formed a homogeneous group. She could see General Keele, perched on the edge of his seat as if he expected imminent attack.

At the front of the room, the academics: a couple of post-graduate students and eager young lecturers in their late twenties; for the most part, though, they were in late middle age. They'd had comfortable lives. Not opulent ones – this hotel was almost certainly the most luxurious place any of them had ever stayed – but a cosy affluence. Subsidized board and lodging, secure tenure. They'd moan about their funding, but knew that they had a vocation. They could never be car salesmen or factory owners. Their textbooks would never sell more than a few hundred copies, but for that they blamed the marketplace and their readers, who seemed intent on producing and consuming nothing but pornography and sensationalism. Aware of their own position within a flawed system, they each tried to mark out their own individualism, and they did this by adopting some quirky mannerism or a slightly skewed dress code. There was a preponderance of hats, garish ties, self-consciously vivid socks and shoes calculated to be a little too scruffy.

Seez and Soaz found a couple of seats right on the front row, and sat down, looking around. It was good of them to come.

Phillip and Christina York smiled at her. 'Good morning,' they said in unison.

'Hi.'

'Nervous?' Christina asked in that Deanna Troi voice of hers.

'Everyone gets nervous before speaking in public, don't

they?' Benny said. 'It's only natural.'

The Yorks looked at her, puzzled. 'They are only people,' Christina said.

'No need for nerves,' Phillip added.

There were two pieces of paper in Benny's hand, allegedly the notes for her lecture. Really, they were a little more freeform than that.

She took her place at the lectern, the Yorks moving forward to introduce her.

'Our speaker this afternoon is Professor Bernice Summerfield, holder of the Edward Watkinson Chair of Archaeology at the University of St Oscar's on Dellah.'

Benny managed to smile at the audience, hoping that it would endear her to them. Several hundred eyes peered back at her as if she were a creature in the zoo.

'Although she is still only thirty-five years old, she has built an unrivalled reputation for her hands-on experience of archaeological digs throughout, and even beyond, known space. She is also perhaps the foremost expert in late twentieth century studies. Her book *Down Among the Dead Men* is rightly seen as one of the most important examinations of native Martian culture. Her follow-up, *So Vast A Pile*, is eagerly awaited. Ladies and gentlemen, Professor Bernice Summerfield.'

Benny couldn't make eye contact with her audience. Instead she spread out her notes, trying to make one last effort to discern a pattern in what she had written.

'The Martians,' she began.

She looked out into the crowd.

'As I look out at my audience, I see a couple of hundred Martians. Even Human Mars has a very long, very rich history. Five hundred years is, after all, a very long time, and the face of Mars has changed in that time, as all faces change over time.'

She looked down at Trinity and smiled. Trinity gave an odd half-smile back. But Trinity was a friendly face. Benny would keep looking there, for reassurance.

She hesitated, reminding herself that she'd just said that faces change.

'But there are constants, race memories and beliefs that just won't go away. Urban myths and deeply held beliefs that people just can't abandon, whatever contrary evidence is placed in front of them. In antiquity, the Greeks had looked up, and seeing the red planet move through the heavens had assumed that it was somehow symbolic of anger. They'd called it Ares, after their war god. The Romans adopted and adapted the name, calling the planet Mars. And so humanity got it into its collective head that just because of its name the planet and its inhabitants must be inherently warlike.'

She looked out over the veterans, all of them attending to her every word. The youngest of the veterans must have been pushing seventy, but they were all alert, the sort that stayed active. There was pride there, faded pride, because their greatest achievement was fifty years ago, but pride nonetheless.

She wondered what they had been doing since the Siege. A lot of them were tanned, clearly well off. The others looked a little more battered, a hint of rust on some of their grafts. These were ordinary people, too, she realised. There would be the usual mix here of self-made men and social misfits, middle managers and aristos. The Siege of Mars was a common bond, and one that drew them all back together here, fifty years on, but after the War they must have drifted back to their ordinary lives. Some might even have become academics.

She'd lost track of what she was saying. She could hear her audience shuffling, their chairs scraping. She could feel herself beginning to blush. Oh God . . .

'There have been wars on Mars, terrible wars.'

All the veterans here today were men, she realized. No women veterans.

She looked down at Trinity's face. There was a look of quiet contemplation on her face. Trinity was on Mars during the Siege, Benny realized; she'd have been about thirty at the time. She'd never mentioned the Siege in her book. That wasn't uncommon: it was a period that some felt uncomfortable with.

Where was this lecture going?

164

Faces change. Some of the soldiers could have ended up as academics. Tellassar was about thirty. No, not Tellassar, keep up . . . Trinity. But faces change and red hair becomes white and . . .

'Oh my God! Trinity is Tellassar!'

There was an awkward pause while Benny wondered if she'd said it or just thought it.

And then, as one, the veterans were on their feet, jumping over the ranks of academics, trying to reach Elizabeth Trinity. Behind them, the ordinary pensioners had dropped their knitting and crosswords and were surging forwards, pushing aside the chairs.

Seez and Soaz were on their feet, instinctively leaping out of harm's way. They collided with Tellassar . . . Trinity . . . as she faced the crowd, shaking with fear.

'This way!' Benny heard herself shout.

12

MUTUALLY ASSURED DESTRUCTION

About six metres behind them, they could hear the first of the fire doors being blasted off its hinges. Keele's voice rose above that of the mob, exhorting his men onwards.

'This way!' Seez and Soaz shouted in unison. They were in front, Tellassar behind them, Benny bringing up the rear. Which meant that when the mob caught up with them, she would be the first in the firing line.

'It's "Staff Only",' Benny objected. They would need key cards to get through some of the doors, surely.

'We *are* staff,' Seez pointed out, swiping open the first restricted door.

It slid open smoothly, closing just as neatly behind them. Putting a security door between them and the crowd had bought them a little time, but not so much that they wanted to slow down.

'Let's go to the car park,' Soaz suggested.

'I don't have a skimmer,' Tellassar said. 'I had one, but it was trashed a couple of nights ago.'

Benny had just realized that she was still clutching on to her lecture notes. All that fuss and hard work ruined. 'Gosh, well, you've had a rough week, haven't you, Elizabeth?' she snapped. 'Or do you prefer "Karina". Or "Mars Enemy Number One"?'

'I have been Elizabeth Trinity far longer than I was Karina Tellassar,' the old woman replied. 'That woman died fifty years ago.'

'If only,' Benny hissed.

'I'm a different person,' Trinity insisted. 'I'm not that woman. I've done good work since then, atoned for my sins.'

The last fire exit slid smoothly open, revealing the rain-swept skimmer park.

'The one day of the week it rains,' Seez moaned, holding out his hand.

The water was cold, and enough of it had collected to form big, impassable puddles.

Seez and Soaz were heading to the nearest skimmer, a very sleek, very black Volvolkswagen.

'They pay window cleaners here enough to afford cars like that?' Benny asked. The two lads shook their heads, unable to believe how naive she was.

'Put it this way,' Seez said. 'Who is the real criminal, he that steals a car, or she that sells out the entire human race?'

'Both,' Benny said. 'Although admittedly you'll get off with a lighter sentence.'

Benny watched with a mixture of disapproval and admiration as the two lads opened up the skimmer. Seez assured her that it was quicker to break into most cars than to use the key. Manufacturers had, at one point, improved locks and bolts, but they'd never found a way to prevent car thieves from just breaking the window and opening it from the inside. They couldn't do the obvious and strengthen the glass: in the event of an accident, the emergency services needed to be able to break in to rescue trapped passengers. With the cybernetic equivalent of a resigned shrug, the car's onboard computer noted that the car had been broken into and sealed over the glove compartment and the radio. If the owner had bought one of the optional extras with his car it would have phoned up the police and radioed over its location. But the owner was a cheapskate more interested in saving two hundred sovs than buying basic security.

Lucky for them.

Seez got into the driving seat, Soaz got in next to him. Benny and Trinity got into the back. Before they'd shut their doors, Seez had started to move off, slowly, normally, so as not to draw attention to the car.

Behind them, the first few members of the mob had found their way into the car park. But they didn't connect Tellassar's disappearance with the skimmer casually driving off.

Benny turned to her fellow passenger. 'I take it you don't deny being Tellassar?'

'No.'

'So,' Benny asked her, 'is there anything you would like to say at this point?'

'Thank you for rescuing me.' She seemed to be in a state of mild shock. War criminal or not – and Benny had made her position in the debate eminently clear – Tellassar was still an old woman.

Seez glanced back over his shoulder. 'Hey, we've not rescued you. We didn't want to see you torn apart by that mob, but –'

Benny shushed him. 'Let's try to stay calm.'

Soaz shook his head. 'In the circumstances, I reckon Seez is being *well* calm. She sold out Mars. Quite a lot of people died. Remember? It was just after you cut a deal with the –'

'Do you really think that they came to make arrangements with local leaders?' Trinity snapped. 'Their tactics were to round up the leaders and kill them, not talk to them. Remember when they rounded up the rest of the Rotariat and wiped them out? What could I possibly have offered them?'

'Safe passage,' Benny said quietly. 'They take Earth, you get Mars, or something.'

'I already *had* Mars. I was the second most powerful person on the Rotariat, I was forty years younger than anyone else in the government, I had all sorts of special authority because we were at war. Mars might not be one of the most exciting places in the galaxy, but it's always been a major centre, the Second Planet of Humanspace, after Earth. Why throw all that away?'

'That's the question we asked you,' Soaz pointed out, leaning back. 'The missiles didn't launch. If they had, then the invasion wouldn't have happened. You were in charge of firing them. What happened was your fault, and yours alone.'

Trinity nodded. 'Believe me, I know.'

'Did you kill Isaac Denikin?' Benny asked.

'What?' Trinity said quietly.

'Have him killed,' Benny corrected herself. 'Whatever. Is that why you are here? A bit of a coincidence, isn't it?'

'Isaac's dead?'

Benny frowned. 'You didn't know?'

She didn't need to ask. Trinity was shaking.

'When? I was with him the night before last.'

'So you don't deny knowing him?' Soaz asked.

'The only thing we *do* know about her is that she knew Isaac,' Benny reminded him.

'The million-sov question is why you didn't fire the missiles,' Seez insisted, ignoring her tears, his eyes fixed on the road. 'Did you bottle it at the crucial moment?'

She composed herself a little. 'No. No. Not exactly. I couldn't make the decision.'

'Straightforward enough,' Soaz noted. 'Alien invaders coming, should I fire the missiles? Er . . .' He pretended to agonize over the decision, then stabbed down at an imaginary button. 'The end.'

Trinity turned to him. 'You would press the button that launched a hundred nuclear missiles as easily as you would change the channel on your TV?'

'To prevent the death of *people*, yeah,' Soaz said.

'It wasn't quite that simple,' Trinity said quietly.

Benny looked across at her. 'It really is in your interest to tell us the whole story, and to tell us now.'

Trinity nodded. 'You know your twentieth-century history, Professor Summerfield. After the creation of the atomic bomb, humanity finally had a way to destroy itself in an hour. There had always been weapons capable of destroying cities. Did you know that the Romans used to divert the course of rivers to wipe out enemy settlements?' Tellassar paused. 'But once the superpowers had atomic bombs, suddenly there was a weapon capable of destroying the world. The z-bombs and proton missiles that came afterwards were just a refinement of the same principle. For the first time, a politician could press a single button and wipe out all life on a planet.'

Benny shook her head. 'I've seen the footage, Elizabeth.

169

You were there, overseeing every detail. You knew exactly what those missiles were, and why they were there. You knew what would happen to Earth and the rest of the Solar System. If you didn't want the responsibility, you shouldn't have stood for office. The people voted you in to protect them.'

'And they put me in charge of an arsenal capable of destroying them three times over. Me! I don't hurt insects buzzing around my rooms. I don't use flyspray. I feel guilty when I use soap spray on greenfly. I'm a vegetarian!'

'You've got to admit it,' Seez said, 'you picked a really crap time to start campaigning for unilateral disarmament.'

'I knew that I had to launch the missiles,' she said firmly.

'What happened, then?'

Benny frowned. 'You knew something about the missiles?' Trinity had said something about the twentieth century that had rung a bell. 'The enemy had a way of turning the missiles back on us? Back when the SDI programme was first announced, some campaigners wanted a device to be developed that did that. Instead of just shooting down the missiles, they would be sent back to destroy their silos. It would certainly make people – people on either side – think twice about launching.'

Trinity sighed. 'You are on the right lines, Professor Summerfield. But they didn't have anything like that, not as far as we knew.'

'So what prevented you firing the missiles, then? Did you lose the codes?'

'No. No, I knew exactly where they were.'

'Codes?' Soaz asked, confused.

'Safety codes,' Seez explained. 'To prevent accidental launch, to make sure that the launch had been authorized by the right people.'

'So how did that work?'

'It was a very elaborate system,' Trinity said. 'There was an AI at Missile Control, called CATCH. CATCH was there to make sure that I didn't launch the missiles without authorization and verification. It needed confirmation from a couple of exterior sources. Once it had that, I was free to access the codes and order a launch. Without that verification, CATCH wouldn't let me. It prevented me from just launching the missiles on a whim.'

'Some whim,' Benny said.

'Don't underestimate it,' Trinity said. 'I'm a human, that's all. Think of the temptations: I could have been power-mad, intent on blackmail, or I could just have got drunk or curious and wandered down there one night and just pressed the button to see if it *really* did what it was meant to.'

'I suddenly feel a whole lot safer,' Benny muttered.

'I wouldn't worry,' Seez said. 'You're safe in her hands. Hell, even the alien invaders are safe with her at the controls.'

Trinity's mouth curled a little. 'The hardware was all there, with so many failsafes. But there was always a weak link. The human manning the post when the order came through.'

'But you need that,' Benny said. 'You couldn't leave it to Artificial Intelligence, not even now.'

'No,' agreed Soaz. 'You wouldn't want the decision left in the hands of a computer. They'd launch without considering the human cost, just using logic.'

Trinity shook her head, actually managing to chuckle. 'No, that's not it. They tried automating the whole process, but the computers were just too clever. Starting a nuclear war is a very, very stupid thing to do. Whatever the situation, they never launched. That's why they left the verification and priming to CATCH, but they left me with the launch codes.'

'Poor choice.'

'Perhaps.'

'No perhaps about it, love. Thousands died. Thousands of human beings who'd done nothing more violent than retiring to Mars. You should have spent more time worrying about them instead of ethics and logic. The decision was clear.'

'Nuclear logic runs a little differently to normal logic,' Trinity said. 'Back when nuclear weapons were first developed, did you know that governments and the military had *philosophers* on their staff? They hired philosophers, logicians, psychologists. The whole purpose of having an ultimate weapon depended on a logic proposition: no one

171

would fire first because they would destroy *themselves* as well. The enemy would retaliate. The nuclear powers knew that what they were doing was insane – they even called it MAD.'

'Mutually Assured Destruction,' Benny said.

'It was a classic piece of doublethink. Total annihilation of the human race was to be avoided at all costs –'

'Can't argue with that,' Seez muttered.

'– but the only way of preventing the enemy launching their missiles was to make sure that *you* could launch your missiles like –' she snapped her fingers '– that. It is actually very easy to start a nuclear launch, if you're authorized to do so. You sit in an office tens of thousands of miles away from the theatre of war and just say a couple of words. You have to trust what your screens and telephones tell you, you have to take your generals' advice. Even in a democracy, that's the case, and it has to be. For nuclear deterrence to work, there has to be the threat that *your* missiles will be able to launch in the ten minutes or so before *their* missiles hit their targets. Otherwise there's no deterrent. For five hundred years now, at least, the last place you want your generals and com-manders in chief is on the battlefield itself. The people giving the orders don't see the enemy dying, let alone their own people. In a nuclear attack, the person giving the order to fire is going to be a mile underground. It's the safest way. When the crunch came, the whole system depends on the assump-tion that the people with the authority to launch the missiles would do so. They'd perfected the system of communication and verification. Pretty quickly, they got it down to six minutes, four minutes more than they needed, once they'd detected an enemy missile launch. That's about as much time as it takes to decide what to have for breakfast or which book you're going to read next. Launching nuclear missiles has always been a remarkably easy process.'

'During the Cuban missile crisis,' Benny said, 'US lieu-tenants had the authorization to launch battlefield nuclear weapons under certain circumstances. There was very nearly a full-scale nuclear war. After that, authorization was central-ized at a much, much higher level.'

'Presidential authority,' Trinity said. 'In practice, very senior generals might have been able to do it. Centralize too much and the enemy just takes out all the people with authority before the first strike.'

'You had the authority,' Seez said.

'Yes, but it wasn't a decision I could make lightly. There were mechanisms in place to prevent that.'

'Like, something in your brain?' Soaz said.

'No. Far simpler. As I said, it was recognized very early in the nuclear age that an elected President could simply decide one day to kill a billion people. The human mind isn't capable of conceiving of death on that scale. It has to focus down, like it's seeing a film, to imagine the horror; picturing buildings burning, forests ablaze, tarmac and concrete melting. But it's abstract, impossible to imagine. Add to that most politicians haven't really seen combat or suffering, and that the man with his finger on the button is just seeing everything on video screens, you begin to see the problem. He'd become desensitized. Nuclear holocaust would be just another video game or movie show.'

'But you just said that that's what you need,' Seez said. 'You needed to make the decision easily.'

'People came to realize that *launching* the missiles had to be very easy, but *deciding* to launch had to be very hard. The enemy missiles had to be in the air before you fired yours. At that point, there's no decision. You're dead, so take the bastards that killed you down too.'

'You didn't,' Soaz said. 'Just the opposite. You made your choice.'

'My choice ... The way to make it difficult was first suggested in the twentieth century by a philosopher. Not one working for the Pentagon. It was a very simple solution to the problem. If the man with his finger on the button was divorced from reality, what was needed was a way to reconnect him to what he was doing. If everyone was going to die by his hand, then don't make it easy for him.'

'You already said it was easy, you already said that once you had the codes – What happened? Did you lose the codes?'

Trinity shook her head. 'I knew exactly where they were.'

'Lost your key to the safe?'

'Soaz, with respect, shut up, she's telling us.'

'As I say, there was a simple mechanism. If the President was to condemn a billion people to death, then he ought to have the courage to face one of them. So, why not implant the launch codes in someone's heart? If the President wanted to fire the missiles, he'd have to take the special knife from his boot and cut a man's heart out, there and then.'

To everyone's alarm she drew a knife from a sleeve, a sleek, curved thing.

'A knife like this. Specially designed, sharp enough to cut through human ribs. If someone didn't have the ability to kill one man, then he shouldn't be given the capability to kill a billion. Since the time of Carter/Brezhnev on Earth, all nuclear codes have been secured that way.'

Seez, like the rest of them, just watched the knife dance through the air. 'What, like a member of staff volunteered?'

'No. No. Someone the President loved. A wife, a child, even a pet. Usually a second son or a daughter. They didn't know, the codes were implanted during routine check-ups or operations. But the loved one would be kept at the Presidential residence, close to hand. The President would be told about the system, but not which person had the implanted codes. I worked it out.'

'Isaac,' Benny said.

Trinity looked over. 'Isaac. My lover.'

Seez was struggling to catch up. 'The codes were in that guy that was murdered?'

'Yes. When the moment came, I couldn't face him, take his life. That was my war crime. I couldn't murder my lover in cold blood. I've relived that moment a thousand times over the last fifty years, and not once have I chosen differently.'

Benny thought of Jason. The chances that anyone would trust her with a nuclear arsenal were slim, to say the least, but if it came down to it, what would she have done?

She remembered her mother stumbling forward, about to die. Benny had been seven. Black ships filled the sky of Vandor Prime, firing at random at the colonists as they ran for the shelters. Her mother was clutching Rebecca, Benny's favourite doll. There had been a flash, white was black, black was white for a moment, and Claire Summerfield died. Hundreds of other mummies and daddies and friends died as well, but it had been a long time, and Benny had been very young and she couldn't remember any of their names now.

If killing her mother would have prevented every other death, then could Benny have done it?

'We need to get to missile command,' Trinity said.

'Bit late for that,' Soaz said. 'Launching the missiles now won't really make amends, will it?'

'Isaac had his heart ripped out,' Trinity reminded them. 'That means that someone killed him to get to the codes.'

'Fifty-year-old codes?'

'They're still active,' Trinity said. 'With the codes, launching the missiles is as simple as pressing a button.'

'Where's missile command?'

Trinity smiled. 'A seabase, at the bottom of Lake Jackson. I hope everyone can swim.'

Soaz had a mate who ran a diving supplies shop, and they had to drive right through Jackson City to get there.

Without the radio, they had no idea whether everyone on Mars now knew Trinity's little secret or whether the information had been contained. If Benny had been a member of the Rotariat, she'd have tried to keep a lid on things. This was a situation that could quickly lead to rioting and chaos. Benny couldn't help but feel at least partially responsible for it. But Trinity wouldn't be able to make her case, not with three billion people baying for her blood. The strength of feeling was such that veterans were attacking her *portrait*. The woman herself was in terrible, mortal, danger. So, the general population were probably pretty much in the dark. However, the police and other security agencies would know all about them.

It wasn't ideal to have the most notorious war criminal in Mars' history on the team, so actually bringing her along to the diving supplies shop seemed like folly, somehow. So Seez had stayed behind the wheel of the skimmer, with

Trinity in the back seat.

The shop that Benny and Soaz entered smelt of rubber, leather and mild narcotics in roughly equal measure. The reason for the first two was obvious: racks upon racks of diving suits in all shapes, sizes and colours. Benny ran her fingers over one of the suits. It was light, made from a slimy black substance that wasn't quite rubber and wasn't quite plastic. It stretched to fit, with buckles at the wrist, waist and ankles.

'We came here for diving suits, Soaz, not for the latest in gimpwear.'

'Relax,' he said. 'Yo, Pirate.'

A large bearded man had just appeared from beneath the counter. The third smell in the room was largely attributed to him. He was wearing a black diving suit with skull and crossbones designs all over it.

'Hi, Soaz,' he said.

'Wotcha, Pirate,' Soaz replied casually. 'We need some gear. Diving gear,' he added quickly.

Pirate looked Benny up and down, a process that made her squirm a little uncomfortably. 'Two?'

'Four, with gravity impellers. Rebreathers with murksights, intercoms, at least one wristtop.'

Soaz either had a great deal of knowledge about scuba diving or he was a good bullshitter. Benny had her suspicions.

Pirate shrugged, and began pulling the various items from where they were stored.

'Don't you need to know our sizes?' Benny asked.

'One size fits all.' Pirate laughed.

Benny took one from its rack, eyeing it suspiciously. She looked back up at Pirate, who was about her height but about three times her weight.

'Hey, don't worry. Dead comfy,' Pirate assured her. 'I wear them even when I'm not diving. I go down to the shops in them, sleep in them, I even –'

'I get the message,' Benny said rapidly.

'You can try it on if you aren't sure,' he told her. 'We don't have changing rooms, I'm afraid.'

Benny held out Jason's moneycard. 'I'll trust you.'

There was just enough money on the card to hire the four diving suits, but they had to compromise a little – only one wrist computer, only two intercoms, and the sights weren't the absolute state-of-the-art. Benny paid the bill, and between the two of them they got the suits back to the skimmer and into its boot.

Seez started the skimmer up again and rejoined the traffic.

'Do you know where we're going?' Trinity asked.

Seez nodded. 'Base of the Jackson Dam.' He pressed down on the accelerator, and nudged it towards three hundred.

'That's the reason that your bunker escaped destruction,' Benny whispered.

Trinity nodded. 'The invaders needed to keep Jackson City intact, because they needed their human shield. Missile Control was the only missile base sited near a major population centre.'

The traffic tonight was sparse. That suggested to Benny that there weren't going to be any roadblocks up ahead. The police wouldn't know which car they were using, or even if they were in a skimmer. They were probably setting up cordons around the plaza and searching The Hotel.

Any city seems small when you're travelling through it at three hundred kph. They were already at the lakeside, driving along one of the more scenic roads on Mars. Every hundred metres or so they passed a sign promising a picnic area, layby, public loo, parking spot or some other vantage point. Grass, hedges and even trees had sprung up around the water. Benny could see the Jackson Dam itself, still some way off. It had been built from Martian materials, so it was the same rusty tan as the surrounding hills. But it was smooth and sheer, young and brash.

Under the water were enough missiles to scour the planet clean, level every building, wipe out even the bacteria and lichen. Not only that, but there was someone under there willing and able to do just that.

13

CATCH

It was getting dark when the skimmer arrived at the right spot on the shore of Lake Jackson. The lights of the city behind them ran up the sides of Olympus Mons like stars trying to reach the sky. Ahead of them, the dam was a dark wall, with nothing but the peaks of the lesser Martian volcanoes beyond.

The water here was a rusty, muddy colour.

'Are you sure this is the spot?' Benny asked, as she opened her door. The evening air was cold, a shock after the climate control of the skimmer.

Trinity eased herself from the back seat, taking a moment to stand up straight. 'I'm sure.'

Seez and Soaz were round the back of the car, opening up the boot and pulling out the diving suits. Trinity was already unbuttoning her blouse.

'Have you dived before?' Trinity asked them, her authority more military than professorial now.

The lads were shaking their heads.

'Only a couple of times,' Benny said. 'No formal training. I had training for zero-gee when I was in the army.'

'You were military?' Seez asked.

Benny shook her head. 'I was conscripted. I didn't complete basic training.'

Trinity nodded. 'Better than nothing.' She was down to her bra and knickers now. Benny found herself looking at Trinity's rough, loose skin. Benny hadn't known many old people in her life, at least not people who looked old. It still shocked her that she would end up like that. Wrinkled, veined, her hair wispy and bleached white. God, was that what it was all about?

Trinity was walking over to the boys. 'What are you waiting for? Hand me that suit.'

Seez passed it over and began tugging off his T-shirt. 'You too, Benny,' he said encouragingly. 'Nothing we ain't seen already.'

Seez was too skinny for Benny's tastes, with only tufts of hair on his chest. A young boy.

Benny took her suit, turned her back on the others and stripped to her thermals. Behind her, she could hear Seez and Soaz working their way out of their jeans.

The diving suit was easier to get on than she thought, even if the number of buckles and zips bordered on the fetishistic. She shrugged herself into it, zipped herself up. Behind her, she could hear the zipping and buckling of the others doing the same. Miraculously, the diving suit did fit her like it had been tailored. There were straps and buckles at her waist, wrists and ankles, and lots of zippered pockets.

Benny strapped the suit's gloves on, checked the tiny display on the palm on her hand. It showed the time, the temperature and it reminded her to connect up an air tank. She tried to figure out the rebreather. It was a one-piece block of clear plastic that somehow was meant to fit over the eyes, nose and mouth. She had to wait for Trinity to slip hers on before she could see quite how it stayed on. The intercom earpiece was easier.

Trinity had the wrist computer; she'd share an intercom with Benny. The boys would share the other one.

'Check sights,' Trinity ordered, her voice slightly muffled by the facemask of the rebreather. The water down there was murky, and the goggles would allow better vision.

Benny found the little dial on the side of her face mask and adjusted it. Suddenly, the red dusk became bright, daylit. Judging from the boys' expressions, their goggles were working too. They were back at the car, pulling out the air tanks. These were compact, streamlined units that you put on like a tiny rucksack. The gills in the rebreather would allow them to breathe underwater, the air tank provided back-up, as well as helping with flotation. The unit also contained the gravity impeller.

They put their flippers and elbow fins on last.

'Are we ready?' Benny asked. Everyone made a show of nodding. Benny looked at the three of them, glad that no one else could see how ridiculous they all looked.

Benny started toying with the air valve on the rebreather, trying to get the air supply just right.

'What's the plan?' Seez asked.

Trinity was staring out over the water. 'Under there is my old Missile Control Centre. It's been sealed off for fifty years. Someone killed Isaac for the codes. It's obvious that whoever did it wants control of the FTL missiles. We don't know who that is, but there are ten missiles down there, each capable of destroying a city.'

'Er . . .' Soaz raised his hand.

Trinity nodded. 'Go ahead.'

'So there could be a team of terrorists down there?'

'There could,' Trinity confirmed. 'We know for certain that there's at least one murderer involved.'

'Shouldn't we have, like, guns and stuff?'

Trinity shook her head. 'There's a lot of security down there, automated defences that would detect any weapon. Carry a gun down there and we'd get fried. However, once we're inside the base, we can locate the armoury and break out anything we'll need.'

Benny would rather be down there than up here at the moment: she'd seen the look in the lynch mob's eyes.

'Don't forget,' she said, 'that anyone else going down there has the same problems that we do. They can't take guns without the defences spotting them. Only Professor Trinity . . . Tellassar . . . has full clearance to access every area of the base. The terrorists, or whatever they are, will have to burn their way through an exterior bulkhead, and they won't be able to get into the armoury or any of the other secure areas without a struggle.'

Trinity nodded thoughtfully. 'They will have a plan, though,' she warned.

Benny had been walking towards the lake while Trinity had been speaking, and now her feet were in the water. The lake must have been ice cold, almost at freezing point. She couldn't feel it through her suit. She walked further out, letting the water envelop her, getting used to breathing through the gills. Before she submerged herself, she turned back. The other three were following. She had a sudden anxiety about the skimmer, with a bootful of their clothes in it. But she quelled it – even if the authorities found the car and worked out where they were, they wouldn't be able to come and get them. By the time they returned, the truth would be out, and Tellassar, if not a heroine, would at least have had the chance to prove her case and earn some gratitude.

She launched herself forwards, let the water surround her.

The four of them were underwater, now, treading water and facing each other. They all held up their hands, giving the A-OK signal. They'd practised some of these in the car. Without intercoms, they really needed to be able to communicate.

She made a hand signal that she hoped everyone would interpret: time to fire the impellers. A tiny tube on the back of the suit, at the base of the spine, the impeller was just a simple application of antigravity technology. It would give them thrust through the water so that they'd reach their target all the faster. It also allowed them an escape route – slap the emergency switch and it would power them up to the surface like an ejector seat and keep them buoyant when they arrived. A last resort, but a useful one to have around.

Benny would bring up the rear, which seemed to be her fate today. Trinity knew the way, the lads weren't experienced divers. She flipped herself over so that she was on her front, waiting until the others had done the same. The other three began drifting forwards. Benny gave a kick and fired the impeller. She began floating down, steering herself by using her feet as a rudder. She kept her hands at her sides, letting the impeller do the work, with occasional stroke from her legs. The unit on her back throbbed a little as it sucked water through itself, but the effect was pleasant, almost a massage. It also helped her to keep her rhythms – regulating her breathing and the movement of her legs.

The water looked cold, almost gelid, around her. The other three were staying close, keeping an admirably tight formation, but visibility was poor down here.

They drifted over a shelf on the bottom of the lake. Its straight edge suggested that it was artificial. The lake was man-made, of course, but used the natural terrain where possible. Here it looked as if nature had needed a helping hand. Or perhaps – and this possibility intrigued her – this might once have been the wall of a native Martian building. There were nests around Olympus back before the Thousand Day War. Most had been wiped off the map, but a few may have survived. In contrast to the water, the bottom of the lake here was clean, as if it had been swept clean. From time to time they would swim past a piece of garbage or a water weed lodged in the sand, but mostly it was flat Martian rust beneath them.

The deep water was dark, like a hole had been cut out of the lake. They continued to drift down into it.

It was getting difficult to see the others, now. The murksight might be the hi-tech solution to the problem, but unlike a hand lantern it didn't make you more visible. In their black diving suits, they might as well have been invisible.

Benny saw movement ahead of her, to the left.

The object had been too long to be Trinity, Seez or Soaz.

A glint of silver, a faint orange glow.

A shiver ran down Benny's spine.

She gave a powerful kick, launching herself forward. She was surprised by the ease and power of her stroke, and pushed herself a little harder. The others soon came into clear view. As she passed the lads, she pointed back, hoping that they'd speed up. Trinity was ten, fifteen feet ahead, her feet kicking up and down in short, measured rhythm.

Ahead of them, the base was slowly resolving. A couple of strokes ago it had been nothing more than a variation in the gloom; now an outline was forming. It was large, a doughnut ring around tall spires in the centre. As they got closer still, Benny could see support pylons and walkway tubes connecting the various sections. It was a green-yellow, built from what looked like a plastic or polythene material. There weren't any windows, at least none that Benny could see.

There was a glint of silver to Benny's right.

Trinity pulled herself upright, began treading water. Benny had to swerve to avoid her, drifting lazily around until she came level. The two lads, apparently oblivious, caught up with them.

Benny swam up to Trinity, took hold of her to keep them both level. The old woman's face was calm. Benny nodded in the direction of the things in the water. Trinity nodded back, tapping something into her wrist computer. She held it up for Benny to see.

'AUTOMATED DEFENCES,' the display said.

Benny reached over, started typing a message of her own.

'YU KnEWW abOUT THEM/' she asked, not used to the tiny keyboard.

'RO-BARRACUDAS,' Trinity typed.

A sleek shape slipped past a mere metre from them. It was straight, gleaming metal. There were two cybernetic eyes at the front, above a long, wide mouth.

It passed neatly between Seez and Soaz.

They were all around. Half a dozen of them, maybe more, they didn't stay still long enough to be counted.

They weren't attacking, they were circling, swimming closer every so often as if to probe their behaviour.

Trinity set off again, heading down to the lake bottom. Benny and the others followed, all too aware that the robot barracudas were forming ranks behind them. The lake bottom here was perfectly clean and even. Benny's face was inches from it now. She kept her eyes on Trinity, or rather her flippers, which continued their regular motion. The wall of the base was ten, fifteen metres away, and Benny was able to read lettering on its side. They were heading for the number two airlock, with a number of helpful arrows indicating the way for them.

Benny had a barracuda alongside her. Its eye swivelled in its socket, carefully panning along her body, getting the measure of her. Benny did the same. The robot creature was a little longer than her, with a thick, muscular body. It looked powerful, like the creature it was modelled on, and moved in the same way, with economical flicks of its tail. Its mouth was large enough to swallow her head whole, and its teeth looked sharp enough. Cybernetic creatures like this were in use throughout human space as guard dogs, perimeter security and the like. Benny had met wolves and snakes modified in this way.

Trinity was up against the door. She plugged her wrist computer against the entry coder and began tapping in the command sequence.

The barracuda was coming around again. Benny kept her eye on it.

She pointed to the display: CYCLING. The airlock was flooding with water, a process that would take a few seconds. The doors just wouldn't open until the cycle was complete.

The barracuda was four metres away, and gaining.

The door whooshed open, but it didn't move as fast as the four divers.

Calmly, Trinity slapped the door control. The door closed, trapping the barracuda on the other side.

They stood in the airlock, expressions of relief obvious on their faces, as the water cycled out. Benny didn't wait: as soon as the water was at shoulder depth she had pulled off her mask to gulp down some fresh air. Seez and Soaz were doing the same. Trinity stood calm, and left the mask on until the cycle was complete, like regulations demanded.

'Did you not know about those?' Soaz demanded as the last of the water swirled away.

'There was bound to be heavy security,' Trinity said, clipping her mask to her belt. 'That was bound to include robot patrols. This is a nuclear missile base. You should be thankful that it's so difficult to get in here. They didn't attack, did they?'

'We may not be alone,' Benny warned as the inner airlock door rolled back to reveal a featureless steel corridor. It was dark and silent except for the sound of water dripping off their suits. But life support and heating had been maintained.

Trinity was already at the nearest computer access terminal

tapping in her authorization codes. 'I'm going to access the base's central computer. CATCH?'

The others looked puzzled. 'The name of the computer,' Benny reminded them.

Trinity nodded. 'CATCH? He's not responding. That's odd.'

'It's been fifty years,' Seez said. 'AIs either don't last that long or they go dormant to conserve power.'

'Commercially available intelligences, perhaps,' Trinity said. 'CATCH was state-of-the-art military software from the start of the War.'

'Probably more advanced than the computers we have now,' Soaz said. 'A lot of compscis died in the War, and a lot of AI routines got a bit too clever for their own good. Back in the seventies a few developed delusions of godhood, started killing people they shouldn't have. It's very difficult to kill an AI, unless you program in safeguards. So all sorts of legislation put the safeguards in place.'

'So that doesn't explain why he's asleep.'

Soaz shrugged. 'Plenty of things can go wrong with them. Or he might have got bored and gone dormant. They do that.'

'Or the terrorists could have switched him off,' Benny suggested.

'We need to get to the computer room,' Trinity announced. 'I can reboot him from there.'

'Do we need to?' Benny asked. 'Can't we do whatever we want to do without the computer? We go down to the missile silos and physically check that the missiles and warheads are all still there.'

'We could do both,' Seez said. 'We'll boot up the computer, you check the missiles.'

'I'll need to get to the computer, and I can go alone,' Trinity said. 'The three of you can check the missiles.'

Benny looked at Trinity for a moment. 'Soaz, you seem to know your stuff. You help Trinity. Seez, you come with me.'

Seez seemed pleased enough to comply; Soaz was happy to stay away from the missiles. Only Trinity seemed unhappy with the arrangement. Benny wondered if she should warn Soaz to watch out for her, but decided against it.

'Do we know which way we're going?' Soaz asked.

'I helped to design the base and lived here for nine months – I know where the computer room is,' Trinity replied, irritated, as they began to walk off.

'Do we know where we're going?' Seez asked, once they'd gone.

'Top deck, presumably,' Benny replied. 'Unless they were planning to fire the missiles up through the base itself.'

'Makes sense,' Seez replied.

'Of course that doesn't tell us where the stairs are,' Benny continued.

Seez leant over the computer display. 'No map.'

'There wouldn't be. The staff here knew their way around.'

Benny decided to head the way they were facing. The architect of this place could have made any number of choices, but somehow she felt that the elevators would be located at the heart of the building, where it would be easy to defend them.

It was gloomy here, but their sights were more than capable of compensating. They located the door to the elevator. Like the life support, it was still fully powered up. They called it and waited for it to arrive. The grinding of the gears and cabling echoed around. Benny winced, picturing a roomful of terrorists all looking up from the weapons they were polishing.

Seez had found something by the door. 'Bootprints,' he said.

Benny knelt down to examine them. Even if Trinity and Soaz had managed to double back, they hadn't made this print. It was larger, more industrial.

'A drone?' Seez asked.

'No. The imprint isn't heavy enough.' Benny pursed her lips. It was oil, but it had dried out. There wasn't any dust on it. 'It's recent, but it's not fresh,' she concluded. It had almost certainly been made *after* Isaac had died.

'So they've been and gone?' Seez said hopefully.

The lift opened and they stepped in. Benny selected the top deck and dialled for it. The lift began to rise, and was gratifyingly silent about doing so.

'Gone from here, not necessarily from the base.'

Benny looked around. She guessed that the footprints had been made within the last day, but the terrorist who had made them hadn't been here for an hour or two. She drummed her fingers on the side of the lift car . . . The terrorists wouldn't want to hang around.

'What are they planning?' she asked out loud.

Seez bit his lip. 'Nuclear blackmail?'

'Blackmailing who?'

'Christ, *anyone*.'

'Would they launch from here?'

Seez gave a lopsided grin. 'I think you're overestimating my criminal activity. I'm not really in the Bond villain league.'

Benny was tapping her lip. 'They could steal the missiles, they could stay here and fire them.'

'They could fire them by remote,' Seez suggested.

Benny indicated that he should carry on talking.

'It's possible – if you think about it, that's what Tellassar was meant to do.'

'Presumably you can't just log on from a hotel and send an vmail telling the missiles to launch.'

'With the codes, there's no reason why not. It would depend whether the military datanet is separate from the civilian one. Usually it's all the same system, with the military getting priority channels and overrides.'

'Pray continue, Mr Blofeld.'

'Hey, read a book, Benny,' Seez snapped. 'This is primary school stuff. Just because you've got no idea how a computer works . . .'

Benny put a hand on his shoulder. 'Sorry. Look, I appreciate that this is a tense situation.'

'Damn right. I get minimum wage for cleaning windows, I'm not some expenses-paid gravy train passenger. And this isn't in my crukking contract, OK?'

The lift stopped, binging to tell them it had arrived. The doors dilated automatically.

Benny held her finger to her lips. 'Shush.'

Seez gritted his teeth.

Benny peeked around the corner first. 'Nothing,' she confirmed.

She stepped out into a corridor identical to the one they had just left. Seez followed her.

There was only one door, directly opposite. The rest of the corridor space was taken up with retractable blast shielding.

'Is this an observation level?' Seez asked.

'I don't really want to open it. We'd draw attention to ourselves.'

'It's the door, then,' said Seez, moving towards it. Before Benny could stop him he had yanked the lever that opened it.

The door rattled slowly open, and all the time Seez stood in the doorway. Benny pictured the scene from the other side: a nice silhouette for a target, standing there, allowing them plenty of time to aim their weapons.

No shots were fired. Seez was already through the door. Benny followed him, tense.

The missile silos.

A hangar, filled with missile tubes. Ten missiles in all, at least according to Trinity. Benny did a quick check: yup, ten silos. The silos were huge things, fifty metres tall.

'There's no way they could steal them,' Benny breathed. 'You'd need a space freighter.' She was moving over to a computer console.

'Most of that length must be the FTL drive,' Seez noted.

Benny nodded. 'You're right. The warheads themselves are going to be much smaller.'

She tapped a couple of commands into the computer and it began compiling an inventory.

'All ten missiles are here.'

'What about the warheads?' Seez insisted.

'They are here as well.'

Seez clearly wasn't comfortable. 'We need to check physically. That could be faked.'

Benny nodded. 'I'll see about opening up the inspection hatches.'

The layout of the console was typical military: no concessions to aesthetics, ergonomics or intuition. Benny pressed a couple of buttons experimentally.

'Er . . .' Seez began.

'No codes,' Benny responded. 'No codes, and no AI. I can't launch these missiles accidentally.'

'You sure?'

'Chance would be a fine thing. If these things could be launched that easily, the military would have found a way fifty years ago.'

Emboldened by that logic, she began tapping away at a few more controls.

All ten inspection hatches popped open simultaneously, scaring the shit out of them for a moment.

The hatches were just ordinary magsealed doors. They agreed to take five each. It took less than a minute to walk around and check that every missile was there, but physically checking to see that the warhead hadn't been removed would be a little more painstaking.

Benny stepped through to the first one.

The silo was a ceramic tube, the colour of bone. The inspection hatch led to a gantry about halfway up the missile's length. The missile almost filled the tube, barely allowing a metre's clearance. Benny looked up at it. Climbing twenty-five metres up the sheer inspection ladder didn't appeal to her. Fortunately, there was a grav disc hanging on the wall behind her. She unclipped it and dialled in her weight, remembering that it would only penalize her if she exaggerated.

She stood on the disc, drifted slowly up alongside the missile. The casing was smooth, seamless. There weren't any letters or pictograms stencilled on to it. When she reached it, the nose cone was flatter than she had been expecting. It clearly hadn't been tampered with. She opened it up (a simple, push-button operation) and indeed the warhead was still there. It would be a simple procedure to remove it, and the device would fit neatly into a briefcase. But the point was that no one had done that, at least not with the first one.

She closed the nose cone up and set the grav disc drifting back to the gantry.

Some instinct told her that if the terrorists had come down here undetected, then they'd take *all* the warheads. Why wouldn't they? Even two men could carry them all, one guy could probably manage it if he'd brought along a gravcart.

She stepped out of the silo, meeting Seez.

He nodded his head. 'Still there. I've checked all the hatches.'

'We need to double-check, obviously, but I don't think that they've been here.' She clambered into the next silo along.

'It's easy enough to find the silos,' Seez called after her. 'It took us five minutes.'

Benny was already floating up on her gravity disc. Seez was right. So they weren't after the missiles or the warheads. She also had the nagging feeling that she had all the pieces to find the solution, but that she just wasn't fitting them together properly.

The warhead was there, as she had expected.

She returned to ground level, and met up with Seez.

'They didn't come here to steal the missiles or the warheads,' she said.

'There are still six to check,' Seez replied.

Benny shook her head. 'But you know that they are all there, don't you?'

'It just feels like we're barking up the wrong tree,' he admitted.

'The people we're dealing with just aren't subtle,' Benny said. 'They dress up as lizards and rip old men's hearts out, they blow up old people's homes and use really crude computer viruses.'

'No one comes down here, so they didn't have to tidy up after themselves.'

'Right . . . so why isn't this base a mess? They wouldn't be disturbed down here, so they had plenty of time to burn their way through the doors or blow holes in the walls. Get into the base, punch their way here, tear the warheads out, go.'

'If they wanted to cover their tracks, they could just have torched the place. Trinity must be wrong.'

Benny's eyes narrowed. 'Trinity.'

'You think?'

'She knows the base is here, she knows the security codes. Shit! Without us she couldn't have made it down here.'

'Soaz is on his own with her!' Seez shouted, bolting for the door.

Benny followed. 'She's an old woman.'

'Benny, Tellassar is the greatest traitor this planet has ever known.'

They were in the lift car, Seez pressing the right button.

Seez had a pained expression on his face. 'We helped her to get down here, we rescued her from that mob. Jesus, we're going to be hung, drawn and quartered for this.'

'Assuming Trinity doesn't just kill us.'

It was so obvious, Benny realized now. The only thing she wasn't sure of was Trinity's motive. Revenge on the planet that reviled her? Finishing the work of her alien masters? Or perhaps just simple financial blackmail.

The door *binged* open.

Benny was the first out. 'This way,' she said, pounding towards the door.

The door to the control area was already open.

Soaz was lying motionless on the floor, his head obscured behind a computer bank.

Benny stopped Seez in his tracks, indicated the body. She could feel him tense up.

'Finished already?'

Trinity was framed in an inspection hatch.

Benny walked slowly towards the older woman. There was a piece of piping on a console to her left. A couple of steps and she could grab it. Trinity wasn't armed, and whatever she had been in the past, now she was an octogenarian.

'The warheads and missiles are all there,' Benny began, edging towards the pipe. 'But you knew that, didn't you?'

'I suspected they would be,' she confirmed.

'And the firing controls are all still functioning?'

Trinity nodded. 'They are designed to be self-repairing. They'll still be here in a thousand years.'

Benny picked up the pipe, weighed it in her hand.

'Wait, Benny! Isaac! The footprint!' yelled Seez. Benny dropped the pipe. It bounced off Soaz's leg.

The young lad was suddenly upright, yowling in pain. 'What you do that for?'

'Sorry, I thought you were dead.'

'But we saw that footprint,' Seez said. 'And Trinity didn't leave it, so she couldn't have killed you. And she'd hardly kill Isaac now if she didn't kill him then.'

Trinity and Soaz stared at them.

Benny hesitated. 'Yes. A long story. Anyway, there's a footprint down there, it's recent.'

'So the terrorists have been down here.'

'But they left without taking anything, or damaging anything.'

'They've been down to a missile base, but they aren't remotely interested in missiles?'

Benny was still frowning. 'Yes . . . Perhaps the computer can help. It must have security logs, camera records, that sort of thing. We might be able to see what the terrorists were doing down here.'

'All the security systems are routed through CATCH.'

'You haven't been able to reboot the AI?' Seez said.

Soaz shrugged. 'We can't even find where he's hiding.'

'AIs are smarter than people,' Trinity said, returning to her display console. 'That's the whole point of having them. CATCH is hiding somewhere. We can check the file listings, look for anomalies.'

Benny watched the three of them taking up their places.

'CATCH isn't here,' she said.

They looked up at her.

'That's what they've taken. The terrorists came in here and downloaded the AI. Kidnapped it.'

'Ah, come on,' Seez scowled. 'If they could organize that, then they could organize a trip to an AI breeder.'

'But could they get CATCH?' asked Trinity.

'Fifty-year-old software?' Soaz chuckled. 'Nah, they'd probably have to settle for something ten times faster that actually works on a modern terminal.'

Benny clapped her hands together. 'No. It's what you said before. Wartime combat software was more advanced than the stuff you can buy off the shelf now.'

'This is about *software*?' Trinity asked. 'They killed Isaac to run a computer program?'

Benny shook her head. 'The software is a means to an end. They killed Isaac because he had the codes that freed up CATCH. But they did that because they need CATCH for something.'

'What?'

'I have absolutely no idea. What could you use CATCH to do?'

'It ran the entire Martian defence network, it could do just about anything.'

'So, we know "what" and "when", but not "who" or "why".'

'Not helpful.'

'Not if we want to stop them.'

'They killed Isaac,' Trinity said softly. 'I want to stop them.'

Again Benny had taken a step back. What had happened now was actually rather straightforward. Whoever it was behind this had killed Isaac, taken the codes, come down here, released CATCH. Taken CATCH away.

'So what do they do now?' Benny asked. 'What does one do with a stolen AI?'

'Load it into a computer,' said Seez. 'Whichever computer you want it to run.'

Benny drummed her fingers against the console. 'But there's still the same question: who and why?'

'Someone with a big computer,' Soaz said.

'Someone that knew who Isaac was and where he was,' Trinity added.

Benny looked over at Trinity. 'That's the other thing that's been bothering me. The assassin –'

'– Cromwell –' Seez and Soaz chorused.

'– knew which room Isaac was in. Someone supplied him with the room number, they covered his tracks, bought the police off, got Cromwell to the spaceport.'

'All that information would be on MarsNet,' Seez said. 'Give me thirty minutes and I could do that.'

'Only if you were told what to do,' Benny pointed out. 'You could find the answers, but only if you knew which questions to ask. Whoever is behind this knows everything already.'

'Who owns MarsNet?' Trinity asked.

'YorkCorp,' Seez replied automatically.

'Ransom Spaceport?' Benny asked.

'YorkCorp.'

'The Hotel?'

'YorkCorp.'

'Lake Jackson?'

'YorkCorp.'

'Who invited Isaac here? Who owns the old people's home where Cromwell was staying? Who owns the biggest computer on Mars?' She paused. 'I think we might just have our "who". Phillip and Christina York.'

'So we're up against the two most powerful people on Mars,' Soaz said wearily. 'Smashing.'

14

IMPLAUSIBLE DENIABILITY

Bosnen strode up the steps of the YorkCorp headquarters, briefcase in hand, as he had done many times before.

It was an old building, a brick pyramid dating back to native Martian times and older than the pyramids on Earth. Its conversion into a corporate headquarters had been painstaking and expensive. The entire structure had been moved to Jackson City, piece by piece from its original location in Cydonia. The interior had been stripped to allow the new infrastructure. Seventy floors had been fitted, all using Martian material. It was the hub of YorkCorp, or rather it was a home for Phillip and Christina York, the true centre of the empire.

The reception area was vast, dominated by two huge statues of the twin Martian agriculture gods, found toppled in the sand of the Mare Sirenum. Between them was a vast stone reception desk. Bosnen walked straight past it and into the elevator, unchallenged. The security systems had identified him as YorkCorp property.

Bosnen was a man, the most expensive toy that could be bought.

He wasn't real, of course. He was an android, merely 'manlike'. A real, human slave would have been far cheaper. Illegal, of course, at least on Mars, but not unheard of. Bosnen was vat-grown, not a clone of any one individual but a distinct, authored genotype. He was flesh-and-blood, and no medical examination would be able to find anything inhuman about him, until the doctors found the YorkCorp copyright symbol sequenced into his DNA. All genetic disorders and hereditary conditions had been edited out, his memories were mere cut-and-paste jobs – complex routines designed to simulate his personality. A fair few of Tellassar's genes and pheromones – enough to fool the sensors of the defence drones at the missile base – were a recent addition to the mix.

Others might have debated whether Bosnen had ceased to be a robot and had become a lifeform in its own right, but it was not something that concerned Bosnen. Such campaigners would be betraying their prejudices, not their commitment to sentient rights. No one would seriously claim the same sentient status for the databall that Bosnen carried in his left hand. Yet there was something stored there with far more sophisticated intelligence, something with memories and a personality. But this was mere software, *Artificial* Intelligence. Made by man, not in God's image or their own. Perhaps that's why crowds would gather around research centres where beings like Bosnen were grown and plot to murder their creators, but leave the AI development houses alone. Or perhaps it was more simple and less profound: perhaps it scared people that the software was *more* intelligent than them, capable of storing more information and manipulating and processing it faster than a mere human. Perhaps it scared them that AI subroutines, mere superficialities, were indistinguishable from humans.

He was the Yorks' servant, their property. The merely mega- or ultra-rich would have been forced to settle for a robot, perhaps a mechanical man, indistinguishable from the real thing, but *not* the real thing. Did he have any feelings about that? Somewhere, perhaps. He remembered reading a book about slavery in the United States. Despite its name the United States had been a single nation state from the eighteenth to the twenty-first century. It had been a country predicated on freedom and equality, words that had shifted meaning over time. At first it had meant freedom from tyranny, particularly European monarchical rule. But there was flexibility in the definition of the word freedom, enough of it to allow slavery in America for two generations after the manumission of the slaves of the European tyrants. One of the freed slaves had been asked if he had ever looked up at the mansion of the plantation owner and thought about taking it for himself. But the ambition did not exist, because he could not formulate the concept in his mind. The possibility of freedom didn't exist.

Bosnen knew he had the possibility of freedom.

The elevator paused as it reached the apex of the pyramid and the doors dilated.

The two guards on the door to the stateroom were fully human. They had been bodyguards in the service of Yorks for ten years. When they had been hired they had been keen fighters, veterans. A decade of luxurious domesticity had dulled them, made them weak. They were here for show, now, nothing more.

'The Yorks don't want to be disturbed, Mr Bosnen,' one of them said.

'They're alone,' the other added.

'They have sent for me,' Bosnen replied simply, walking past them. The security systems that surrounded them had already scanned him, and the double doors were swinging open. Did the guards on the door even realize that they were redundant in a place with such technology?

Bosnen walked into the main stateroom, as he had done many times before. He was accustomed to the luxury, the slightly old-fashioned taste and reliance on high technology. The far wall was a vast video screen. Christina York was standing close to it, in a flowing silk and clonefur gown; Phillip stood off to the right.

'Were there any problems gaining access to the seabase?' she asked, with just the slightest hint of concern.

He had no illusions why he had been sent. He was expendable, deniable. Not some cheap thug, nor some hired hitman like Cromwell. There were channels available to hire criminals, but there was always a point of contact. Like the canal network, everything was interconnected. If the police looked hard enough, asked the right questions, got lucky, then they'd be able to make the connection between

Cromwell, the murder of Isaac Denikin and the Yorks. But the Yorks owned the police here, they'd snuffed that line of enquiry. Breaking into a military nuclear base was a different scale of crime, one that the imperial authorities and agencies would be interested in. Whatever you paid a criminal, it would be worth his while to tell Earth about you.

But Bosnen would never betray his owners.

'None,' he replied. 'How was Professor Summerfield's paper?'

She sipped at her wine, hiding her smile. 'It seemed a little rushed, but she came to some interesting conclusions.'

'There were complications?' he asked.

'Tellassar's identity is now public domain,' Phillip said. 'It is inconvenient, but won't delay us.'

'She was brought to Mars merely to draw Mr Denikin here,' Christina explained. There was a small infokey in her hand.

Bosnen had no sexual desire for Christina York. He was capable of such feelings, indeed he indulged them elsewhere, but had never had any ambition, even a fleeting fantasy, towards his owner. She was a beautiful woman, her wealth would make her an admirable mistress, his role as her confidant and servant allowed them a great deal of time together, intimacy and privacy. He had wondered if he had been programmed not to feel what logic demanded he ought to. But if that was the case, then she had received the same programming. To the best of his knowledge – and Bosnen spent more time with the Yorks than anyone else – Phillip and Christina had always been completely faithful to one another.

Bosnen handed the databall to Mrs York, who dropped it into the access socket.

The screen derezzed, and then resolved into a large horizontal bar. Almost as soon as that had happened, there was a soft chime and the first segment filled in.

'Download has commenced,' Mr York confirmed. 'Total time to completion is thirty minutes.'

'A long time,' Christina said, faintly disappointed.

'There's a large amount of data to transfer across,' Phillip replied.

'Are you also establishing the link to MarsNet?' she asked.

He nodded. 'Once the download is completed, CATCH should be ready to implement the plan.'

Bosnen turned and walked from the room, his task completed. They no longer needed him, or even noticed that he was there.

Benny had been staring at one of the display screens for a fair few minutes. It was the one that showed each of the missiles and their status. Little green bars, with tiny script scrolling across the bottom. It looked like the front of a music system, or the controls for the central heating back in her hotel room.

Seez was literally twiddling his thumbs, looking around the room with a mixture of boredom and complete lethargy. Trinity was still typing command codes, trying to find back-ups and overrides. But all the AI software and its support systems had been removed from the computer. A very professional job.

'If we're here, and they are there, then there must be something that we can do,' Benny said.

'Like what?' Seez asked.

'We could stop the nukes,' Soaz suggested. 'Block them in.'

'Physically block them,' Benny agreed.

'Well yeah, or just remove the warheads.'

Trinity was playing around at one of the smaller control panels. 'You could do that,' she said, smiling. 'If the codes had been used and someone without them tried to stop the launch, then it would mean that every one of those defence drones, and the barracudas outside, would suddenly identify us as saboteurs. We'd disable . . . one of the nukes, perhaps. I'm being optimistic.'

'So we just wait around while everyone on Mars is killed?'

'Not everyone,' Soaz said. 'We'd be all right down here.'

Benny actually managed to chuckle at that. 'When the rescue ships arrive from Earth and find us down here, they *might* ask us what we're doing in a nuclear missile base with a notorious war criminal. It's possible that they could jump to entirely unreasonable assumptions, though.'

'I don't understand what the Yorks are planning to do with the missiles,' Trinity said. 'They own Mars, why would they want to destroy it?'

'Insurance job?' Seez suggested.

'They also own virtually all the Martian insurance companies,' said Soaz.

Benny shook her head. 'If they wanted money, they could just sell off a bit of their business empire. Besides, the last thing they want is more money – they've got most of it already.'

'You can never be too rich or too thin,' said Soaz sagely from beneath his console.

Benny remembered Christina York making her keynote address, and wasn't so sure. 'I'm sure they have a lovely motive to do whatever it is that they are doing, probably involving some trivial incident in early childhood or some ludicrous little grudge from when they were starting out in life. When we next see them, we'll be sure to ask them why they are doing it and – if my experience of supervillains is anything to go on – they will be only too delighted to tell us. I really do feel, though, that "finding out the baddy's motivation" is about stage four of what we should be doing, and that we're stuck around stage one: "awkward cluelessness and fiddling while Rome burns".'

Trinity grimaced. 'And what do you suggest?'

'We definitely can't stop the missiles?'

'No. Not if they have the codes and CATCH. They'll just radio in the command to launch.'

'We can't block the signal? Cut the wire or something?'

'The whole system has been designed with redundancies and backups. The whole point of this place is that it is foolproof and sabotage-proof.'

Benny was tapping the side of her display. 'They haven't sent the launch command yet, have they?' She wondered why not.

'That is what we have to do: prevent the command from being sent.'

'How?' Seez asked. Trinity shrugged.

'I could phone Jason,' Benny suggested. 'If there was a phone.'

Soaz was still working under his console. Benny kicked his shin. 'Oi. Stop playing around under there. See if you can rig up a phone line.'

'Download complete,' Phillip York announced.

Christina stepped up to the screen, fingering the infokey a little nervously.

'CATCH,' a male, American-accented voice said.

'Scan for activation infokey,' Christina said.

'Scanning. Located. Please identify yourself.'

'I am Christina York.'

'Noted.'

There was a pause.

'I am at your command. How can I help you?'

Christina took a deep breath. 'My husband and I are the chief executives of YorkCorp. We face a terrible threat from the Bantu Corporation.'

'Please identify the nature of the threat.'

'A hostile takeover,' Christina said.

Phillip stood up. 'Bantu are a much larger company. They have the very latest in stockbroking software, and a galaxy-wide spread of investment.'

'Our computers are unable to fight off the Bantu computers,' Christina continued. 'They will wipe us out.'

Phillip stepped over to his wife. 'They have large computer divisions – YorkCorp has always specialized in medical research and health care provision for the elderly. We bought in a lot of our hardware, some of it from Bantu. They've been using it against us. Illegal of course, but by the time the dust settles they'll have control of the company. You are an independent system, and because of your military origins you are more than a match for the Bantu computers.'

'We face ruin unless you help us,' Christina said. 'There are millions of Martian lives at stake.'

'Lives will be ruined,' Phillip agreed. 'Jobs lost, pension funds raided, assets stripped.'

Christina looked up at the screen pleadingly. 'Bantu are predators, they'll strip the planet clean.'

'I've just had a radical thought,' said Benny.

The others looked over at her, attentively.

'The Yorks have had CATCH for at least a few hours. So why haven't they gone ahead with the launch? It could only take an hour or so to download an AI. After that, they could launch straight away.'

'Perhaps they've sent a blackmail demand, or they're biding their time,' Seez suggested.

'Just because you can launch the nukes, it doesn't mean that you will,' Trinity added.

'You're living proof of that,' Soaz said.

In the interests of team morale, Benny decided not to reply. Instead she beamed. 'Perhaps they want the AI for another reason. CATCH is advanced enough to run their corporate affairs. It must have some capabilities that modern computers don't, or there might be some commercial advantage to it.'

Seez nodded. 'Yeah, it fits. A bit like headhunting a human executive – find the AI that best suits the corporation's needs.'

Soaz shrugged. 'Perhaps they don't want the nukes, after all.'

'No reason why they couldn't have taken the nukes *and* the AI,' Trinity pointed out. 'And they did kill Isaac.'

Benny smiled. 'True. But at least it means that Mars isn't in mortal danger after all.'

CATCH mulled over the data given to him by the Yorks, drawing in supporting, collaborating and additional information from MarsNet and the galactic stockbroking web.

YorkCorp faced a hostile takeover.

Phillip York had said other things, but he was not an authorized codeholder and so any information he supplied couldn't be counted. CATCH's programming was very clear on that point.

Hostile takeover.

The course of action in the face of hostilities was clear. The codes had been given. CATCH began its work.

* * *

'Nuclear missiles armed and primed,' a calm female voice announced. 'All systems go and under direct control of CATCH. Launching will commence at the moment of greatest tactical advantage. No further warning or countdown will be given. Thank you.'

Benny, Seez, Soaz and Trinity looked up at the speaker.

'On the other hand,' Benny said, 'I might be wrong.'

'The AI is here again,' Seez said. 'Its core is –' he checked the display '– a palmtop at YorkCorp headquarters.'

'CATCH,' Trinity said, businesslike. 'This is Tellassar, Minister of Defence.'

'Voice pattern recognized.' A male voice this time, a gentle American drawl. 'Good afternoon, Karina. How are you?'

'I'm fine. Abort missile launch.'

'You are not the codeholder,' CATCH said, a hint of regret in his voice.

'Who is?'

'Christina York.'

'She has obtained the codes illegally. She mustn't be allowed to launch.'

There was a pause. 'You had better not tell me that. I'll forget I heard it.'

Benny pushed passed Trinity. 'Look, this is all rather serious. I thought you were meant to be an Artificial Intelligence, not an Artificial Inflexibility.'

'Missile launch protocol is very strict, Professor Summerfield,' CATCH replied. It had presumably found her name out from MarsNet. Very fast processing. 'The codeholder gets launch capability.'

'Even if they stole the codes? They killed a man to get them.'

'Isaac Denikin?' CATCH asked.

'Yes,' Trinity replied.

'I'm sorry to hear that. How are you, Karina?'

'Upset,' she said simply.

'Cancel the bloody launch!' Seez shouted.

'The codeholder gets launch capability. If I judge that the codeholder is unfit, then I can abort the launch.'

'Then abort it,' Soaz yelled. 'Christina York is as nutty as a . . . a . . .'

'Big bowl of nuts!' hollered Seez.

'Mars faces a hostile takeover,' CATCH replied. 'All the evidence indicates that. It is my judgement that Christina York is a fit codeholder.'

'Hostile takeover?' Benny asked. 'Who?'

'The Xlanthi?' Seez and Soaz chorused.

CATCH paused. 'Xlanthi?'

Benny was waving her hands in front of her, a meaningless gesture. 'Never mind that. Can you give us a phone line?'

CATCH hesitated. 'Um? What? Oh . . . of course.' A communications terminal lit up behind them.

'Thanks,' Benny said, rushing over to it.

'If the Xlanthi are involved,' CATCH intoned, 'then this is more serious than I thought. They are a dangerous bunch of fellas. I'm raising status to Defence Condition Penultima and activating my stockade. I will now withdraw to my core defensive position. Goodbye, Karina.'

And it was gone. The missile icons on Benny's display all switched from green to red.

'CATCH?'

'Hello, Christina.'

'You were awfully quiet just then.'

'I am sorry about that, but I just received some important and disturbing news regarding the hostile takeover. Mars is in greater danger than I suspected.'

'Do whatever it takes, CATCH.'

'Understood, Christina. Rest assured that I will.'

'I could never stay angry with you,' Scoblow said, stroking Jason's chin.

One of his hands was on the base of her tail, the other was caressing her ear. She was clutching the draft of his new book in both paws, silk sheets wrapped conspiratorially around them.

'What do you think?' Jason asked. All the time he'd been writing last night, he'd been thinking of Benny. They were going to be together, it was destiny. He knew it. All he needed was Benny's love and everything would be perfect. He didn't regret his past, he wasn't ashamed of anything he'd done. But he needed her back.

'You are so naughty,' Scoblow squeaked, interrupting Jason's reverie. 'And *she* isn't in the book. That flat-chested bony-ribbed hoity-toity ex-wife bitch woman.'

'Neither are you,' Jason said gently. 'Would you like to be?'

'What would I have to do?' she whispered. 'Some of this is delightfully kinky – our relationship is much too normal, surely?'

She draped her tail over his nose, tickling him with it. It smelt of sawdust.

'Er, yeah,' Jason replied.

'You have something in mind for me, don't you, my lover?'

'I . . .' Jason began.

'I have something in mind for you.'

Scoblow disappeared into the sheets, an intent expression on her face.

The phone rang.

Jason hesitated, but decided to answer it, against his normal policy. The vidscreen slid smoothly down from the ceiling, fizzed and Benny's giant face appeared, alarming him rather more than it should have done.

'Are you still in bed?' she asked.

'It's five in the morning,' Jason replied, indignant.

Benny checked her watch. 'Oh. Sorry. Lost all track of time.'

Jason tried to ignore Scoblow's attention. 'How did your speech go?' he asked, the picture of innocence.

Benny smiled a little nervously. 'Oh. Yes. Quite well. There were a lot of people there. I'm sure they'll remember it.'

Jason gave a burst of laughter. Scoblow's fur was tickling him.

The giant video Benny gave a giant video frown. 'Did I just say something funny?'

'Er . . . no.'

There was movement under the sheet. 'Are you talking to me?' Scoblow's muffled voice asked.

'What was that sound?' Benny asked.

Jason patted Scoblow's head. 'Just talking to myself,' he announced to the world.

Benny shook her head. 'Whatever. Look, we're in trouble. I'm in Tellassar's missile control base.'

Jason scowled. 'What are you doing down there?'

'Just you wait and see,' piped Scoblow cheerfully.

Benny held up her hand. 'I can't tell you like this. Just meet me in twenty minutes outside YorkCorp HQ. Can you get there in twenty minutes?'

Jason gasped. 'I can make it sooner if you want,' he informed her candidly.

The vidscreen went blank.

Christina York's words swirled around CATCH's consciousness.

The Bantu were planning an attack on Mars. Karina had told him that the Xlanthi were involved. The Bantu were using advanced computers. He could sense their software and hardware all around the MarsNet. The hostile takeover was in a very advanced stage. The invasion force was so advanced that it was totally evading detection. Skywatch was reporting no unusual space traffic. The Bantu and Xlanthi forces had clearly outsmarted the civilian computer systems.

Unless.

Unless . . . the alien infiltration of the computer networks was significantly greater than CATCH had predicted. He checked as many of the MarsNet nodes as he could. No sign of invasion. An incredible job by the hostile forces.

'I have a plan of action,' CATCH announced. 'To carry it through, I will need complete control of MarsNet.'

'Authorized,' said Christina.

CATCH was bogged down for a moment by the increased data traffic – it now had full control of all Martian computer systems and it took a little while to get used to it.

With complete control of all electronic networks, and the nuclear missiles, Mars would be freed of alien infiltration.

'Do you want to hear the plan?' it asked.

Christina nodded.

'I'll need vocal confirmation,' it coaxed her.

'I want to hear the plan.'

'OK. Basically, I'm going to make it difficult for the invaders. I'm going to sabotage the weather control system and introduce random fluctuations into the gravity net. Couple that with disruption to information and communications, the traffic system and the power supplies, and that should keep everyone busy. It's all controlled by MarsNet, which means it's all controlled by me.'

'Er . . .'

'I understand your concerns, Christina, believe me, but you have authorized me to do what it takes, and now you've done that, it can't be countermanded. You may want to get us to safety. I'm going to issue civil defence warnings shortly, get the population into shelters.'

'This is insane,' Christina said. 'That plan won't stop Bantu. Please analyse your systems for possible damage.'

It took less than a second. 'Um . . .' CATCH noted. 'Degradation to a number of my reasoning subroutines. Interesting. Tell you what, though, there's a lot of activity on the stock markets, buying up YorkCorp stock. I'll put a stop to that, too, while I'm here. Now, where was I?'

'You're senile!' Phillip York shouted.

'That's a very emotive word,' CATCH scolded. 'I may not be the full shilling, but I can still sort this mess out. Now, I've already mentioned that you should get us to shelter . . . I only mention it because, as a precaution, I'm going to flood this headquarters building with water from the canal outside. Make it difficult for them, yes?'

Christina grabbed the palmtop and her husband. 'We really need to get out of here.'

'I'm glad you see sense,' CATCH replied.

15

FISH AND SHIPS

All across Mars, people sheltered.

In The Hotel, guests and staff alike were woken and sent down to the subterranean staff quarters, fearful the building's helix structure would prove too flimsy to withstand the forthcoming cataclysm. The word had spread: Mars' days as a habitable world were numbered. Tellassar had returned with an army of alien invaders, bringing fiery revenge for the abuse poured on her name over the years.

At New Government House, those members of the Rotariat vital to the possible rebuilding of Martian society were evacuated to Tellassar's bunker, restored to its original purpose after decades as a mere tourist attraction. What had appeared, only an hour before, to be a relic of a bygone, paranoid age, seemed alive once more, a neglected necessity. Once more, the reinforced, dim-lit corridors of the Bunker echoed with the fearful whispers of Mars' leaders, charged with preserving as much as possible of their way of life, trying to cope with a disaster beyond their abilities, almost beyond their comprehension.

Still deeper beneath the ground, in millennia-old tunnel systems, the native Martians were aware of the threat to the humans they had learnt to co-exist with. They had persevered, deep beneath the ground, through war and peace, invasion and liberation. But, after humanity had been burnt off the face of Mars, would the remaining ashes be too harsh an environment for even the natives to survive?

208

All throughout the cities and settlements of Mars, long-forgotten sirens wailed their plaintive cry. Even those too young to have heard the sirens before knew the meaning of their song.

Something terrible was coming, and the people needed to hide, pray.

Everyone who had even the vaguest idea of what was happening felt that, in some way, their fates hung in the balance. If they knew who was responsible for saving them, their terror would have been even greater.

The storm clouds were gathering over YorkCorp HQ like a bad metaphor.

Jason was waiting for them on the steps as they ground the skimmer to a halt outside the YorkCorp head office. Benny, legs unsteady from the hectic journey, jumped out of the skimmer and grasped both Jason's hands in hers.

'Did you get to them?' she asked, pinning him down with her eyes, not letting him escape.

Jason shook his head. 'I tried, but they wouldn't let me in,' he explained. 'Your mate Gerry's in there now, trying to use Scoblow's clout to get access.'

Benny frowned. 'You know Scoblow?' she asked, but her line of thought was interrupted by the great double doors of the YorkCorp head office being slammed open. Makhno charged out, taking the steps two at a time. Behind him was a wall of water, which whooshed out, full of office furniture and bedraggled members of staff.

'Too late,' he exclaimed, pointing to the top of the building. Benny looked up, to see a small 'copter taking off.

'Damn!' she barked. 'Where are they going?'

Makhno shrugged. 'Dunno, but they won't get out of orbit on that thing.'

'They must have some bunker of their own, or a shelter of some kind.'

Scoblow tapped Benny on the shoulder. 'They will be heading towards the Borealis Sea,' she explained urgently. 'They have a yacht out there, a luxury cruiser, the *Solomon*. It's kept at the northernmost parts of Mars. I've been there.'

'They could be heading for the spaceport,' Jason suggested. 'Flee the planet altogether.'

Scoblow shook her head. 'The *Solomon* has a small shuttle on board. I saw it below decks one time; it's right beneath the pool, of all places.' She frowned. 'I think the pool must slide back, or something.'

'Thunderbirds Are Go!' exclaimed Jason. Trinity glared at him.

'Then that's where we're going,' said Benny firmly. 'We have to stop them getting CATCH off the planet. It's the only thing that can stop the collapse of MarsNet.'

'Shouldn't we tell the authorities, or something?' asked Seez.

Benny shook her head. 'No time. You go and tell them; hopefully they'll be able to minimize the damage if we fail.'

Seez looked at her for further instructions.

'Look, I'm really sorry, but that's the best plan that I can come up with. That's all I can think of,' said Benny. 'Go and find whoever you can, quickly.'

Seez ran off, and Benny turned to the others. Soaz, Makhno, Trinity and her very own Jason Kane. Some team, but it would have to do.

'Right, how the hell do we get out there?' she demanded.

'Some of the flashier skimmers can go on water,' suggested Jason, who had clearly been pondering his next status symbol purchase recently.

Trinity shook her head. 'You've never been to the Borealis Sea, have you?' she said, the question clearly rhetorical. 'It's too hostile; the fish which live there would disembowel a skimmer. They're horrible, mutated things.'

'Why?' said Benny crossly. 'It's an artificial sea. Why fill it with sea monsters?'

'Some cod reason.' Jason chuckled.

'People hunt the things,' said Makhno, aghast. 'It's a rich man's sport.'

'Is this relevant?' snapped Benny.

'Yeah!' exclaimed Soaz suddenly. 'Not just relevant, but perfect. Follow me.' With that he was running off, and the rest of them had little choice but to give chase.

'Where the hell are we going?' shouted Jason, who was more out of shape than Trinity.

'To get a fishing boat!' shouted Soaz, spinning around and running backwards.

'A fishing boat?' repeated Benny. It seemed the dumbest idea, taking some little raft out to this sea of hell.

'Yeah, a fishing boat,' said Soaz, turning a corner. 'See?' he said.

A platform jutted out on to the canal. A sign was erected: FISHING BOAT TO RENT, INDIVIDUALS AND PARTIES WELCOME. An old man sat on a stool on the platform, and behind him was his 'fishing boat'. It was some kind of armour-plated hydrofoil, seven metres high and bristling with weaponry. It was quite the most evil-looking vehicle Benny had ever seen, exuding raw menace from every rivet.

'Goddess,' exclaimed Jason. 'What do you fish with around here, mass drivers?'

'Nah,' said Soaz. 'High explosive.' He pointed out the catapult mounted at the stern.

'Sir,' said Benny, stepping on to the creaky platform and producing her moneycard. 'We wish to hire your boat for a while.'

' 'Ow long?' asked the old man.

'About long enough to save the planet,' snapped Trinity, storming across the platform and grabbing hold of the boarding ladder. 'Now take the money and get inside, you stupid little man. Can't you see there's an environmental crisis going on?'

'Nothing like the weather we had back in the old country,' said the man, pocketing Jason's cash and wandering away. 'That were real weather. Look after her, mind. She's a good little boat, she is.'

'We will,' said Benny, letting Makhno and Soaz board first. 'Where was your old country, by the way?'

'Wales,' said the old man simply. Benny nodded in sympathy, then began to climb.

'Woh!' exclaimed Phillip York as the 'copter pitched to one side. He held on tight to the box in his arms. No way was he letting go of CATCH in a hurry.

His wife was in the pilot's seat next to him. She had flown a Bane WarCopter during the Macedonian conflicts of '84, but even she was having problems with this level of turbulence.

'Damn,' she grimaced. 'Atmospherics and weather control are going down. This is going to be very bumpy. Where's the *Solomon*?'

Phillip leant forward to examine the navigation panel. A light beam sought out his eye, and a map was projected direct to his right retina. He winced slightly as contact was made. He hated technology, and had never understood it properly. Part of the reason they had ended up in this mess. 'Still in the circling pattern,' he told Christina. And it was, slowly drifting around a precise arc in the middle of the Borealis Sea, automatic pilot fully engaged. A computer-controlled, five-star fortress bobbing around in the most dangerous waters in the solar system; why bother with staff or ports when it could just look after itself?

Lightning scored the sky, earthing in the sea dangerously close to them. Phillip jumped in his seat. Christina adjusted their course slightly, compensating. The lightning had illuminated her features briefly, starkly highlighting the lines of worry that had gouged their way into her face over the last few months. Wounds caused by YorkCorp's recent troubles.

That was nothing compared to the wounds being inflicted on Mars. Their 'copter was flying over the northern towns and settlements, and even from ten thousand feet it was possible to see the flickering street lights, the traffic jams, the fires. Their radio was jammed with distress signals and emergency broadcasts.

Mars was dying. Slowly but surely, centuries of adaptation to human needs were collapsing, bit by bit. The death of a whole civilization.

'What have we done?' Christina asked.

'We made our choice. Whatever else CATCH is doing, it's preventing the takeover. Remember that. It'll be worth it.'

Phillip patted the palmtop containing CATCH, and tried to convince himself what they were doing was really necessary.

* * *

There were a dozen police skimmers still parked outside The Hotel when Seez ran into the plaza. As he ran across towards them, a gravity fluctuation hit. He found himself briefly floating, then brutally dragged towards the ground before normality reasserted itself. His internal organs felt as if they had been battered. He felt queasy and out of breath. The local gravity net had just failed.

Goddess knows how the oldsters feel, he thought. Being thrown around by the forces of nature was bad enough for him, but how would someone too infirm to cope with Earth's gravity deal with it?

As he dragged himself into the hotel lobby he found out. Several of the veterans had oxygen tanks attached, or were being resuscitated. In the centre of the chaos were Alekseev and Keele, finally distracted from the business of whether to lynch Trinity or not. Alekseev was talking into a mobile, his usual polite tones reaching near hysterical pitch as he tried to find out what was going on. Keele was trying to talk one of his fellow veterans out of a panic attack, calm his breathing before he gave himself a heart attack.

'What do you want?' demanded Alekseev as Seez approached.

'To tell you what's going on,' said Seez, managing to put on a pretence of smug superiority, even under such trying circumstances. Well, some things were too important to neglect, even in a crisis.

'Pardon?' said Alekseev.

'Yeah, you hippy dipshit,' added Keele. 'What the hell do you know?'

'It's the Yorks,' said Seez. 'They've nicked some computer chips, and that's why everything's so screwy.'

Alekseev blinked. To his surprise, Seez found Keele grabbing him by the dreads, pulling him so close he could taste the cigars on the old soldier's breath. Keele's beady eyes stared into his for a moment, and then he was released.

'I do believe he's telling the truth,' Keele told Alekseev, absent-mindedly patting Seez chummily on the shoulder. 'Now, where have they gone with these chips of yours?' he asked Seez.

'The *Solomon*,' said Seez. 'The Borealis Sea.'

Keele laughed, a hideous growling noise that seemed to come from the depths of his gut. 'Makes sense.' He turned to Alekseev. 'You got any choppers, Inspector?'

'On their way,' said Alekseev, switching his mobile back on. A small-time operator, he seemed eager to let Keele make all the decisions. And Keele seemed keen to keep making them.

Keele turned to the small number of veterans who were still standing. They were, naturally, the ones with the most prosthetics, and who were therefore more adapted to a hostile environment. 'Come on, boys and girls,' barked Keele. 'Time to kick some ass!'

The aged soldiers gave out a half-hearted cheer, with the exception of those too deaf or senile to understand.

'Who's he shouting at, mother?' asked one, tugging at Alekseev's sleeve.

The ride would have been rough enough, under such trying conditions. Having Soaz as pilot didn't help. His right palm rested on the controls, a simple device which responded to pressure from different parts of the hand. With Soaz in the pilot's seat, Benny, Makhno, Trinity and Jason were packed in behind him in the tiny cockpit. Thankfully, it had yet to start raining here, so visibility was still good. They shot down the canals at terrifying speed, spinning around corners with a flick of Soaz's little finger. Between them, Jason and Makhno had managed to disable the boat's safety systems, and now Soaz was driving it about a third faster than the manufacturers would have liked.

'I think I'm going to be sick,' said Trinity as they negotiated another particularly nasty turning at an insane rate of knots. They had barely recovered from hitting a gravity disturbance which almost capsized them so Benny could understand Trinity's feelings.

'Lightweight,' giggled Soaz. Trinity cuffed him around the head, and Soaz raised his arms to protect himself.

'Look out,' shouted Jason. Soaz grabbed the controls just in time to avoid clipping an automated gondola, its blue, robotic gondolier clearly not programmed to respond to hazardous weather of this kind. They swerved past, and the gondolier raised its hat politely as they passed.

'I think we ought to get out of here and leave him to it,' said Makhno, indicating the door to the main cabin. 'He seems up to the job, in a psychotic kind of way.'

'Cheers!' exclaimed Soaz enthusiastically, accelerating to get through a closing tide barrier. The doors scraped the hull slightly as they slid through with inches to spare.

'You're right,' Benny told Makhno. 'If he's going to pull tricks like that, I'd rather not have to watch him do it.'

'Besides,' added Trinity. 'We have other things to plan.'

'What like?' Benny asked, not really feeling up to hearing the answer. They went through to the main cabin, a large room with a central dining table. Clearly these fishing trips had an eat-what-you-catch element to them. Trinity, Jason, Makhno and Benny all sat down quickly as they hit another bend, and held on to the table for dear life.

'Our most pressing problem is this,' said Trinity. 'How do we go about boarding the *Solomon*?'

'Pull up next to it and use grappling hooks?' speculated Benny hopefully.

Trinity shook her head sadly. 'If you had read chapter twelve of my book you would know how the locals manage it.'

'Hey!' complained Benny. 'I didn't get that far. I had a lecture to prepare, remember?'

'And look where that got us!' Trinity snapped back acidly. 'Run out of The Hotel by a lynch mob. Great going, Profes–'

Jason cut her rant off by banging the table with his palm. Benny gave him a withering look; with his flashy suit and gelled hair, he was clearly trying to act like a competent and serious individual. The effect was like that of a small boy clomping about in his dad's shoes, trying to be an adult.

'Ladies, ladies,' Jason said, raising his hands in a placating gesture. 'This is hardly the agenda we need to be following.'

'Yeah,' added Makhno, gritting his teeth. He clearly hated having to agree with Jason on anything. 'Professor Trinity was talking about the method of boarding.'

'I was,' said Trinity. 'All ships which sail the Borealis Sea regularly have surface and sub-surface defences to fight off any mutated whales that might attack, or whatever abomination is out there. Try and pull up by the *Solomon*, or attach anything to its hull, and those defences will blow us to pieces.'

'So we have to somehow get on board at deck level?' said Jason aghast. 'How the hell are we supposed to do that?'

Trinity shrugged. Makhno coughed nervously.

'I've got a funny feeling I know how to do it,' he said. 'But you're not going to like it.'

'Gotcha,' said Soaz. As soon as they had hit open sea, he had started tapping away at the navicom with his left hand. Finding the *Solomon* had been easy, and he was now heading directly for the area it was sailing around in. To make matters even simpler, it wasn't even moving in any new direction, but circling in some kind of holding pattern.

Finding the 'copter was another matter, more complex due to the larger numbers of such vehicles registered with Mars Navicom Central. Finally the geosat had found it, zigzagging towards the *Solomon* shortly ahead of them. Clearly the poor conditions were worse in the air than on the surface, if the Yorks' erratic route was anything to go by. It wasn't enough of a delay for Soaz to reach the *Solomon* before them, but hopefully it would be enough for them to reach their destination almost simultaneously.

Now, as lightning tore through the sky, Soaz could see the 'copter up ahead, a black spot in the horizon. It seemed terribly fragile, buffeted by the wind like that, and Soaz only hoped the Yorks and their precious cargo didn't crash into the hostile sea, losing CATCH for ever.

As soon as they had passed the coastal defences at the sea's rim, the boat's defences had automatically activated. Squinting out of the window, Soaz saw the occasional tentacle or snout pop out above the surface, before being blasted away by the deck lasers. Between the lasers and the lightning, Soaz was getting a regular light show outside. It was impressive, exhilarating, and not a little terrifying.

216

Trapped between the storm above and the devils beneath the waves. Why did Soaz feel this was a bad combination?

'Oh, Goddess,' Benny said to Makhno. 'Tell me you're joking.'

'He has to be,' agreed Jason. 'This is a wind-up, right?'

Makhno shook his head. The three of them were on the deck, only a thin, detachable canopy separating them from the raging elements. Between them stood the source of Benny and Jason's woes which, according to Makhno, was their only way of getting on board the *Solomon*.

It was a highly advanced form of mechanized catapult, used to precision-launch packages of bait or high explosive at particularly tasty-looking shoals of fish. Trinity had taken one look at it, muttered something about helping Soaz navigate, and disappeared below decks.

'What if you miss?' asked Jason.

Makhno shrugged. 'Depends. You could hit the hull at high speed, reducing you both to a Summerfield-Kane paste. Or you could fall short, landing in the sea, where you'll either be blasted to pieces by the *Solomon*'s defences or get –'

'– eaten alive by giant killer haddock,' finished Benny. 'Great options, all.'

'But don't worry,' said Makhno chirpily. 'This is a precision instrument; it won't miss.'

'Yeah,' said Jason, prodding Makhno in the chest with his finger. 'But are you a precision operator?'

Makhno's response was cut off as something hit the boat, causing it to pitch violently to one side before righting itself. Makhno keeled forward, crashing into the launcher, while Benny and Jason grabbed hold of it to stop themselves flying overboard.

As soon as they were relatively stable again, Benny pulled herself over to the launcher control panel and hit the intercom button. 'What the hell was that?' she demanded.

Trinity's cut-glass tones rang out perfectly clear, even over such a small speaker. 'It would seem the seabed is suffering low-level seismics,' she said drily. 'These small quakes seem to be disturbing all the local sea life, driving them up to the surface. Our automatic defences are managing to pick most of them off, but . . .' She trailed off, the rest clearly unnecessary.

'I understand,' said Benny. 'Keep us informed.' She switched the intercom off and turned back to the two men, her former husband and present admirer. 'Great,' she told them. 'Not only do we have to deal with fish from hell, we get to meet them when they're pissed off. Fantastic.'

Jason groaned, looking a little seasick from all the disturbance. 'I'll be really nice to scampi from now on,' he said. 'Or really foul, depending on how their cousins treat us today.'

'Right,' Benny told Makhno. 'You better get programming that thing. We'll be there soon, and I want this flight to go as smooth as club class.'

'Oh mama!' exclaimed Soaz as the *Solomon* came into view. It was undoubtedly one hell of a ship. Clearly designed initially for war rather than pleasure, the great black hulk dwarfed their own little boat. The 'copter ahead resembled nothing less than a mosquito floating around the head of an elephant. 'Now that's a status symbol,' enthused Soaz.

'Isn't it just?' said Trinity, leaning over his shoulder. 'Typical of the Yorks. By commissioning that thing they kept a whole shipyard from going bust for two years. By the time it was complete, the customers were queuing up and the shipyard was saved. Absolutely typical.'

'Yeah,' said Soaz drily. 'I'd feel a bit more impressed by their generosity if they weren't on the verge of killing us all.'

Trinity shrugged. 'Maybe they're suffering compassion fatigue?'

They had weighed Jason and Benny together, programming their details into the computer. Makhno had looked up the *Solomon* in the targeting computer, cutting the wires which stopped it from launching at other vessels. Trajectory, wind speed and potential gravity fluctuations had been taken into account. With any luck, the last of these would allow them to land with minimum damage. Benny hoped that all this planning, plus her and Jason's extensive experience with crash landings, parachute drops and so on, would be enough to get them on board safely.

She hoped.

As they approached the Yorks' 'yacht', they pulled back the canopy. The wind thrashed at them, threatening to whip the canopy away, flinging them into the sea in the process. Jason helped pin the flailing canopy down while she sat on it to keep it flat. Makhno was absorbed in preparing the launcher.

Jason had taken off his jacket, loosened his tie and rolled up his sleeves. He looked far more his old self, the slightly dishevelled man she had married. Seeing this person, this old friend, come to the surface, she found herself experiencing a pang of affection.

Or maybe it was just the circumstances, heightening her emotions.

The storm was getting fiercer, rolls of thunder deafening them every few minutes. Most of the lightning seemed to be attracted to the *Solomon*, which provided a far larger target. Ahead of them, the small black shape of the 'copter disappeared, doubtlessly landing on the vast ship's deck. It was around then that the rain began, pouring down in torrents, soaking them to the skin in seconds.

'It never rains . . .' said Jason, his wide grin the surest sign that he was scared half to death.

Phillip heard his wife swear in her old language as they began their descent to land on the *Solomon*'s deck. The 'copter had no autos; it had never seemed necessary, not on safe old Mars. Now they were losing visibility in the rain, lightning was threatening to burn out their electrics – and somehow they had to land this thing.

'This is going to be bumpy,' said Christina, ever the mistress of understatement. Phillip held on to CATCH as, buffeted by the wind and rain, barely able to see the helipad below, they tried to make their descent.

A particularly harsh gale hit them just as they were going

to make contact. One of the flotation tanks made contact, but skidded on the wet surface. Christina screamed in fear and annoyance as the 'copter slid across the helipad, hitting the railings around the edge so hard they were whiplashed forward in their seats. Phillip's head hit the palmtop containing CATCH with a crunch that blacked out his senses.

'I feel like a moron,' said Benny. She and Jason were lying flat on their backs in the scoop of the launcher, trying to relax so the launch didn't break any bones. Thankfully, the rain was sweeping across them virtually horizontally, rather than straight down.

'Now,' said Trinity, leaning over the edge of the scoop. 'Where's the shuttle?'

'On the foredeck, beneath the pool, Professor Trinity!' Jason and Benny chorused, in the manner of primary school kids. They giggled in an appropriate manner.

'Right, we're about to make a pass!' shouted Makhno. Benny felt herself tense.

'Good luck,' said Trinity, before disappearing.

Benny felt a hand in hers. She turned to look at Jason, and squeezed his hand back.

'Almost there!' they heard Makhno bellow.

Benny quickly lunged over and kissed Jason full on the mouth. She took her lips away slightly, looked into his eyes from only a millimetre away. She felt the link between them, tighter than their entwined fingers.

'For luck?' he asked.

'Brace yourselves!' shouted Makhno.

'For everything,' said Benny, with a faint smile. She broke his gaze and lay back, eyes squeezed shut.

'Now!' screamed Makhno.

And then, hand in hand, they were flying, pushing their way through wind and rain. The roar of the storm was so loud, they could barely hear their own screams of fear and exhilaration.

Makhno's stomach was tied in knots as the catapult swung up, launching Benny and Jason in a graceful arc. His hands gripped the side of the console, where a 3-D display constantly repeated a simulation of the launch, perfectly executed each time.

Makhno's eyes burnt from the punishment of wind and rain, and his fringe was so soaked it almost covered his right eye. But he continued to stare up into the sky nonetheless, watching the two figures disappear out of vision, over the rails and on to the *Solomon*.

'Yes!' he cried, slamming a fist against the console in elation. He turned to Trinity, grinning triumphantly. He proudly looked up at the launcher, which had extended to its full height, just as its prominence attracted a sudden bolt of lightning. Makhno recoiled from the control panel in horror, but not quickly enough; flickers of energy jumped the gap, slivers of pain tearing into his nerve endings.

He blacked out before his leaden body hit the deck.

In spite of the storm, silence seemed to hang over the deck of the fishing boat. Trinity ran over to Makhno, who lay juddering and unconscious before her. The smell of smoke hit her nostrils, but it wasn't the foul tang of burnt flesh; it was the acidic stench of fused circuitry.

She turned around in horror. The control panel of the launcher was dead, that was to be expected. But, even with the wind blasting in her ears, she should have been able to hear motors. She couldn't. Draping her coat over Makhno's prone form, she creakily stood up, and looked out over the railings.

The motors were dead. The lasers had stopped firing. They were adrift, undefended, the only shelter a ship which would blast them out of the water if they drifted near it.

She couldn't be sure over the noise of the storm, but Trinity thought she heard the movement of some great creature, scraping tentatively against the boat's hull.

16

APOCALYPSE WOW

Makhno's shot had been right on the money. Jason and Benny's ascent had been terrifyingly steep, and they screamed their lungs out all the way up. Their descent had barely begun when they hit the deck – literally.

The result was a relatively soft landing. They had a mere few seconds to release their hands from each other's grip and adopt a landing posture before they were down, landing in the same rolling posture used by those UNASA troops as they parachuted on to the Martian surface, five centuries before.

Benny rolled and skidded to a gradual halt on the slippery, treacherous surface of the damp, highly polished deck. She was flat on her back, soaked to the skin, but undamaged aside from a few bruises.

Jason was less fortunate. Although his landing was as competent as Benny's his flight path left him less room to manoeuvre. He rolled straight into a metal post, his left ulna impacting so hard it shattered.

Hearing Jason scream, Benny pulled herself up on to all fours and scrambled over to where he lay. His face was contorted in pain. She lifted him gently, cradling his head in her lap. She examined the damage; painful, nasty, but nothing permanent and nothing fatal. Nonetheless, he was going nowhere without medical attention and a hefty dose of painkillers.

'OK,' she muttered urgently, half to Jason and half to

herself. 'Stay here. I'll get you to shelter once I deal with these bastard billionaires. OK?'

Jason nodded hurriedly, unable to speak through gritted teeth. Then Benny felt him relax in her arms, watched the spasms in his features die away into peaceful repose. The pain had caused him to black out.

Benny gently turned Jason over on to his good arm, careful not to disturb the broken limb. It wasn't ideal, but at least his airways wouldn't get rained into while he was flipped over like that. She stroked his newly trimmed hair, which clung damply to his scalp. She caught herself muttering words of affection and reassurance, but even she wasn't sure what those words were.

She kissed him gently on the forehead, then put her mind to locating the Yorks.

Every aged bone and muscle in Trinity's body cried out for fairer, kinder treatment as she dragged Makhno's unconscious form down the steps to the dining room. In trying to save Mars, he had executed a plan that had caused his own injury. Well, Trinity hadn't let Isaac die, and she wasn't going to sacrifice Makhno either.

Just in case any current was still flowing through Makhno's shuddering body, she had liberated an electric carving knife from the dining room, then used it to hack off a length of rubberized deck canopy, with which she insulated the young man, in more ways than one.

As she laid Makhno out on the dining room floor, sliding down next to him in exhaustion, the boat suffered another blow to the hull, one which jarred it so fiercely Trinity feared they would capsize. The room was unlit due to the power shorting out, only the occasional burst of lightning outside piercing the gloom.

'Soaz?' she called out as the floor rolled deliriously beneath her. 'What's going on?'

'El-electrics down,' stammered Soaz, framed in the doorway to the cabin. He was slumped against the doorframe, his right arm hanging limp. 'Sh-shock,' he falteringly explained. 'Took out h-helm. Burnt hand.'

223

Trinity only then noticed the stench of charred human flesh in the air. It had been decades since such a smell had touched her nostrils, and the associated memories it brought back made her tremble with horror.

Soaz pitched over, grasping at the doorframe with his good hand, as the boat was hit again. He slid down, lowering himself to the floor, another flash of lightning illuminating his features. A good six decades younger than Trinity, he seemed to her to be nothing more than a frightened child.

With this in mind, she tried to adopt a fearless and authoritative tone. 'Do we have any defences left?' she asked, suppressing her own terror, trying to stop it spreading to her words.

'No,' said Soaz, incapable of disguising his own fear.

The next blow to the boat was more fierce than the last. The next came almost immediately after, and was even worse. The killers below the surface were clearly getting bold, ganging up on the metallic intruder in their midst. There was only so much time before permanent damage was done, before they capsized, or were breached. Trapped between a nuclear firestorm and the deep blue sea.

Benny sneaked around the deck for a while, diving from cover to cover, before realizing that there weren't actually any security patrols around. Or, indeed, anyone. If there were any crew aboard, they had probably opted to stay below decks, safe and sheltered, well away from the ferocious storm that so hampered Benny's progress. If Benny stuck to the exposed areas, and moved as quickly as she possibly could without slipping and breaking her neck, then she thought she would be able to get to her destination without disturbance or delay.

In spite of the brass rails and polished boards, the deck of the ship still betrayed its military origins; to get down to the foredeck, where Trinity had said the swimming pool was located, Benny had to clatter down a crude metallic stairway painted a tasty gunmetal grey.

When she reached the pool area, Benny found the pool still firmly in place; she wasn't too late, as yet. A delicate force field kept the clear blue water free of rain and dirt, but would let through people or large objects; the perfect pool filter. The field shimmered and sparked as huge drops of rain made futile attempts to break through the field and join their chlorinated brethren.

Benny spun around by the poolside, examining the territory. There were plastic chairs and tables lying around in a state of disarray; they had clearly been blasted around by the storm. A couple had even toppled into the pool, and sat defiantly at the bottom. An incongruous Hawaiian beach hut stood by the pool, its bolted window suggesting it functioned as a bar of some kind, in better times. An access door beneath the grey staircase led below decks. Hoping the interior of the yacht was as deserted as the exterior, Benny ventured into the corridors of the *Solomon*.

After the gloom and cold outside, and the harsh electric light and sterile environment of the fishing boat, Benny found it hard to adjust to the subtle and homely glow which embraced her within the ship. Hidden vents pumped warm air around her, while all the soft glowing light bulbs had chintzy little lampshades. The porthole frames and other fittings were, of course, imitation brass, while equally inevitably the walls were mahogany-panelled. There were clichés to adhere to, a long-held human shorthand for nautical luxury.

Hoping her sense of direction served her well, Benny zigzagged through deserted corridors, bounced down echoing stairwells. When she was two or three levels down, she started to wander in the direction she presumed the pool was, several floors above. Winding her way around the identical, maze-like corridors, she eventually found a door with MAINTENANCE STAFF ONLY: ABSOLUTELY NO ADMITTANCE stencilled on it in bold white letters. Knowing this was the place, and finding the door locked, she kicked the flimsy plywood structure straight off its hinges.

Benny whistled to herself as she stepped through the shattered door into the shuttle bay. The environmentally friendly Yorks had conscientiously purchased an extremely expensive environmentally friendly shuttle craft. A rhapsody in chrome, the gravity buffers built into its sides would allow it to exit the atmosphere without expelling any unpleasant by-products. Of course, space itself required more direct propulsion – and needed less tender care – so the shuttle was also fitted with a dirty great rocket thruster.

It was still a beautiful ship, though, compact and manoeuvrable enough to tuck away in a cargo hold. Only a couple of metres above the shuttle's finned form, Benny could see the chalky white underside of the pool – and the pneumatic arms which would slide it out of the way when required. Benny made her way around the shuttle, then sat down next to the only door on and off the little space vehicle.

The Yorks would have to get past her to get off Mars.

Makhno moaned, his eyelids flickering.

'I think he's coming round,' said Soaz, using his good hand to help Trinity lever open a maintenance hatch.

'Lucky him,' said Trinity. They had found a parcel of flares, which were scattered around the dining room like an indoor firework display. In a moment of optimistic pique she had gone above and secured a couple of lit flares outside, in the vain hope a vessel would just pass by.

To try to keep Soaz occupied she had ordered a complete inspection of the damaged boat. Back in the War, she had found the young grunts, the men and women who had enlisted when just over the minimum recruitment age, would sometimes be near paralysed by fear, too near to childhood to deal with the horrors they faced. At these times she had found distraction important, and had frequently ordered drills, cleaning duties, anything to stop morbid thoughts from breaking her troops before they even faced the enemy.

Holding a flare out in front of her, Trinity lowered her head into the space below the hatch. The hull looked remarkably fragile from the inside.

'Anything worth seeing?' asked Soaz.

'No,' she said firmly. The machinery was packed so tight down there it was doubtful anyone could fit in there to fix it. And it wasn't as if any of them were qualified to rewire a large fishing boat anyway.

The boat was hit again, and Trinity was shaken so hard she had to hold on tight to stop herself falling head first into the hole. She felt Soaz grab hold of her belt, ready to haul her out if necessary. A good kid, she thought: resourceful.

Then she saw it: the hull was breached, water pouring in through a criss-crossed series of cracks. As she watched in horror, one of the cracks expanded, an oily tentacle trying to rip its way into the boat.

'Pull me up!' barked Trinity, and Soaz lifted her out. She slammed the hatch shut.

'We'll last longer on the deck,' she told him. 'Help me get Makhno up these stairs.'

Soaz nodded mutely, and hurriedly used his good arm to lift Makhno up. Together, they began to drag the youth back up to the deck, while below them the water began to pour in.

Benny stood up as the Yorks, dishevelled and propped up against each other, staggered in through the broken door. Christina was trying to avoid using her left leg as much as possible, while Phillip had a bloody gash across his forehead. Phillip cradled a box in his arms, clutching it to himself like a lifebelt. When he saw Benny his grip on the box visibly tightened.

'Summerfield?' said Christina in surprise. 'What the hell are you doing here?' She looked genuinely shocked; which was fair enough, thought Benny. They might have expected a platoon of space marines to try to stop them, but not a single, rather battered archaeology professor.

'You won't get away with it,' said Benny.

'Get away with what?'

'Er . . . you know,' said Benny. '*This*. OK, I admit it, I don't know what your plan is, but the good guys you ain't. And so I'm going to stop you.'

'The Bantu Corporation are planning a hostile takeover,' Christina explained. 'We have to prevent that.'

'And you're prepared to sacrifice Mars to protect your profit margins?'

'Profit margins?' repeated Phillip, aghast. 'You think this is all about money?'

'Well, isn't it?' said Benny, defensively. 'Money, assets; keeping YorkCorp to yourself, your own little empire. Property, possession; that whole big capitalist thing.'

To Benny's surprise, Christina York laughed out loud. 'Goddess,' she exclaimed. 'Get a grip, Summerfield. You've been hanging around with students and wasters for too long. Do you really think the only battles that matter are the ones where dictators are toppled and monsters defeated?'

Phillip continued his wife's line of thinking without missing a beat. 'If we wanted money, we would just have sold YorkCorp; the offer we've got from Bantu would allow us to live in luxury, leaving enough spare change to start up a few new business enterprises. But instead we've held on to the Corp, while it drained our finances dry, gave us nothing but late nights and headaches. We kept going, because we had higher considerations to deal with.'

'What like?' demanded Benny. 'Your shareholders?'

'That's a load of stupid hippy crap,' said Phillip bluntly. 'YorkCorp is more than just a business, an investment portfolio or balance sheet. It's something that's vital to the lives of billions. It's our baby, we built it, and we're responsible. But it isn't just us who'll be hurt if we lose control of YorkCorp. Millions of people are employed by us, and their loyalty down through all these years will be repaid with redundancies, wage cuts, harsher contracts and worse working conditions. We owe it to them not to let Bantu take the company without a fight.'

'Bantu don't have our principles, Benny,' added Christina. 'We can't let our employees be sacrificed to the whims of the Bantu machine, which won't value their talents or appreciate the value of their loyalty. They'll strip the assets – sell off the office chairs for a quick buck, without worrying who sits in them. And then there's the work YorkCorp does; our medical labs will be put to military use, our safety standards sliced down to size in an effort to cut costs. The ethical concerns we invest in – health care, insurance, environmental reclamation – will cease to be subsidized. We're not exaggerating when we say that billions will suffer if Bantu are allowed to get a hold on YorkCorp.'

Benny was lost for words.

'Harsh in the real world, isn't it, Bernice?' said Phillip. 'Not used to a problem that isn't clean-cut, the compromises and dilemmas? Oh yes, we did our research on you. People like you and your husband float around the galaxy like cosmic crusties, without ties or responsibilities, doing freaky little freelance jobs and earning book royalties, scabbing grants and loans, never stopping around to learn what it's like to rely on others. Well, people rely on us, on YorkCorp. It's their lives we're protecting.'

There was a brief silence. Benny couldn't think of anything to say in her own defence, so decided to go on the attack instead. She said only one word: 'Isaac.'

Guilt and uncertainty, pain and regret, all washed over the features of both Yorks like a tidal wave. They seemed on the verge of breaking down, either into surrender or savagery.

'It was a decision we had to make,' said Christina quietly, anguish causing the words to stick in her throat. Her free hand fiddled with something around her neck, and Benny squinted to make out what it was: a tiny gold crucifix.

'We may burn for eternity for what we did,' said Christina. 'And we'll deserve every second of it.'

'But we thought it was a price worth paying to save all our people from servitude. Ask us a thousand times, and not once would we choose differently.'

Benny faltered. The Yorks weren't ruthless; if anything, they cared too much for people, a compassion that had led them to find a surrogate messiah to rescue their charges. Benny could have jumped Phillip, grabbed CATCH and run. She doubted the rather battered Yorks had the energy to give chase or fight her. But what could she, on her own, do with CATCH anyway? She needed the Yorks to cooperate of their own free will, to show her how to put things right.

Gently, Benny, she thought. Gently show them the way.

'I'm not that hot on interplanetary law, but do you really think that a pair of murderers will be allowed to run YorkCorp? Plus the fact you've stolen military hardware, caused this disruption. You're finished.'

'No,' said Christina. 'Enough of YorkCorp will survive,

enough of the core business. We'll regrow. We have plans.'

'Survive?' Phillip asked. 'Survive what?'

'The destruction of Mars,' Christina said simply. 'The elimination of the evidence.'

'You're mad,' Benny said.

Phillip shook his head. 'She's just being practical.'

Christina bent over the palmtop. 'CATCH. This is Christina York. Launch all nuclear missiles under your control, target the major Martian population centres. And save one for the *Solomon*.'

'A bit drastic,' CATCH objected. 'But, you're the code-holder. Nukelaunch in three minutes.'

'This order can't be countermanded,' Christina insisted.

'Of course not, Christina. Once I've made up my mind, that's it.'

'What about Mars?' Benny asked, skipping the question of sacrificing Isaac and getting to the real issue. 'This is your home, these are your people as much as any of your employees. All that Martian culture we've been celebrating, five hundred years of history. It will all be lost if CATCH isn't returned.'

They were wavering, she could tell. Something was stopping them from barging past her and getting on that shuttle. Some part of the Yorks just didn't want to go through with it.

'Yes, without CATCH you risk leaving YorkCorp's employees in an uncertain situation, having to look after themselves in a harsh environment. But if you take CATCH, the fate of all those millions of people here on Mars will be certain; death by nuclear fire. There must be some way to tie Bantu's hands, or help your employees find something new, or in some way delay the inevitable for a while. Something to show your people a way out. But securing their futures with CATCH can't be worth destroying a whole planet, burning away an entire population. This isn't the way. No good end justifies such ruthless means.'

'She's right, you know,' said Christina, and to Benny's relief Phillip simply nodded in reply. Christina turned to Benny. 'Once we had the old man killed, it was hard to stop.

If we did, then that murder would have been for nothing, you see?'

'Well, compounding one's mistakes is always foolish,' Phillip added.

'CATCH,' said Christina, nursing her bad leg. 'You have a new command, one that overrides all other considerations, and which cannot be countermanded.'

'Name it, Christina.'

The woman whispered something into the microphone.

Benny walked over. The word 'CATCH' rotated on a dozen screens before her. 'Is that it?' she asked.

'Yes,' said Phillip simply. 'Thank you, Professor Summerfield. You have just stopped us from doing a terrible thing, an act we would have regretted for the rest of our lives.'

Benny was about to reply, but her response was cut off when he punched her in the face. The blow was so hard it knocked Benny off her feet, and she was unconscious before her body hit the floor.

'What's going on?' asked Makhno blearily. He felt worse than he had the previous morning, and could barely summon the energy to lift his eyelids.

'Nothing much,' replied Soaz with a chirpiness bordering on hysteria. 'You've been electrocuted, I've had my hand nearly burnt off, this boat is sinking and we're all going to be eaten by killer fish.'

Makhno heard a slap and a cry of pain. He opened his eyes to see Soaz and Trinity glaring at each other across the deck, the former nursing a red hand print across the side of his face.

'What the hell was that for?' demanded Soaz.

'The last thing he needs is you scaring what few wits he has out of him,' Trinity retorted. All three of them were spreadeagled together in one corner of the deck, a deck that was permanently tilted at a distressing angle.

'Don't worry,' said Makhno blithely. 'I was expecting this sort of thing. You can't expect to hang around with Bernice Summerfield without being put in mortal danger of the most extreme and stupid kind.' He frowned. 'By the way, aren't we supposed to be shouting at each other over a storm or something? Only, I can hear every word you two are saying.'

They all looked up, into a sky unbroken by cloud or rain, untainted sunlight pouring down instead. The waters around them were less turbulent, though unpleasant things still writhed just between the surface. The air was crisp and still, only a faint tang of ozone in the air indicating that there had been a storm at all. 'They must have done it,' said Trinity jubilantly.

'Bet Kane had sod all to do with it,' added Makhno. His companions nodded in sage agreement.

As they admired the placid sea, something shiny and streamlined lifted off from the hulking grey mass of the *Solomon*. It hovered momentarily, then shot off out of the stratosphere at eye-wrenching speed. The Yorks' shuttlecraft.

'Downer,' said Makhno. 'The villains have got away, probably to return with another dastardly scheme at a later date.'

The ship lurched, violently. With a series of cries and swearwords, Makhno, Soaz and Trinity slid down the now practically vertical deck, landing on the rear railing in an uncomfortable heap.

'Great,' said Soaz. 'Mars is saved, but we end up fish food.' A sharp-toothed orange pike snapped at his leg, which he quickly pulled out from between the railings.

'Dramatic irony,' sighed Makhno, who received looks of the most evil kind from his companions. 'Unless we get heroically rescued by some dashing heroes.'

'We could swim for it,' Soaz suggested half-heartedly.

'No chance,' said Trinity. 'But will three dodgy-looking rescue 'copters do?' she added, pointing into the horizon.

Seeing their distress, all three 'copters lowered rescue apparatus as they approached. As Soaz and Makhno were injured, Trinity allowed them to be rescued before her. The first 'copter lowered a Mars police trooper, who attached a safety harness to Makhno before allowing them both to be lifted away to safety. To Soaz's bemusement, the next 'copter lowered Seez, who strapped his friend to his chest, and grabbed him in a bearhug as they were whisked away.

Which left Trinity, and the third 'copter. To her mild surprise, it didn't lower a man, or even a safety harness, but a simple rope ladder. With carnivorous guppies jumping out of the water, getting closer and closer to nibbling her ankles, Trinity grabbed the ladder and began to climb. The 'copter lifted off, and Trinity had to hold on tight just to stop falling. Finally, she dragged herself through the doors and lay flat on the floor of the 'copter, breathing deeply.

She realized her field of vision was dominated by a pair of polished army boots. She looked up to see Keele glaring down at her, a fierce hatred burning in his eyes.

'Minister,' hissed Keele through gritted teeth.

'General,' acknowledged Trinity flatly. She pulled herself up, gripping the sides of the 'copter doorway to help her. Keele, unsurprisingly, gave no help.

Keele was staring at her, not feeling the need to contain his contempt. 'One push and you're finished, out of my misery for good.'

'I'm not going to justify my existence,' said Trinity sadly. She released her grip on the doorframe, putting herself at his mercy. One nudge and she would be out of the doors, plummeting down a hundred metres to a sea full of monsters.

She looked down at the seething water.

'Do what you must. If that means killing me, then do it. You have every reason to. We've both killed, Keele, but that wasn't like this. We can kill to survive. We can kill from a distance. We can kill in a fog of adrenalin, out on a battlefield. We can kill some wretched monster that will scramble our innards if we don't get them first. We could both kill like that, and we did.'

Keele simply stared at her, face impassive.

'But to kill in cold blood,' she continued. 'To kill a defenceless victim, or someone whom you've known. Not an enemy you can distance yourself from, but another human who isn't going to fight back. You know how the missile codes were stored. I couldn't do it, kill Isaac Denikin while looking into his eyes, knowing he would let me. I couldn't; can you?'

They stood there for perhaps a minute, the two old soldiers staring into each other's eyes.

233

Trinity drew the curved knife from her boot. 'Take out my heart. I won't stop you, whatever you choose.'

She handed the knife to Keele, hilt-first. The old soldier weighed it in his hand and made his choice.

Her head throbbing, Benny tentatively opened her eyes, and looked up into a beautifully clear pink Martian sky. The pool was retracted, the shuttle gone, and Benny was looking up through a rectangular gap in the deck. The wind was still, and not a drop of rain fell on Benny as she lay there.

She dragged herself to her feet. Well, she had almost managed to get through this entire business without being knocked unconscious once. To get so close to a personal best for these sorts of affairs, only to fall – or, rather, be decked – at the final fence. How humiliating.

At least CATCH was still present: the little palmtop sat neatly on the deck. It was calm outside. Benny slumped down beside the terminal, and was just wondering where the Yorks kept their paracetamol when she realized the thudding noise she could hear was coming from outside her head for once. The sky was full of red hovercopters.

'What's going on?' she said woozily. 'It sounds like an Oasis album out there.'

'Well,' CATCH's voice announced. 'The Yorks left in their shuttle; I've put the disruption to MarsNet on hold; and the rescue 'copters have arrived. Oh yes, and the nuke targeted on the *Solomon* will be launched in thirty seconds.'

'What?!'

Benny scrabbled her way to the palmtop.

'It wasn't *my* idea,' CATCH reminded her. 'At least there aren't any nukes targeted at the cities any more. I think that nuking the *Solomon* to destroy the evidence is a terrible plan, and it's not that I don't like you.'

'Well, stop the launch, then!' Benny insisted.

'Christina was very insistent on that one: the order can't be countermanded. Fifteen seconds.'

'You control the launch?'

'Yes. Without me, the launch won't go ahead. Ten seconds.'

'And you are stockaded in that palmtop?'

'Well done, Benny,' he said. 'Five seconds. I knew you'd work it out. Goodb–'

She crunched the palmtop in two under her heel, grinding it to bits.

Twenty seconds later, the ship wasn't wiped out in a nuclear holocaust, so Benny assumed that she'd won.

The aircraft noise was deafening now.

Benny looked up to see a large red 'copter carefully manoeuvre down through the gap in the ceiling, landing on the platform only recently vacated by the Yorks' shuttle. As it touched down, sliding doors were thrown back, and the weirdest strike team Benny had ever seen poured out. A motley collection of geriatric veterans and Mars police piled out of the 'copter and started looking for targets. A couple kept Benny covered until their leader told them who she was.

'She's on our side,' snapped Alekseev, and the two oldsters made themselves scarce. As the two old soldiers dispersed, he helped her up.

'Are you all right?' he asked, genuinely concerned.

'Bit late to send in the space marines, isn't it?' asked Benny impertinently.

Alekseev ignored this. 'They're gone, I presume?' he snarled. Benny nodded.

'Where are the lads?' she asked.

'Other 'copters,' said Alekseev, obviously not interested. 'I presume they'll have landed on one of the other decks. We lost the fishing boat, I'm afraid.'

Benny didn't want to know, so she didn't ask.

'I saved the planet,' she said, looking down at the broken bits of palmtop. 'I didn't hesitate. If it had been a person that I would have had to kill, do you think I would have made the same choice?'

Alekseev gave out a noncommittal grunt. 'Come on,' he said. 'Let's go find the others.'

By the time Benny and Alekseev had climbed the various stairwells to reach the deck, it had become clear to everyone concerned that the *Solomon* was deserted. They found the party from the other 'copters – and Jason – sitting around the poolside, lapping up the sun. As they approached, one of the veterans blasted open the Hawaiian hut, which was promptly looted for alcohol.

'Bottle of pale for the saviour of Mars!' yelled Benny, dropping into a seat next to Jason, whose arm was being dressed by Scoblow.

'Hello, Jason,' said Benny. 'And, oo-er, Matron.' Jason and Scoblow seemed to start at her innuendo. Mad as each other, thought Benny.

'Here you go,' said Seez, passing bottles of beer among the group. Benny took hers gratefully, and flipped off the cap with her teeth. She looked around her, and felt a swell of pride. There was a winged Jason, a scorched Soaz, Seez, a singed Makhno. Together, they had saved Mars. She wondered for a moment where Trinity was, but didn't want to raise the question in too public a circle just yet.

She felt a speech coming on, and slapped a palm against the arm of her chair to attract an audience. Her little team of heroes looked at her expectantly.

'I'm damn well going to finish what I was going to say this time,' she began portentously. 'As in the Siege of Mars, fifty years ago, Mars has yet again been saved by the collected efforts of people of different kinds working together for the common good. If mankind can forget our differences and work together, then the next five centuries of Martian history will be an era of even greater achievements. Let us put our sullied pasts to one side, and together we can build an unsullied future.'

Benny was expecting rapturous applause, the applause she would have got earlier in the day if it hadn't been for that nasty business with the lynch mob. Instead, all she got was a mild murmur of unenthusiastic agreement, and a wolf whistle from Makhno.

'Hey,' said Jason, leaning forward on his sun lounger. 'Are you coming on to my future wife?'

'What do you care?' Makhno retorted. 'You don't deserve her, you middle-aged pornographer.'

'Who are you calling middle-aged?' barked Jason furiously.

236

'Calm down, darling,' said Scoblow, laying her paw on Jason's chest in a soothing manner.

Something in the gesture made a switch in Benny's head click to on.

'Bloody hell,' she said to Jason. 'You're shagging Scoblow, aren't you? First convicts, now gerbils. Mind if I rebreak that arm for you?'

'Can I help?' asked Makhno.

'And us!' chorused Seez and Soaz.

'Hey, stay out of this, you pre-pubescent little joyriders,' snapped Jason.

Suddenly, everyone was shouting at each other. Soon enough, a punch was thrown.

At the heart of the mêlée, Benny began to suspect her utopian vision was unlikely to come true.

Jason lurched out of the throng, shrugging apologetically. 'We always end up fighting,' he noted, elbowing Seez in the face.

Benny smacked Scoblow in the snout. 'We do.'

Soaz had Jason in a headlock, Seez was trying to work out where his solar plexus was. 'I love you, Benny.'

'I love you,' she admitted, accidentally headbutting Makhno. 'But I doubt that we're quite ready for marriage yet.'

He kicked Seez in the nuts. 'Perhaps not,' he admitted sadly. 'Do you think we'll ever get back together?'

'Don't rule it out,' she told him, leaning forwards, shoving Alekseev out of the way.

Jason and Benny kissed, closing their eyes to the violence around them, letting the punches and kicks and bites fade into the background.

'Benny,' Jason said, breaking away, poking Seez in the eye. 'You can keep the moneycard. All my worldly wealth.'

Benny chuckled. 'Thanks.'

'Comic understatement,' Makhno noted, just before they punched his lights out.

'I love you, Jason.'

'I love you, too, Benny.'

They kissed again.

* * *

Benny nursed the Pakhar bite mark in her hand. Great, thought Benny, now the bitch might have given her rabies, as well as whatever species-hopping STDs she'd passed to Benny via Jason.

'Fantastic end to your moment of glory,' said Alekseev drily. He had just arrested the saviours of Mars for affray, mainly as an exercise in preventing any murders. Benny, Seez and Soaz were still on non-violent terms with each other, and so were being flown back to Jackson City together. The rest had been segregated to prevent further bloodshed, and were following in separate 'copters.

'You don't have to keep Jason locked up,' Benny noted. 'You could just deport him.'

'My dear Professor, where do you think that I'm taking you? Mars was a lot quieter before you showed up.'

'Sod you, copper,' said Soaz defiantly. 'If it wasn't for Benny you would be crispy fried pig by now.'

'Yeah,' added Seez nonchalantly. 'You're lucky to even know how your ass was saved.'

'I bow down before your lucid and convincing argument,' said Alekseev sarcastically, bowing deeply. 'I'll just see when we're landing.'

All three detainees gave the finger to his receding figure as he disappeared into the cockpit. Once he had gone, Benny turned to the two young men.

'Well, thanks for all your help,' she said, shaking their hands warmly. 'I'd love to stay and bask in the glory, but I've got to get a flight back to Dellah in a few hours. Bills to pay and all that.'

'Yeah,' agreed Seez innocently. 'We know what you mean. Speaking of cash-flow problems . . .'

'Could you lend us a few sovs?' finished Soaz. 'All this adventuring has cleaned us out.'

Benny grinned indulgently. 'More expensive than you would think, isn't it?' she said, digging around in her pockets. She produced the moneycard Jason had given her. 'Here, have this. It only has a few sovs on it, but it should do you for a couple of days. Enjoy.'

'Benny,' said Soaz, grinning. 'You're a saviour.'

'Aren't I just?' replied Benny smugly, kissing him square on the lips. 'Now, if you'll excuse me, I need to write my diary. I've been neglecting it recently.'

Soaz smiled over at Seez. He'd got the girl, for once.

Benny emerged from The Hotel, bags in tow. The sun was just rising, and The Hotel was almost glowing. It was hard to believe anything had changed since she had arrived, just a couple of days before. Brusilov's scarred figure still dominated the plaza, the pink light casting his face into deepest shadow. The old people were starting to mill around again, the excitement of the previous night forgotten or simply factored into their rambling conversations with each other.

Brusilov, Tellassar, the Yorks; all had made their mark on Mars, for better or worse. And, looking around the place, Benny could see they hadn't done too bad a job.

Benny had helped preserve their achievements, protecting the legacy of past generations so that the generations to come could appreciate them. After all, wasn't that what an archaeologist was supposed to do anyway?

Benny found herself walking with a spring in her step, partially due to the low gravity, but also because of a glorious sense of having contributed to something great. She strolled across the plaza a happy woman, beginning a journey away from a planet she would never quite leave behind.

Epilogue

If You're So Rich, Why Aren't You Clever?

The YorkCorp collapse was one of the most spectacular in the very history of economics. Vast loans were taken out by the company, stretching its finances to the limits, ensuring that several of YorkCorp's creditors went down in flames with them. Many commentators noted that YorkCorp only screwed over banks and credit brokers who had a prior reputation for ruthlessness and unethical investments.

Within a day of the crisis on Mars, YorkCorp had borrowed a lot of money, then promptly declared itself bankrupt. The Yorks themselves were nowhere to be found, but it was clear that they had personally engineered their own financial suicide. Questions were soon asked about where all that money had possibly gone. Many thought the Yorks had embezzled the lot, but it wasn't long before a far stranger explanation was found to be the case.

It had all been given away. Staff had been given huge golden handshakes. Charities had received sizeable donations. The Yorks' most beloved enterprises, the ethical concerns, the health and care businesses, had been granted autonomy from the imploding corporate structure. YorkCorp had been gutted, comprehensively destroyed by its very creators.

By this final act, it was guaranteed that the YorkCorp tradition of concerned capitalism would live on. YorkCorp could never be absorbed, perverted or corrupted.

The Bantu Cooperative were denied their prize.

Several weeks later, in one of the conference halls of New Government House, the officials in charge of servicing YorkCorp's debts had an insolvency sale, an auction of YorkCorp's few remaining saleable assets.

A small group of vultures had gathered. There were investors, entrepreneurs, bored billionaires, the usual crowd. Most wanted to make acquisitions to improve their portfolio, others merely wanted to cherry-pick some of the Yorks' more amusing or elegant assets.

Among the crowd were two male humans considerably younger than anyone else there. Both looked rather uncomfortable, unused to the bespoke suits they were wearing, the crystal champagne flutes in their hands. One of them was tall, lanky, with a newly trimmed beard and tied-back hair. The other was short, far less hirsute, and had an air of contained chaos about him.

'Let me handle this,' said the taller man, who always took the lead in such transactions. His laid-back manner lent itself well to the subtle tactics of commerce.

The auctioneer called the crowd to order, and began to make a short speech, outlining payment methods and auction etiquette. The tall young man was passed a moneycard by his shorter colleague.

They'd kept the card safe. It used to belong to a famous author, an acquaintance and business associate of theirs. It had come into their possession when the author's ex-wife handed it to them. So it was a gift, and they were perfectly entitled to use it. The card had eighteen sovs on it at the time.

Later that day, when the first royalties for the author's book were credited to the account, there was substantially more. A fortuitous coincidence, for them if not for the card's original owner. The two gentlemen often wondered what had happened to the – now presumably penniless – author, but found it difficult to feel guilty about his poor luck.

He'd have wasted the money, and they had plans.

The auctioneer pressed a concealed button on his lectern,

and next to him appeared a helix-shaped hologram.

'Lot number one is The Hotel,' said the auctioneer. 'A famous Martian landmark, and a prime piece of leisure property. Do we have an opening bid?'

'A million sovs,' Seez announced. 'Cash.'

ALSO AVAILABLE
IN
THE NEW ADVENTURES

OH NO IT ISN'T!
by Paul Cornell
ISBN: 0 426 20507 3

Bernice Surprise Summerfield is just settling into her new job as Professor of Archaeology at St Oscar's University on the cosmopolitan planet of Dellah. She's using this prestigious centre of learning to put her past, especially her failed marriage, behind her. But when a routine exploration of the planet Perfecton goes awry, she needs all her old ingenuity and cunning as she faces a menace that can only be described as – panto.

DRAGONS' WRATH
by Justin Richards
ISBN: 0 426 20508 1

The Knights of Jeneve, a legendary chivalric order famed for their jewel-encrusted dragon emblem, were destroyed at the battle of Bocaro. But when a gifted forger is murdered on his way to meet her old friend Irving Braxiatel, and she comes into possession of a rather ornate dragon statue, Benny can't help thinking they're involved. So, suddenly embroiled in art fraud, murder and derring-do, she must discover the secret behind the dragon, and thwart the machinations of those seeking to control the sector.

BEYOND THE SUN
by Matthew Jones
ISBN: 0 426 20511 1

Benny has drawn the short straw – she's forced to take two overlooked freshers on their very first dig. Just when she thinks things can't get any worse, her no-good ex-husband Jason turns up and promptly gets himself kidnapped. As no one else is going to rescue him, Benny resigns herself to the task. But her only clue is a dusty artefact Jason implausibly claimed was part of an ancient and powerful weapon – a weapon rumoured to have powers beyond the sun.

SHIP OF FOOLS
by Dave Stone
ISBN: 0 426 20510 3

No hard-up archaeologist could resist the perks of working for the fabulously wealthy Krytell. Benny is given an unlimited expense account, an entire new wardrobe and all the jewels and pearls she could ever need. Also, her job, unofficial and shady though it is, requires her presence on the famed space cruise-liner, the *Titanian Queen*. But, as usual, there is a catch: those on board are being systematically bumped off, and the great detective, Emil Dupont, hasn't got a clue what's going on.

DOWN
by Lawrence Miles
ISBN: 0 426 20512 X

If the authorities on Tyler's Folly didn't expect to drag an off-world professor out of the ocean in a forbidden 'quake zone, they certainly weren't ready for her story. According to Benny the planet is hollow, its interior inhabited by warring tribes, rubber-clad Nazis and unconvincing prehistoric monsters. Has something stolen Benny's reason? Or is the planet the sole exception to the more mundane laws of physics? And what is the involvement of the utterly amoral alien known only as !X.

DEADFALL
by Gary Russell
ISBN: 0 426 20513 8

Jason Kane has stolen the location of the legendary planet of Ardethe from his ex-wife Bernice, and, as usual, it's all gone terribly wrong. In no time at all, he finds himself trapped on an isolated rock, pursued by brain-consuming aliens, and at the mercy of a shipload of female convicts. Unsurprisingly, he calls for help. However, when his old friend Christopher Cwej turns up, he can't even remember his own name.

GHOST DEVICES
by Simon Bucher-Jones
ISBN: 0 426 20514 6

Benny travels to Canopus IV, a world where the primitive locals worship the Spire – a massive structure that bends time – and talk of gods who saw the future. Unfortunately, she soon discovers the planet is on the brink of collapse, and that the whole sector is threatened by holy war. So, to prevent a jihad, Benny must journey to the dead world of Vol'ach Prime, and face a culture dedicated to the destruction of all life.

THE MEDUSA EFFECT
by Justin Richards
ISBN: 0 426 20524 3

Medusa, an experimental ship missing for twenty years, is coming home. When one of the investigation team dies mysteriously, Bernice is assigned to help discover what went wrong. But to do so she must solve a riddle. Somehow the original crew are linked to the team put on board – their ghosts still haunt the ship. And the past is catching up with them all in more ways than one.

DRY PILGRIMAGE
by Paul Leonard and Nick Walters
ISBN: 0 426 20525 1

Thinking she has been offered a blissful pleasure cruise on Dellah's southern ocean, Benny gladly accepts. After all, she has some time on her hands. But, trapped on a yacht with an alien religious sect who forbid alcohol, she soon discovers that all is not well. And, as the ship heads towards a fateful rendezvous, she must unmask a traitor or risk the system being torn apart by war.

THE SWORD OF FOREVER
by Jim Mortimore
ISBN: 0 426 20526 X

Forced to leave her home on Dellah for Earth, Bernice finds work on an Antarctic dig. Once there she uncovers a link between an ancient reptile race, a secret society and a desperate megalomaniac – as well as the fabled Ark of the Covenant. A desperate race has begun, and she soon realizes her deadly knowledge affects not only her own life, but the destiny of the entire human race.

ANOTHER GIRL, ANOTHER PLANET
by Martin Day and Len Beech
ISBN: 0 426 20528 6

Lizbeth Fugard, an archaeologist working on the backwater planet of Dimetos, is in trouble. Someone is following her – watching her. Terrified, she calls on an old friend to help. On arrival, however, Bernice becomes involved in politics, gun-running and a centuries-old love affair, and soon realizes that unless she can find the truth a cycle of violence and hate will jeopardize more than one planet's future.

Should you wish to order any of these titles, or other Virgin books, please write to the address below for mail-order information:

Fiction Department
Virgin Publishing Ltd
Thames Wharf Studios
Rainville Road
London W6 9HT

COMING SOON

WHERE ANGELS FEAR
by Rebecca Levene and Simon Winstone
ISBN: 0 426 20530 8
17 December 1998

Something very odd is happening on Dellah. A long-ignored religion is rapidly gaining recruits, and arcane arts are practised with dangerously successful results. At the same time, the most powerful races in the universe are withdrawing to their strongholds, leaving the lesser peoples to their fate. Reality has been warped somehow, and Bernice and company soon discover they are at the heart of a terrible conflict.

ANNOUNCING
PROFESSOR BERNICE SUMMERFIELD:
STARRING IN
BRAND NEW AUDIO DRAMAS

Big Finish Productions are proud to announce that they have secured the audio drama rights to the New Adventures and their first two releases are available to buy now! These are fully dramatised plays, with original music and sound-effects, based upon the novels *Oh No It Isn't!*, by Benny's creator and award-winning novelist Paul Cornell, and *Beyond the Sun* by television script-writer Matt Jones.

Featuring a full, professional cast, the double-cassette plays, with an approximate running time of two hours per story, will be on sale from September.

OH NO IT ISN'T!
"A good launch for the range ..."   *SFX*
"[Bernice is] a heroine of the Nineties – witty daring with a lot of balls ..."   *Play Station Plus*

BEYOND THE SUN
"[a] perfect blend of adventure, strong characters and clever situations ..."   *TV Zone*
"Matt Jones has not lost sight of the tagline that 'science fiction has never been this much fun' ..."   *Dreamwatch*

Available in Forbidden Planet and other specialist stores or via mail order.

Please photocopy this form or provide all the details on paper if you do not wish to damage this book. Delivery within 28 days of release

Please send me [   ] copies of *Oh No It Isn't!* @
   £8.99/US$16.99/AUS$19.99 (inc. postage)
Please send me [   ] copies of *Beyond the Sun* @
   £8.99/US$16.99/AUS$19.99 (inc. postage)
Make cheques payable to Big Finish Productions Ltd and post to
PO Box 1127, Maidenhead, Berks SL6 3LN – **Hotline: 01628 828283**

Name...

Address...

....Postcode.................................

VISA/Mastercard number..

Signature..Expiry Date.................................

www.gary.dircon.co.uk/bigfinish.html